Until I Saw YOU

DIANNA ROMAN

WILD ONE PRESS

Published by Wild One Press
Cover design by Wild One Press

Images:
Lens flare, white flare light by Mario Szafran from QUQA Design / Canva.com
1128134789 by Tyschchenko Photography / Shutterstock.com
485380684 by Dean Drobot / Shutterstock.com
Print by Burhan Kapkiner / Canva.com

ISBN: 978-1-959553-01-4 (Trade Paperback)
ISBN: 978-1-959553-00-7 (eBook)
ISBN: 978-1-959-553-02-1 (Large Print Paperback)

Visit the author at www.diannaroman.com

This book includes a content advisory.

PRAISE

This book is one of those you never forget. I promise you, this book will grab you and not let you go. – **Cathy Christmas**

I LOVED it. Humor, warmth, acceptance, healing, friendship, and hope. One of the best books I have read this year. – **Tracy Ann**

You haven't seen what Dianna Roman can do until you've read Until I Saw You. – **Larissa, Love Bytes Reviews**

Dianna Roman proves once again that she is the queen of MM romance that is both emotional and hauntingly beautiful. – **Amity Malcom, author of Beautiful Games**

Have tissues but also be ready to laugh out loud! – **Rhonda, Bookbub**

One of the best books I've read this year, if not ever!!! – **Bkwrm24, Goodreads**

A beautiful book of two men, both damaged in their own way, trying to come to terms with life experiences and circumstances that were beyond their control. – **Donna Dee, Goodreads**

With every touch,
Riley is returning
a piece of me
I didn't think
I'd ever get back.

I honestly don't know why God
gave me eyes
before you came along,
because I didn't use them
for a damn thing...

Until I Saw
YOU

CONTENT ADVISORY

This novel contains the following topics and terms that may trigger sensitive reactions in some readers. Please read at your own discretion.

- Off-page sexual assault, discussions of sexual assault
- Physical and emotional domestic abuse
- On-page physical altercation
- Both preferred and slang terminology regarding low vision and sighted persons
- Explicit consensual sexual content
- Adult language, profanity

A DOG NAMED LARRY

This book contains a dog named Larry, who is also referred to by the following names during the story:

- Jedidiah
- Jed
- Zeke
- Boomer
- Eisenhower
- Copernicus
- Kevin
- Barkus Maximus
- José
- Bruce
- Bartholomew
- Marlon
- Bogart
- Russell

Dedication

To victims of abuse—

You are neither what they say you are nor how they make you feel.

You can be what they say you can't.

You can do what they say you can't.

You ~~can't~~ **can**.

Chapter 1

RILEY

The blonde blob shifts in my field of vision, cascading a halo of silver-gray light with shards of white around it from the vanity bulbs. She's been standing at that mirror for thirty minutes. I never paid attention to how long it takes her to get ready until I had nothing to distract me during the wait. That's all I seem to do these days—wait like a piece of carry-on luggage, idly standing by an occupied traveler.

I don't really know why I'm standing here, staring into this murky abyss that I could literally see by looking at anything else in the apartment. Maybe because she seems like one of those science documentaries that you can't understand. Why else? I mean, what's the point in watching, if you don't get to see the reward? And who in the hell is she primping for because it sure as shit ain't me?

The audible sound of her lips smacking precedes the clatter of more beauty crap on my counter. It's probably best that I can't see how much of my bathroom she's taken over. I'm constantly knocking things onto the floor whenever I wash my hands or try to find my razor. Speaking of which, she swears she didn't use it on her legs and that the nicks I can feel on my face must be because of my inability to shave properly now that I'm blind. I'm calling bullshit on that one.

"Almost done, babe," she says yet again. "Then we'll get you ready."

I respond with a grunt from the doorway like a good piece of luggage. I can get myself ready just fine, but it's one argument I've learned to avoid. They say when you lose your sight that it doesn't heighten your other senses. Whoever believes that hasn't heard Valerie's sighs when I commit the heinous crime of rummaging something out of my dresser myself. I can't work anymore. What the fuck is so wrong with sweatpants and t-shirts when you've got nothing to do but lounge around the house all day?

When Val said she was coming to stay to help me out three months ago, my dumbass kind of thought it was for the weekend. My buddy, Rob, said because we'd been dating for eight months at the time, that should have been a red flag—code for moving in. I still owe him twenty bucks, but fuck if I'm owning up to that oversight. I mean, how the hell did he call that shit? The guy hasn't had a girlfriend that lasted longer than a week in the ten years I've known him.

I think I'm standing here hoping I can see proof of my twenty-dollar loss. That, and if I'm going to be gifted with a precious moment of vision, I want to know what my half an hour of leaning on this door frame resulted in.

I saw her yesterday. It was only for about a minute when I woke up in the morning. It's the first time in two weeks since the last time it happened. The doctor said he doesn't expect it to last, but Val has hope.

I think there's some universal rule that says you're supposed to cherish people who have hope in you, but it's not really hope in me. Is it? It's just hope that I won't be a helpless liability anymore. It's hope that I'll be the guy who can tell her she looks beautiful, the guy who can fly her through downtown on my motorcycle instead of the one she has to buckle into the passenger seat of her *Prius*.

I hate that fucking *Prius*, and if I ever find that vanilla air freshener she has in there, I'm pitching it out the window on the freeway. The only acceptable vanilla scent comes from cookies. Everyone knows this.

I didn't tell her this time. Not about the air freshener, about seeing her drooling on my pillow, her purple eye mask askew over her eyes, clear as day in the morning light for sixty seconds. I should have been happy. Right? I got to see my girlfriend's face. I don't resent her, but there was nothing—no warm fuzzy feelings other than the brief joy of getting to see a person, any person.

She's doing the best she can. Val's been handed everything in her life. I don't think she even had a pet to take care of growing up. I tell myself that's the problem, that she's overcompensating. I tell myself what the doctors say—that this is going to be a big adjustment. This restlessness I feel can't be all her fault. I know it's just a shit show that I have to get used to, but I mean, I should have *wanted* to look at her. Right?

Sixty seconds, give or take, and I honestly didn't care that it was the woman who says she loves me lying there. I'd have been happy just to stare at a homeless man. Happier even, possibly. It would have been something new. There is no more *new* when you go blind.

Want to know a secret? I only spent about thirty of those sixty seconds on Val. I scrambled out of bed and flipped open my photo album on the dresser, scanning every picture I could before the tunnel vision was replaced again by the blurry light people see in visions of the afterlife. And then I cried.

I cried because I'd already seen those pictures of me and Brent as kids, of Mom and Dad laughing at Christmases. Those are already memories I can pull from when I'm eighty. I wasted my sixty seconds.

I should have searched my phone for the Taj Mahal or some famous artist whose work I've never seen. I should have checked my messages for pictures of my brother Brent's kids, but that's a joke. No one sends me pictures anymore. Why the fuck would they?

I need to make a list, in case I get another sixty seconds, another ten. Anything. I've seen movies where they ask people on death row for their choice of a last meal. What do you choose to see though, knowing it might be the last thing your vision ever manifests? How do you know what that one glorious image is when you've never seen it before?

"Alright." Val sighs, shuffling her crap around on the counter and zipping something. "Let's get you dressed."

"Can you get me one of my black V-necks to go with my leather jacket?"

"Riley, no! It's a luncheon, not a rock concert, and you need to change your jeans," she huffs, shuffling past me.

My foot catches on something just inside the door to the bedroom, outside the master bath. It gives, bowing like it's made of plastic. My toe snags inside a circular opening, causing me to drag it as I stumble. There's a *thud* when something hits the floor.

"What the fuck?" I mutter, reaching down to feel what I've knocked over.

My hand connects with the soft feel of fabric and the hard, rubbery texture of a clothes basket. When the hell did she put that there? The woman leaves shit all over the place, never in the same spot. I have a twelfth-floor penthouse with a laundry room, and she's got mounds of clothes in every room like a snake that sheds its skin where it lies.

"Oh, just leave that. I'll get it later," she calls from somewhere over by my closet. I can hear the slide of hangers on my railing, making my skin crawl at the thought of being her life-sized Ken doll.

"I'm not wearing dress slacks for lunch at a friend's house. It's Marco and Jill, not a five-star restaurant," I point out, chucking her shit back into the basket.

"I never said anything about dress slacks, but you can at least wear your *Calvin Klein's*."

"What's wrong with the jeans I have on?"

"Those are stone washed. The Calvin's are crisper, dark navy. They look nicer."

13

"I'm not changing my jeans. These are fine. Just grab me a shirt, and we can get going. I'm freaking starving."

That sigh. Here we go.

"Riley, it's April. It's Spring. It's a housewarming party. If you're not wearing khakis or slacks, you should at least go for business casual. It won't kill you to make a little effort."

"They're *jeans!* Blue jeans are blue jeans. I don't think a guy who used to crush beer cans on his forehead will give a shit what kind of jeans I'm wearing to his house for lunch."

There's a stagnant silence before she mutters, "He doesn't do that anymore."

I hate that I've become an embarrassment that I have no control over. Her criticism feels like scolding a Kindergartener for not being able to know how to spell. And part of me gets it, that whole big adjustment thing.

I can't see my clothes. I can feel their texture. Some days, I can differentiate if they're dark or light. I know if they're in my drawer or closet, they're clean. Before my vision went to shit though, my wardrobe wasn't complex—blue jeans, graphic t-shirts for casual events, and dressier V-neck tees, Henleys, and sweaters for nights out. I've got the obligatory khakis, dress shirts, and even a half dozen suits for the launch parties we had at work. Everything I own is blue, gray, or black. So, no matter what I grab, the odds that I won't match are slim. My wardrobe is basically embarrassment-proof, in my opinion. Why is this always an ordeal?

I can feel her staring at me. What I'd give to know if it's a pout on her face or disgust. That's what's so unfair. I can't mask my emotions, but literally everyone else is a mask to me. That leaves me ever exposed, wearing my reactions on my sleeve.

"I'm just trying to help, babe," she finally says. "I don't want people talking about you."

My teeth grind. There it is. Charity that I didn't ask for and don't need, but yet charity I can't shun because how many people in a newish relationship stick with someone with my kind of problems? Why did she have to tell me that my socks didn't match when we went out last week? I never would have known. I never would have cared. Why do I care now?

Folding my arms, I concede, "I know. How about I wear my black blazer with one of my V-neck tees. Dinner jacket screams prestige."

The guttural noise her throat makes tells me she thinks I'm being sarcastic or that I never lived in the world when my eyes were open. "Seriously? It's like you're not even hearing me."

"What? I always wear a jacket when we go downtown. You never complained before."

"It was cute at first, Riley, but I assumed you didn't dress like a music scout all the time. Here," she says, thrusting something at me. "Keep the stone washed, but at least wear a polo."

Grabbing the hanger from her, I run my fingers over the fabric, some horrid poly blend that is sure to make my back sweat within five minutes. "A polo? Where the hell did you find this? I don't even own any polos except for the ones I get from conventions and Christmas, but I'm pretty sure I threw them all away. I haven't worn polos since my internship."

"It's the one I got you for Christmas."

Fuck. Yeah. I remember now. She said it was salmon. It was hideous and deserved to be banished to the back of my closet even though I thanked her like a good boyfriend.

"Oh, yeah. Forgot about that one. Um, didn't you get me a black one too?"

"What is it with you and black?" she grumbles. "It's like you exude mortician. What part of Spring says death?"

Oh my God. We live in Chicago. It's so windy it never feels like Spring. Plus, my stomach is literally eating itself from all the bird food she's been force feeding me, and she wants to argue over seasonal swatch choices? Seriously, I haven't had a pizza in like two weeks, and I fucking know she lied about us being out of *Better Cheddars*. Her distaste for cheese is unnatural. She should have disclosed that information on the first date.

"Val, I don't want to spend all day at a fashion show. I'm starving. I'll wear a freaking polo, so I don't embarrass you, but give me the black one, and let's go. This is getting ridiculous. They're our friends. If they're going to judge us for our clothes, then we need new friends."

Sighing, she wrenches the shirt out of my hand. I hear the squelch noise of hangers being angrily slid across the closet railing.

"I don't understand what the big deal is. It's not like you can even see what you're wearing. Why do you care?"

Do adjustments mean you have to get used to being treated like a child? Do they mean you have to give up all of your free will and hand your balls over to a woman who you can't even remember why you were attracted to in the first place?

Pressure builds in my lungs, in every vein. I don't want to snap because then I'm not just a blind guy, I'm an *angry* blind guy who can't match his fucking socks or find his snacks.

"I've never worn pink in my life, and I'm not wearing it now. *I'll* know I'm wearing pink. I can picture it in my head, so it's the same as if I could see it."

If she turns on the fake sniffle thing she does, I'm not going. I'll happily stay here and have a talk with my *Rita* app to hook me up with the greasiest pizza delivery place in our zip code. And you know what? I'll be happy. I can't remember the last time I was happy, like truly happy. I used to always be happy.

The sound of her annoyed inhale makes my muscles clench, but she clips out, "Fine. Here. Black it is."

A hanger pokes me in the sternum, and I grab it before it falls to the floor. More polyblend fabric. Yay.

I don't even freaking care at this point. At least I salvaged a modicum of my dignity. A person should be allowed to wear whatever the hell they want. I honestly don't care what I wear, but that's not the point. She tells me what to eat. She's always messing with my hair. My hair is self-sufficient. I comb it, and it lays where it wants to. It's always been like that, a floppy, sandy blonde mess that I can finger comb out of my eyes. She doesn't let me do anything and talks to me like I'm an idiot. I know being blind isn't supposed to be fun, but something tells me it shouldn't suck this much either. I should be allowed a few opinions like what color shirt I want to wear. I can't see, but I'm not brain dead.

Twenty gag-inducing vanilla scented minutes later, Val knocks on the door to Jill and Marco's new apartment. We're greeted by Jill's cheery voice as she lets us in.

An elbow nudges me in the ribs, followed by Val's harsh whisper. "Glasses off, Riley."

Her and my sunglasses. God forbid I give the appearance that I can't see. Let's not give a damn about sudden changes in light still giving me splitting headaches. Complying so I don't have to guess what kind of sympathetic looks she'll get from the house guests if I argue, I hang my shades on the neckline of my stupid, stretchy polo shirt.

"Hi, Riley! How are you doing?" Jill says three decibels louder than necessary because, don't you know, when you lose your sight, you lose your hearing too.

"Great! How are you?" I yell back.

Judging by the silence that follows, it's okay for them to yell but not me, and I assume there will be words later from Val. Jill offers to take our coats and hesitates when she asks to show us around their new place. I have no desire to be led by the arm or pushed in between my shoulder blades the way Val does to me, nor to bump into anything and break it in Jill and Marco's new digs.

"The food smells good," I offer, giving Val's shoulder an affectionate squeeze. "Why don't you have a look around, while I grab a bite. I know you've been dying to see the place."

"Oh, sure!" Jill enthuses, likely relieved I've saved her from having to try to figure out how to show a blind guy around her new house. "We've got a buffet table set up just to your right there in the living room. Help yourself, Riley."

"Great!" I give Val a peck on the cheek. She loves public displays of *coupley* shit, but my lips connect with the skin next to her nose when she turns her head at the last second.

"I'll just be a minute, Jill. Let me help Riley get a plate and get situated, then I'll take you up on the tour."

Val's hand closes tightly around my bicep. Her other one presses to my back, urging me forward into the blurry unknown. It's like being shoved into a haunted house, not knowing what's going to pop out at you in the dark. I've told her countless times, it's easier when she goes first and leads the way, but she says then she feels like she's leading me like a dog. She hates the cane the doctor gave me because she says I hit too many things and it makes a lot of noise, but I kind of thought that was the point. Whenever she walks by my side, I bump into her. It's not my fault she swings her hips and flips her hair every thirty seconds, so shoving me it is.

"Alright. There's an armchair just a few steps ahead of you, if you want to go sit down. I'll make you a plate," she says, amidst the clank of ceramic presumably being drawn from a stack of dinnerware.

"What have they got?"

"Club sandwiches and appetizers. What do you want to drink?"

"What kind of appetizers? Anything good?"

I smell fried food. Please, let there be fried food.

"Don't be rude, Riley," she hisses. "I'm sure it's all good, and what was with the yelling? Are you trying to embarrass me?"

Reaching out toward the table, I ignore her. If I can't walk around and mingle, I'm damn well going to enjoy the food. Her hand slaps mine just as mine connects with what feels like deep fried pastry dough.

"Stop! You're going to make a mess. I said I'd get you a plate. Can you just go sit down?"

"Are those crab rangoon? Grab me some of those. Will you?"

"You'll get flakes all over you the way you eat."

"What do you mean *the way I eat?* Like a hungry person who hasn't had lunch yet?"

"No. You just shovel everything into your mouth like a pig, and now that you can't see it's worse, because you don't know when you have crumbs all over you."

"I'll dust off my chest," I grit out, reaching for the rangoon again.

A hand clamps over my wrist. "Riley, don't! Just let me get it for you."

"I literally just touched them. I can grab my own food. Okay? Just go do your thing."

"There's tongs, okay? Clearly, they don't want people touching everyone else's food. Don't cause a scene. I'll grab you one."

Snatching up two of the crusty appetizers, I veer my hand to the right, feeling the plate in her hand and drop them on its surface. "There. I only touched the two I want. My hands are clean. Quit freaking out."

"Oh my God. I can't do this today. You're being impossible on purpose."

Sliding my hand under the plate, I grab its edge with my other one. "I'm not being impossible. I'm being self-sufficient. Just go talk to Jill."

"Riley, don't," she seethes, tugging at the plate.

Now, I'm on a mission. There is no way this woman is getting this plate from me. Slipping it from her grip, I take a step down the table and reach out for the next cloudy blur in the center of my vision. Bringing my hand down like one of those claws in a toy arcade game, I make to scoop up whatever bounty I find. My palm connects with something gooey and cold at the same time Val lets out a loud gasp.

Macaroni salad is my best guess. Squishy with perhaps little chunks of bell peppers chopped up in it.

Fuck it. I like macaroni.

Making like an ice cream scooper, I cradle my fingers, sheer off a handful of the sticky pasta, and slab it onto my plate. Bringing my thumb to my mouth, I suck the sauce off, then set to cleaning my other digits as I inform Val, "See? I'm good. Can you grab me a beer though, babe?"

"Hey! Hey!" an amused greeting comes from my right. "You can have mine. I just grabbed it. I'll go get another one," my buddy Rob says.

Thank Christ. Someone sane to talk to.

"Rob," Val grits out. "I didn't know you were coming."

"Uh, yeah. I mean, I work with Marco too so…"

"Mm," she grunts. "Well, watch him, and you two stay out of trouble."

I wait for the clip of her heels to storm off and then turn around and edge the toe of my shoe toward the direction where she said there was a chair. When I find it, I sigh, dropping down into its cushiony padding with my plate.

There must be an end table to my right because I catch the distinct sound of a beer bottle hitting wood as Rob pats me on the shoulder. "Be right back, bro."

I've successfully de-sauced my fingers by the time he returns and plops himself down in a chair to my right, filling in the spatial gaps of my surroundings. A napkin brushes my hand, so I take it.

"Thanks, man," I tell him. "Is she gone?"

"Yeah. Out on the balcony with Jill."

"Thank God."

"That bad?" he asks.

"Let's just say, I might have to keep that twenty bucks I owe you to put toward my bail money. Was she always this bad?"

"Uh, no comment." He chuckles, but I can't share in his amusement.

She's never made her dislike of Rob a secret. Who couldn't like Rob? He's the happiest guy I've ever met and harmless as a puppy. Sure, he's not the brightest bulb in the box, but he's always the first one there when you need something.

There's a crinkle of paper. I track him setting something on the side table next to me. "I'm glad you made it. I brought your birthday present with me just in case."

Smiling, I reach for what's clearly a lumpy, haphazardly wrapped package. "Dude, my birthday isn't until Wednesday next week. Aren't you coming to the party?"

"You're having a party?"

My fingers pause mid-tear through the wrapping paper. Val's been talking about throwing me a birthday party for three weeks. She even sent out paper invites like I'm a twelve-year-old rather than turning thirty-two.

"Didn't Val send you an invite?"

"Uh, no I didn't get anything. Maybe I missed it in my mail. Sometimes the mailman drops my stuff in 4D instead of 4B."

Good old Rob. So good he's naïve. I have a feeling about where my best friend's invite was dropped—right in the fucking trash can of my apartment if it was even written out.

"Yeah, well, um…six o'clock. Don't be late or I'll eat all the good food."

"You got it. I'll be there."

Tearing open the package, I smile at the feel of a t-shirt. It's our classic gift exchange. Rob always finds the coolest t-shirts. I try to outdo him, but I'm pretty sure he's the winner at this silly tradition we've had going since college.

Spreading it out over my knees, I run my fingers over the design, detecting what feels like the symbol of a bat in the center. "What's it say?"

"It's black, and there's a bat symbol. It says, *blind as a fucking bat*, then a there's a comma, and then the word, *man*."

I crack up, holding it up in front of me, even though I can't see the damn thing. "Blind as a fucking bat, *man*," I declare. "Oh my God. I love it! Val's going to fucking hate it," I add absently.

"Oh, shit. Sorry. I didn't even think about that."

"Pfft. Don't worry about it. You didn't buy it for *her*," I joke.

"Yeah," he concedes, but then adds, "She freaking hates me."

"No. She just hates joy."

I'm starting to think it's true even though I was just trying to get a laugh out of Rob and put his mind at ease. She hates our love of comic book heroes, and how we used to have video game nights and geek out over new app designs we were collaborating on at work. I'm a geek with an athletic build. Apparently, she underestimated the geek part when she first met me.

"Well, I'm glad you like it," Rob says, clinking his beer against where mine is sitting on the table.

Retrieving it, I return the gesture. "I do. Thanks, man."

Leaning back, I take a desperately needed pull and sigh. Rob starts talking about the most recent Bears game. He has a way of describing the plays that I appreciate, unlike some of our other friends who just tell me what the score was or that it was a bust or a blowout. I picture the plays in my mind but get distracted by the distinct whisper of Val's voice, talking with Jill.

"How are you holding up?" Jill asks.

"It's hard. It's so hard. I've tried everything, but he's just so depressed about his situation and…I mean, I'm a positive person, but it wears on you. You know?" Val replies, making my stomach roil.

Depressed? I've never been depressed a day in my life. Sad, on occasion, like when my grandpa died two years ago. Annoyed, sure. Daily. Why the fuck is she telling people I'm depressed? There's nothing wrong with being depressed. It happens to people, but depressed isn't me.

"Well, they say intimacy is a good mood booster," Jill suggests playfully.

"You'd think so," Val tells her. "But that's a whole other problem."

I feign a laugh at Rob's enthusiastic recap of the game, my eyes fixed toward him as I bring my beer to my lips. She *is not*. She is not going to fucking talk about me like I'm not here and about our personal shit to top it off.

"Really?" Jill gasps. "I thought people say that when you lose your sight that sometimes it can heighten intimacy. Like it increases the focus on the sensation of touch."

"I thought so too. Believe me, I've tried. It's not for lack of effort on my part, but it's like he wants nothing to do with it. He doesn't initiate anymore, and he used to be all over me. Now, even when I initiate, he has…problems."

"Wait. You mean…he can't…"

I assume Val confirms that embarrassing factoid non-verbally because Jill follows up with a sympathetic sound. "Oh, you poor thing. Well, keep trying. Give it time. I'm sure things will get better. Has he tried talking to a counselor? Or maybe it was something to do with his accident. They have pills for that."

I can't fucking take it anymore. The fucking macaroni salad is protesting in my stomach along with the blood in my veins. My dick works just fine, but there's something about feeling molested in the dark by the fashion police that makes it not want to stand up and do its job the way it used to.

Jerking off in the shower? Not a problem. Val's voice, whispering and asking me if I can feel every touch as her hands roam all over my body that I can't see feels like an advantage that I no longer can share.

We screwed plenty of times when I could see. I don't understand my stage fright, but I sure as shit don't need Jill's opinions on it or a freaking pill. What else has Val been telling people? And why does it feel like she's going for an academy award for most distraught caretaker?

It's suddenly very hot in here. Tugging at the stupid polo shirt, a bead of sweat runs down my back. I knew this poly-blend crap was going to do that.

"Riley? You okay, man?" Rob asks.

As Val digresses over my list of crimes in the background, doling out her tale of woe, things shift into perspective. I want a fucking pizza. I want to trip over shit that's only there because I left it there. I want to wear sweatpants if I want and scratch my balls even if someone's looking. I want to go to my doctor appointments by myself without someone nagging the physician about some new treatment or procedure they must be forgetting to cure me of this inconvenient life change. I want my best friend to come over whenever he wants without getting shit from my girlfriend because she thinks it was his idea to go rock climbing in Belize and therefor is to blame for me losing my sight. No matter that it had anything to do with getting an eye infection in a remote village before I fell off the face of that cliff and detached my retinas.

"Yeah. Tell me something though. What color is this shirt?"

"The shirt you're wearing?" Rob asks, sounding confused.

"Yeah."

"Uh…it's kind of a pinkish-peach color, I guess."

Mother. Fucker.

I live with the devil.

Slamming my beer down, I dig out my wallet and hold it open for Rob. "Grab a twenty out of there. Will you?"

"Wh-why?"

"Just do it. I owe you."

After he rifles a bill free, I close it up and stuff it back in my pocket, then rise. "Can you give me a ride?" I ask.

"Y-yeah. Sure. Where do you need to go?"

"Riley?" Val calls. "What's wrong?"

"Anywhere. I don't give a shit," I inform Rob, whipping the polo over my head.

"Riley? What the hell are you doing?" Val whisper-squeaks.

Palming Rob's gift, I slip it on over my head. Angling toward Val's direction, I inform her, "I'm done embarrassing you, that's what I'm doing. Have a nice life. Jill, thanks for the macaroni. Say *hi* to Marco for me." I latch onto Rob's bicep, grateful that he's already on his feet as Val sputters. "Come on, buddy. Let's hit it."

"Dude, are you...doing what I think you're doing?" he whispers.

"Riley!" Val shrieks.

"If you find me a pizza, there's another twenty in it for you."

Chuckling, he claps a hand over mine and starts for the door. "I'll buy you three pizzas, *Batman*."

"Hey, that's blind as a fucking bat, *man*."

Chapter 2

HARPER

Six weeks later

There is no victory in escape when you built the walls of your own prison. There's no victory because escape doesn't equal freedom. I never meant for this to happen, and that's the most terrifying part.

More terrifying than fists. More terrifying than the sound and sensation of my ribs cracking against the coffee table. More sickening than my body feeling like it's being ripped apart. If I never meant for this to happen, but it did anyway, will it happen again? *What if* is my new prison.

I still can't decide which was worse—that time our neighbors called the police, followed by weeks of Dallas' retribution after they left as though I was the one who had brought the law to our home, or the mix of amusement and disgust from the responding officers at finding out the call was a dispute between a gay couple. I was used to Dallas' disgust by that point, but I'll never forget the look on those police officers' faces. They were looks that said men don't need help. They were looks that said I wasn't a man, not because I'm gay, but because I was the weaker of the two.

That was four months ago. I should have left then, but I wanted to be a man. I wanted to pretend Dallas' ugly disappointment in me wasn't real. That his rage and his fists weren't real. That all the bills I paid and romantic dinners I made would one day be rewarded with the love I have in my heart to give. I wanted the feeble memory of first touches and kisses, flirting and kindness, to re-materialize and for all the sickening horror to evaporate like a dissipating storm cloud. I never got to meet those aspirations. Instead, I met my worst enemy tonight.

His name is Harper Reid. His battered reflection is staring back at me in the breezeway doors of my employer's office. Brown hair, five-eleven, a hundred and ninety pounds of lean muscle. I used to think he looked physically capable, but he was no match for a six-foot-four, two-hundred-and-sixty-pound wall of fury.

Marcy, our agency receptionist, is going to have a heart attack when she comes in to open up and finds me like this, but I've got nowhere else to go. Daniel's working at the bar tonight. I'm in no shape to take the bus across town to his apartment. Besides, that'd be the first place Dallas would look for me. My oldest friend doesn't deserve to have that kind of drama brought to his doorstep. If Daniel sees me like this, I can't even imagine what he'd try to do to Dallas. *Try* is the operative word, although I'm sure Daniel would refute that point.

No. I'll just be another Chicago casualty. Better to die here in the breezeway of Home Reach on the itchy brown carpeting under the corkboard full of resource flyers we post for our clients. There's even some for people in my situation. They're taunting me. I'm not sure if it's denial, pride, or the inability to move, but I refuse to go to a halfway house even if only for one night.

I can't be half of me. It feels like Dallas already took half or rather, I gave it to him. I worry that if I walk in to one of those shelters, I'm signing my own defeat and might never get the other half back. I've taken so many steps backward; I can't afford another. At least, Home Reach isn't likely to skimp out on my life insurance policy if I croak on company property, so my life is still worth something.

Damn it. Dallas is listed as my beneficiary on my policy.

That's enough motivation to make me stop entertaining morose fancies of dying. No way will I give him that satisfaction. I handed him my life on a platter, a buffet for his pickings, and look where it got me.

Sleep. I just need to sleep for a little while.

Drawing my tongue across the crack in my swollen lip, I taste the metallic flavor of my own blood. I always hated how Dallas and the fighters in his circle used illegal drugs, but for once I think I actually understand it. The pain is slicing through me at so many angles, I don't even know how I could sleep without the aid of a substance while tremoring this much. My muscles have been convulsing since I scrambled out of the apartment and into the cab. The cabbie's reaction to my state was testament to the moment it hit me just how bad off I was. It sounded oddly like an accolade.

"Jesus. Someone fucked you up good, man."

Fucked-up-good is not a life prize I ever wanted to win, but I conceded with a grunt. Unfortunately, I think he was right. Fucked-up-good sums up the makeover Dallas gifted me for telling him he spent too much on this last trip of his. If I'd kept my mouth shut, I wonder about all the other things I could be doing right now.

Shifting against my duffel bag, a sharp blade of pain cuts through my core. It's my body's way of telling me there is no possibility of finding any comfort. Hugging my kneecaps, I let my head rest against the wall. At this angle the cool air from the a/c vent hits my puffy cheekbone and eye, staving off the warm June air seeping into the breezeway through the gap in the doors.

Okay. I can manage to sit like this for a little while. At least I can do that. One small victory. One wise decision after so many bad ones. Maybe it will diminish the swelling by the time Marcy opens up the office in a few hours.

I don't trust Dallas to not check for charges on our joint account and come looking for me at a hotel. I can't imagine showing my face to a reception clerk right now anyway. They'd either tell me to get lost, assuming I'm trouble, or call the police to get me an ambulance.

"You fucking little bitch. Where's that mouthiness now, Harp? What do you got to say?"

His voice in my ear, his fist in my hair, holding my cheek to the counter are still on replay. How can this be the same man who nervously leaned in to steal a kiss behind Daniel's bar one night almost two and a half years ago? His body, splitting me in two, mercilessly taking what I'd once gladly given him, and that's all I could think. That and, *this isn't happening. This isn't happening.*

Another wave of nausea, thick and sticky, creeps up my throat. This glass box of purgatory is tilting, or maybe it's me.

God, it hurts.

Nothing's ever hurt so bad in all my life. My ass, my insides, my guts, my scalp, my fingers. Even my gums. It's like he shoved a grenade inside me and let it detonate.

The carpet scratches against my cheek as I sag to the floor on my side. I can feel my heartbeat in every throbbing wound like it's trying to escape but hasn't decided where to make its exit yet.

"Clean up this fucking mess before I get back. You brought this on yourself."

How could I possibly clean up the carnage of our apartment when I was barely able to clean up myself before the shock set in? Why am I finishing the argument with myself? Am I losing consciousness?

The cab. Thank God for that cab. Thank God for the hundred bucks I had left in my wallet.

Where am I going to go? I can't go back. I don't know anything other than I can't ever go back. If I don't die tonight, he'll kill me next time.

Next time.

The thought sends a violent shudder through my already trembling body. I can't take a next time. There never should have been a *this time*...or the last time, or the time before that.

What have I become?

"Stupid. So stupid," I mutter like an oath, the wiry carpet fibers catching on my split lip.

I am stupid. Stupid for ever dating him. Stupid for believing anything he ever said. Stupid for trying to make it work. Stupid for staying. Stupid for ending up on this floor.

I never meant for this to happen.

I send up the apology to my former self, the one who didn't know the path of love was far less glamorous than the world leads us to believe. Maybe in another life, he won't take the one I did.

I never meant for this to happen, but it did. I'm not a man. Men don't cry. Men can defend themselves.

And I'm not free. Freedom doesn't hurt this bad.

Chapter 3

HARPER

"Jesus, Harper! Why didn't you call me? Holy fuck!" Daniel's voice is like an anvil strike to my skull.

Rousing on Marcy's couch, I turn my head toward him. How can eyelids weigh so much? The one I manage to crack open reveals his stupidly perfect face, crystal blue eyes, and pitch-black Superman hairstyle. Wonderful. I've almost managed the impossible, rendering his playboy face less handsome by inflicting that horror-stricken expression on it with my appearance.

"Marcy, you're a traitor," I accuse my savior, but it comes out pathetically weak and unthreatening, the defining character traits that got me into this mess.

"I don't care. You wouldn't let me take you to a hospital, and I refuse to leave you here alone like this. Here. Let me get you some more ice." Marcy's hand retrieves the melting freezer bag that's draped over my frozen face before she abandons me to Daniel's scrutiny.

Whipping off his black leather jacket, Daniel drops to his knees on the floor next to the couch. As his eyes scan my body, I close mine. I don't want to see his sympathy.

"I'm gonna kill him. I'm gonna fucking kill him," he mutters.

"No," I get out around a hard swallow. "You're not. He's crazy. You can't kill crazy."

He answers with a scoff. "How long, Harper? How long has this been going on? I want the fucking truth this time."

Pinching my good eye closed tighter, I give a single, defiant shake of my head. I've had enough shame for one day. I can't take anymore by divulging the confession Daniel wants.

"You're not going back there. Ever. I swear to God, if you even think about going back—"

27

"Daniel, I'm done. I won't. Just…stop yelling, please. My head hurts." More to myself, I add, "Everything hurts."

"You need a doctor, Harper," he scolds, lifting the hem of my t-shirt.

I don't have the energy to stop him, so I just lie still with my forearm clutched across my ribs to hinder his investigation. Whatever he can see of my midriff can't be that bad.

"Mother fucking shit! Damn that son of a bitching psychotic fuck!"

Or maybe it can.

"What?" I pant, the effort of glancing down stealing my breath.

A warm hand presses to my side and rolls me forward. Molten-white pain sears up my tailbone and mushrooms into my gut, ripping a cry from my lungs.

"Huh-ah! Don't!" I plead. "Don't touch! Please," I gasp.

My teeth grind as he eases me back. Blinking through the pain, I catch Marcy's concerned face where she's stopped beside me on her return from her kitchen. It's quiet, so quiet. Such a change from all the fussing a moment ago. Something tells me it's not a reprieve. Glancing over at Daniel, the sight stuns me enough to mute my pain for a moment.

I don't think I've ever seen him cry, but he looks damn near on the verge of tears. Hands gripping his hair, teeth bared in barely checked emotions—that look he's giving me sends a chill up my spine.

"Harper, what the fuck did he do to you?" he whispers.

My eyes slip closed. I have to force myself to swallow against a clogging lump of shame at the back of my throat. "I'm fine," I assure him, hating that I can't even control the tremble in my voice. Dallas is still controlling me even though he's not here.

"You are so fucking far from fine," he scathes.

"I'll *be* fine," I argue.

"Yeah, because I'm calling you a fucking ambulance, and you're going to the hospital."

"No!" I shout with considerable effort, grabbing hold of his arm before he can stand. "No, I can't."

"What do you mean you can't? You need to see a doctor."

"They'll call the police, and they'll want to know how it happened, and then they'll arrest Dallas."

"Good! He fucking belongs in jail!"

"He'll be there one night at most before one of his crew bails him out, then they'll all come looking for me. You think this is bad? Imagine how much getting arrested will piss him off."

"I don't fucking care! They're all a bunch of meatheads. I'm not afraid of them."

Pinching my eyes shut, I shake my head feebly. As difficult as the action is, it's easier than admitting that *I am*. I'm terrified of what essentially a bunch of cloned, pissed off, drugged up Dallases would do to me.

"Harper," Marcy interjects soothingly, "I told you that you're welcome to stay here. Dallas doesn't know where I live."

"Thanks," I rasp, taking the fresh bag of ice from her. "Can I...talk to Daniel for a minute?"

"Sure. If you're staying Daniel, I can head back to the office, clear out my cases for the day, and be back in a couple of hours. Emily doesn't get home from school until four."

"I'm not going anywhere," Daniel affirms.

"Marcy, I'm fine. Go on and go," I reassure her. "And thank you again for helping me."

"Harper, don't you dare thank me. You're camping on that couch until you're a hundred percent. You hear me?"

Giving her a semblance of a smile, the last of my pride dies. I'm officially a couch-crasher at a widowed mother's crackerjack box apartment with all of my worldly possessions in a duffel bag at my feet. I've barely got a cent to my name, and knowing Dallas, anything left in our account has probably vanished since last night. To top it off, I don't even have my bicycle, which means I can kiss the bike messenger job I picked up on the side for extra cash goodbye. Not that I could even ride my bike right now if I tried, but the fear of the unknown has me taking stock of precious assets. I have to start all over. Twenty-seven and I have nothing to show for the life I've lived up to this point.

Daniel says nothing as Marcy gathers up her keys and purse. Maybe he's going to drop his hero complex for once and leave me to wallow in peace. When the door closes on Marcy, I sigh and close my eyes. It's bad enough I've already imposed upon her, asking her to give me privacy in her own home so I can confess the embarrassing parts to Daniel only adds to this mortifying day.

"Alright, so I know a guy," Daniel says, leveling a sage look at me.

Has he lost his mind?

"What? Like a hitman? You can't be serious."

"No, a paramedic who comes into the bar, but I think I like your idea better."

Right. The whole medical attention thing. How could I forget? I would actually love some medical attention. I just don't want everything that comes with it. Bills, retribution, judgement.

"And you just happen to have the phone numbers of all your patrons?" I venture to distract him.

Shrugging, he glances at the window. "I fucked him a few times. Okay? Whatever. I can call him and have him look you over. Proper

29

first aid, maybe some decent pain killers, not some dime store band aids and peroxide."

When I don't answer, he threatens, "It's either that or I'm calling you an ambulance. This isn't up for debate."

"Fine. Call your hook-up." I'll agree to anything at this point if he'll just let me pass out again.

"Why didn't you call me?"

"Because I knew you'd flip out."

"Of course, I'm flipping out. You didn't even call the police."

"They'd do a police report, but nothing would happen. We were in a relationship. They'll think I let him."

"Would you listen to yourself? Nothing about the way you look says consensual."

And that's it. That one word strips me bare.

"I'm not…a victim." The way my voice breaks is hardly convincing, so I try to add with more conviction, "I can't be."

Daniel gently draping himself over me in a delicate hug is both another blow and a desperately needed comfort. "I am so fucking done with all of those guys," he whispers. "Him and his whole crew. The next time I see them in the bar, I'm going to take a club to his head."

"Daniel, no! Don't do anything. He'll deny it. He won't out himself in front of the guys. And they're trained fighters. You wouldn't stand a chance."

Scoffing, he relinquishes his embrace. "Thanks for the faith."

"I'm serious. Promise me you won't do anything. You're the only friend I've got. I couldn't stand it if something happened to you."

"Look who's talking."

"Daniel, please."

He looks at me like I'm speaking in tongues and shakes his head. "This is so fucked up. You're really not going back there this time. Are you? Please tell me you're done being that dickhead's punching bag."

Hearing the bold accusation makes me cringe. How long has he thought that? "I won't. I can't. Not anymore."

"Thank God," he says on a breath of relief. "You can stay with me. I'll take the couch."

"No. As soon as he realizes I'm not coming back, he'll go looking for me, and of course, he'll think I'm staying with you. I'm not bringing you any trouble. If he comes around, don't even answer the door."

Damn it. I've said too much. The way he's gaping at me is an indication he's piecing together the depth of Dallas' relentlessness that I've always hidden from him.

"I'm not scared of him, Harper. And you shouldn't have to be. He belongs in jail."

"I don't feel like getting prodded and stared at," I mumble, closing my eyes in the hopes it will signal the end to this discussion. I wish I was brave like Daniel.

He must take pity on me because he asks, "Do you need me to go get your stuff?"

"No. Just leave it. It's not worth it."

"You paid for almost everything in that place, Harper. You shouldn't have to buy all new shit for a new apartment."

"I'll go get more clothes as soon as he's on the road again. Okay? But I don't want anything from there. Promise me you won't go over there."

Our three-eyed stare down lasts a painfully long beat as I vision Dallas tossing Daniel's body around the apartment the way he did to mine.

"Fine," he huffs. "But you're not going there alone. You got it?"

I nod. I'll do anything to end this debate, anything that gets me closer to sleeping for three days straight.

"Look, there's that discount place on Vine. We can go get you a bed and find something over in my neighborhood."

My face heats through the sting of the swelling in it. Of course, he'd assume I can easily afford discount furniture and an apartment. Daniel lives in a less affluent neighborhood than I do. I have a decent job. I live in a higher end apartment in a middle-class neighborhood. There's so much I've never told him. That should have been the first red flag that I was in for trouble. If you can't tell your friends about your life, it's not a life you should be living.

"I...Marcy said I can stay on her couch for now."

"Yeah, but you're going to need a place. This is almost as small as mine, and there's *Cheerios* stuck to the pillow."

Squinting, I focus on the crustaceous cereal remnant stuck to the throw pillow under my head. Nothing is as small as Daniel's efficiency that he's holed up in since college in order to bank every dollar that he can, but I don't care about size or cereal at the moment. Either option is charity I don't deserve. "I don't...have enough money for a place right now."

"It's cheaper over by me. I'm sure it's half the price for first and last than over by you, and I can loan you some money."

"No. You've been saving forever to buy the bar. I'm not ruining your dreams. I...can we talk about this later? I just really want to go to sleep."

Pursing his lips, he nods. "Fine. Let me call Jade."

"You screwed a guy named after a precious stone?"

"You're one to talk. Is going for cities any better?"

The pinch I feel in my expression must have given me away because he mutters, "Sorry."

I didn't mean to pout over his playful comeback. Grunting, I shake my head and let out a long breath. Anything I had left is completely drained.

Daniel must notice the shift in my resilience too because he adds, softly before leaving the room, "Hey, you'll get through this, man. Everything's going to be better from now on."

I'm usually an optimist, but I'm also a realist. Life has taught me that more often than not, things get worse before they get better. I really don't want to find out what's worse than this.

Chapter 4

RILEY

The sound of the dart needle connecting with a *thunk* sends a rush through my blood. I sunk another one. I'm the king of the world. I haven't had this much fun in months.

"What did I get?" I ask Rob.

"Uh…you missed."

"Like hell I did! I heard it hit," I argue, taking a swig of one of the beers he brought over.

"Y-yeah," he chuckles. "Um, it hit the wall again."

Chewing on my lip, I consider the report. "How far away from the dartboard this time?"

"Mm, like three inches to the left?"

"Oh, fuck yeah! That's pretty good. You watch. I'll be sinking bull's eyes in no time."

Snickering, he walks to retrieve the darts where we've been hanging out in my home gym that doubles as a rec room. With the patio doors to the rooftop open, the warm June air spilling in makes me imagine I'm at an outdoor bar. The doorbell resounds, instigating a growl from my stomach.

"Pizza! Finally!" I groan, setting my beer down on the pub table by the wall.

"I'll get it, man," Rob offers, clapping me on the shoulder.

It shouldn't relieve me that I don't have to deal with getting to the door, unlocking it, and interacting with a delivery person I may have never met before, but it does. Life has been so much better since Val has been gone, but there's things I probably won't ever get used to.

Aside from Rob taking me out a few times, I've pretty much been holed up at home. It's liberating not having someone dictate my day, but I wonder how long I'll be content being a homebody. The walls seem closer every day, like they're starting to close in around me. Sometimes

33

it's so fucking quiet, I swear to God the clock stops. You don't realize what a life you had until you can't do the things you used to enjoy doing. Dancing at clubs, jogging through the parks, joyrides on my motorcycle.

Fuck. I miss my motorcycle. My fresh air nowadays consists of the time I spend on the rooftop patio outside my bedroom. The freedom it offers is another fleeting gift just like my sight. How long will I be able to afford my twelfth-floor penthouse apartment now that I can't work? The question is another set of walls closing in.

I can wait to mull it over in the dark silence after Rob leaves. No way am I squandering what little social life I have left on worrying over problems that will still be here tomorrow.

A woman's voice floats through the doorway. Did he let the pizza delivery person in? I wonder if she's hot? Wait. This is Rob we're talking about here. He wouldn't know how to flirt if a chick motorboated his face.

"What is that smell?" the woman says, sounding disgusted.

Fuck. Oh, fuck. She drove all the way from Carol Stream? That's like an hour-drive in traffic.

"Mom?" I call out, feeling for the doorframe.

"Riley? What have you been doing in here? Isn't your care worker helping you keep things cleaned up?" My mother squawks amidst the crackle of potato chip bags and what sounds like an aluminum can that just got kicked across the floor.

"I...I can help with that, Leigh Ann," Rob flusters, followed by the rustling of a trash bag. "I was going to help him take the trash out before I left."

"Mom," I call accusingly, "What are you doing here?"

"I came to bring you some cookies we had left over from the bake sale, but I don't even know where I can put them."

"Cookies? You've got cookies?" I sniff and head toward the sound of her voice. "Here. I'll take them." Finding her shoulder, I extend my other hand.

She sighs. "You might as well. Your entire counter is covered with snack boxes."

When I hear her rummaging through them, I pause the cookie I have halfway to my mouth. "You're not messing with my food, are you? I have a system."

"A *system?* Half of these are empty, and some still have food in them. How do you even know which ones are full or still good?"

Grabbing a box, I hold it up and shake it. When it fails to rattle, I kick my foot out to locate the trash can and shove the box down on the top of it. Judging by how much I have to squish it down, the sound I hear is something that overflowed and hit the floor. Honest mistake. Happens to people who can see too, so I keep my poker face, hoping the eyebrow I raise sends my point home.

"There. See? *Empty*," I inform her.

The guttural noise she makes tells me she's not impressed with the new uses of my sensory skills. "I'm going to call that Home Reach agency again and tell them that they need to replace this worker. They should be helping you with some of these things. Is she even here?"

"No! Don't call them. It's fine. I can get it. Rob and I were just hanging out. I was going to clean up later."

She's quiet for a moment, which is a good indicator she's sizing up the results of the last two weeks I've left unattended. I was celebrating, so I may have not been too concerned with the state of my kitchen. That care worker had to go. She smelled like my great aunt Linda... at her funeral.

"Riley, I worry about you," Mom says in that fretful tone she's adapted since my accident, cupping my face. "I know you don't want your mother around all the time infringing on your privacy, but it drives me batty wondering if you're okay. You should have told me this one wasn't cutting it. You have every right to request a new worker. That's what you pay health insurance for."

Groaning, I pinch my eyes closed. "Mom, I let the worker go. I don't need one."

"You what?" she shrieks.

"I've got it covered. I'm fine. She was worse than the last one. It felt like I was suffocating all over again like when Val was here."

"Riley, it'll only be for a little while just until they help teach you how to adapt. That's what their agency coordinator said. You promised you'd stick with this one."

"Not when they follow me everywhere and ask if I need help taking a leak or showering," I counter.

That has her gasping. I can just imagine her covering her mouth the way she does when she's shocked. "Did she touch your...without your consent?" she stage whispers.

"Oh my God," I grumble into my hand and then turn my head toward the sound of Rob. "Why did you let her in?"

"I can hear you, you know," Mom scolds, swatting my arm.

"Sorry ma'am, I wasn't talking to you," I add, patting her arm and address Rob again. "Why did you let her in? If you can't follow the rules, you can't come over and hang out anymore."

"Riley!" Mom's swat to my arm hits harder this time.

"Ouch! Hey, that's abuse to the disabled!"

"You're going to give me gray hair, I swear."

"That's what that dye you use is for."

"I do *not* have gray hair! That's just to brighten up my natural color."

I really shouldn't, but she's just too easy to rile, and it's not like there's many people I get to talk to in person. "Leigh Ann Davenport, are you lying to a blind man? How could you?" Turning to Rob, I whisper, "She so does. Gray hairs everywhere."

His snicker is cut off when Mom snaps her fingers. "That's enough, you two. Robert, come over here with that bag. You hold it open. I'll start pitching the empties in it."

"No! Mom, you don't need to come over here to work. I said I'd get it. I'm not going to die just because I didn't take the trash out."

"Riley, there's spaghetti sauce stuck to your wall."

Crap.

"I can explain that," I offer. "I…dropped a can of sauce, and it splattered on the wall. That's why Rob and I have a pizza coming any minute. We got to talking, and then you showed up before we could clean it."

There's silence as her blurry brown hair remains still in my field of vision. "It's fossilized," she emphasizes.

"It's…this new quick drying sauce they have. We've got it handled," I assure her, trying to still her arms from pillaging my snacks.

Sighing, her body goes slack. "I can't in good conscience leave with this…this…pigsty the way it is right now. What kind of mother would I be? I'll call your father and tell him I'm spending the weekend."

I love my mother, but my stomach takes a dip. What…the fuck…is happening? She is not serious.

The door buzzer sounds. Rob calls out like he's relieved by the distraction, "I'll get it."

"Mom, you can't stay here."

"What do you mean, I can't? If you fired another worker, then your guest bedroom is free."

"No, I mean…what about Dad? You're just going to abandon him all weekend?"

"Oh, he'll be fine." She pats my cheek, mistaking my warning as thoughtfulness. Why is she so damn good? It's infuriating.

Dad might be fine, but *I* won't. I can already imagine her *Leigh-Anning* the shit out of my apartment all weekend. She spent two hours hand scrubbing my bathroom from floor to ceiling, jabbering on about all her neighbors when Val moved out. I can't go through that again. I'm too young to lose my mind.

One thing I've learned since losing my sight is that my phone is my world. Palming it out of my pocket where I keep it at all times, I scamper down the hallway and address my Rita app.

"Rita, call Dad."

He finally answers on the third ring. "Yeah?" he asks absently, noise in the background.

"Charles, this is your first-born. I have a code red emergency here."

"Riley? What's wrong?"

"There's a woman in my apartment. She looked sweet at first, but it was probably just the plate of cookies. Rob didn't know any better and let her in."

"Riley, I'm watching the game," he grumbles.

"How wonderful for you! Let me guess, it's peaceful, relaxing, maybe even entertaining. Hm, I'll bet it has something to do with the fact that your incredibly-giving-to-an-obnoxious-fault wife isn't there. You know the one. Five-six, dyed gray hair, comes bearing homemade baked goods to gain entry."

"Did she bring you all the bake sale leftovers? I asked her to save me some snickerdoodles," he laments.

"Dad, she's elbow deep in my trash can right now. Get your snicker out of the doodle and focus! You need to tell her to stand down."

"Let her be. She worries about you all the time. It's all she talks about. How bad can it be?"

"The last time she started cleaning, she was here for three days. She bleached my light fixtures! Who does that? Tell me the truth— am I adopted?"

"What? She always makes me take ours down for her. Wait a minute. You'd better not let her on a ladder!"

Ah ha! I've got him now.

Rounding the corner, I speak toward the sounds of the "trash panda" that's rustling another garbage bag open. "Leigh Ann! You're in *big* trouble," I warn, waggling my phone.

"What? Why am I in trouble?"

"Charles says you better get home ASAP," I caution, putting the phone back up to my ear so Dad can hear my master plan.

Let her be? Where's the allegiance? What has happened to the sacristy of man-code?

"He's hurt that you've been climbing ladders over here but won't lift a finger at home to help him with the light fixtures."

"Riley!" Dad barks in my ear just as Mom gasps.

"That is not true! Who do you think does all the dishes and the laundry?" she defends.

"I'm kidding," I concede. "He said he wanted to take you out for dinner."

"God damn it, Riley!" Dad yells. "This is the first time I've taken a shit in peace after work in thirty years *and* gotten to watch a game by myself."

"What's that, Dad? Reservations?"

I'll contemplate feeling guilty about his heavy sigh later. This is mission critical right now. "Put her on the phone," he demands.

"Thank you, kind sir. Hold please." Covering my phone, I address the panda. "Mom, relax. Get home to Dad before you hit rush hour traffic. Rob and I got this. Don't we, Rob?"

"Yeah. Pizza clean-up party, Mrs. D. We're on it," Rob assures her.

"Fine, but I'll be back tomorrow to help fold your laundry. You know, I wish you'd consider moving back home even if it's temporary. You could—"

My lungs seize up as her maternal instincts regale a horror tale to my ears. I just regained a scrap of my freedom. I'm not giving it up just because I can't see. Since my accident, she's gone all protective on me. She can show her concern all she wants with baked goods, but when she starts folding my laundry and envisioning me in my childhood bedroom—well, a man has to draw the line somewhere.

"No. No! Not necessary."

"But Riley, you need—"

"A new caregiver. I know! But if you fold all my laundry, then what are they going to do all next week?"

"Next week?"

"Yeah, when the agency sends a replacement over. Leave the clothes for them to handle. That's what health insurance is for, right? You said so yourself."

"Oh, that's wonderful news! I'm so glad you called them," she coos.

Did call, will call—is there much of a difference?

"Yeah. See? I've got everything under control. Here," I hand my phone to her. "Talk to Dad, and don't let him go cheap on that dinner date."

"Hi, Charlie. No, I'm not on a ladder! Why didn't you tell me you wanted to go out tonight? Tomorrow? Oh, I thought he said you wanted to go to dinner tonight. Well, sure. I can heat up some meatloaf when I get home." As Mom rattles on and Dad digs his way out of leaving me hanging, I hedge my way around the island counter until I sense Rob.

"Pizza me," I whisper pleadingly.

I can hear him chewing. The bastard. He didn't even wait for me.

"Here you go," he says, handing me a plate.

"Thanks, traitor."

"It was your mom! I couldn't close the door on your mom."

"Save it. You're dead to me for ten minutes."

Sighing, he sips his beer as I moan around a bite of lukewarm pizza. I love pizza. Even when it's cold, it loves you back.

"So, you've got another person coming next week," Rob ventures. "That's cool."

"No," I whisper after tracking Mom pacing in the hallway off the living room. "As soon as we get Leigh Ann out of here, I need to call freaking *Home Breach*."

"*Home Breach?*" he chuckles. "Nice one, but...it's not actually a breach if you allow them into your home. Right?"

"Like I have a choice? You heard her. If I don't at least look like I'm getting support, she'll either be over here all the time or hounding me to move back home."

Judging by Rob's silence, he understands my predicament. Good. At least he gets it. I can always count on Rob to be in my corner, unless...it has to do with barring my mother from entering, of course.

"I mean, it'll be nice to have someone here in case you need anything though. Won't it?" he adds. "Like they can't all be as bad as the last two. Maybe it just takes some getting used to."

What...the hell? He's gone rogue on me!

"Am I actually hearing this? Add another ten minutes to your you're-dead-to-me sentence."

Why is he laughing? That wasn't a joke.

"Well, you said you get kind of bored, and you could use the help cleaning up around here."

Unbelievable. He's been poisoned by my mother. Setting my pizza down, my gut twists from this unforeseen serving of reality check. Even my best friend thinks I need help? Of course, I need freaking help, but he's supposed to be the one person who still thinks I'm just regular old Riley, the Riley who knows when he's got spaghetti sauce on his walls.

"My housekeeping skills are fine," I challenge. "I've just been...busy."

"Busy? Um...doing what?"

Well, fuck him. Blind people can be busy. What's with the twenty questions tonight?

"Working out," I blurt, recalling my new favorite past time. It does keep me busy. I'm desperate for busy, and if that's the only way I can get it, so be it.

He snorts at me. "Uh, yeah. About that...dude, you're starting to look a little shredded. I think you can ease off the gym time. You're going to make me look bad when we go out together."

"Somebody has to be the pretty one, and how shredded exactly?"

"Like leaner, more muscular than when you played in college even."

Soccer. One more thing that'll forever be just a memory. I don't even care that I'm in the best shape of my life. My vanity left me when I hit the ground after falling off that rock face.

39

"I'm good with that, but if I start getting all veiny like a body builder, let's have this talk again," I say casually. It's the classic Riley, sophomoric humor I feel obligated to dispense.

I don't know how to shut it off. It's become my armor against the concern everyone has for me. If I pretend to act like pre-fall Riley, maybe they'll treat me like pre-fall Riley because more than seeing, I just want to be me again. I'm the one losing his sight, but everyone else seems to be having vision issues. They treat me like I disappeared.

"Deal," Rob says with a laugh.

Mom finally makes her exit after collecting my bills to process and unloading her usual concerns on me. Rob talks about people from our department for a while, making me realize the disconnect is growing between me and my old place of employment more and more. New projects I'm not a part of, new hires, new policies—the world is going on without me. He puts up a valiant effort when I insist that he doesn't need to take my trash to the garbage chute. In the end, I concede when I realize he might need to feel useful as much as I long to. Because let's face it—what's so great about being my friend anymore?

Of all the people I know, Rob's the last one that would abandon our friendship. I don't doubt his loyalty or sincerity, but we used to go on adventures, adventures spearheaded by me. What in the hell is the appeal of hanging around me now? All we'll have is our shared memories and the new ones he brings to me like a kid dropping feed flakes in a fish tank for me to thrive on. He's being cheated, but he's just too damn good to know it.

As soon as the door clicks shut behind him, my heart skips a beat. It's just me and the kaleidoscope of distorted lights across my eyes, just me and measured steps, searching fingers.

I could hop on the treadmill again, but the fear of Rob's "shredded" warning is too real. I ran for three hours before he showed up earlier anyway. Workout and nap. That's all I do, besides sit on my rooftop.

"Rita?"

"*Yes, Riley?*"

"What's the word for a fear of being alone?"

"*Monophobia, or autophobia, is the fear of being alone.*"

Huh. I guess it actually is a thing. That's not reassuring. If it exists, it can happen.

I'm not there yet. I just…wondered. I mean, this can't be it.

How can God or the universe or whatever the hell people believe in take away one of the main ways a person can function and expect them to exist through old age? How old am I going to live to be?

Aunt Loretta lived to be ninety-six.

Fuck.

I need to do something. I am not spending sixty-six years at my parents' house. Well, of course, I can't. They won't live that long.

Shit. Not reassuring either and too depressing to fathom.

I can't go live with my little brother, Brent, and his wife and kids. I know he'd let me, but who wants to be a family's third wheel?

I can do this. I have to do this. The freedom party is officially over.

"Where the fuck did Val put my cane?"

I'm sick of hitting my toes on shit. With my luck, she probably threw the damn thing away. Fuck it.

Feeling inside my closet, I find an alternative. And here I thought I'd never swing a baseball bat again. Who knew?

One thing I can't do yet is clean the way I probably should be able to. Mom's right. If insurance will pay for it, I might as well take advantage of extra help while I can. Better that it's a stranger than someone I know I feel like I'm burdening. There'll just need to be ground rules this time. I'll make that clear.

"Rita, call Home Reach."

"*Calling Home Reach.*"

Chapter 5

HARPER

"It's alright, Marcy. Really. I know it was out of your hands," I assure her, handing her another plate to dry.

"Could you at least stop doing my dishes while I crush your dreams? That'd make this a whole lot easier. You should be lying down, resting anyway."

Glancing into the living room where Emily is belting out the lyrics to a *Frozen* song on her karaoke machine, I stifle a laugh at Marcy's good intentions. Even though I'm up and moving now after three days in the fetal position on her couch, my energy is a distant memory. I'm certainly not going to interrupt Emily's time to unwind after school by trying to reclaim the couch. I don't want to get comfortable here. I can't. It's not right to not stand on my own two feet. That seems of the utmost importance, the key lesson I was meant to learn after my fight with Dallas. I'm never depending on anyone again nor putting myself in a situation where I'm taken advantage of.

"It's not your fault the senior center asked to keep Madison on as their VRT. That's what I get for being gone for a few days. Mr. Boswell never liked me very much, so it's not a surprise. I'm just grateful you were able to cover my shifts, so the agency didn't lose the position."

Rolling her eyes at me as she grabs a dish towel, she jerks the wet plate out of my hand. "It's Mr. Boswell's fault that he's a pervert who prefers having a female therapist on their staff to a male one." Sighing, she frowns. "I'm sorry, Harper. There's only a few follow-ups, nothing long-term or full-time right now."

"Maybe...I can find a private listing somewhere. Advertise for services and go get my bike from the condo, so I can—"

"How the hell can you ride a bike right now? You can barely walk to and from the living room without hobbling?"

My face burns with shame. She's not wrong, but hearing it rebrands the label that's been searing into my soul the last three days—*helpless*.

Her hand clutches my arm, and as if my complexion and silence haven't embarrassed me enough already, I flinch from the innocent contact. "I'm sorry," she whispers. "Just…you know what I mean."

"I do. It's alright," I assure her. "I just…I'm so grateful to you, Marcy, but I need to find something. Dallas…cleaned out the account."

"Are you kidding me?"

Scoffing at her widened eyes, I let loose a sour laugh, scrubbing the macaroni pot with more vigor. "I wish I were."

"Oh, Harper," she lets out on a sigh.

We wash and dry in silence. My mother always used to say the key to happiness was finding something to be grateful for. As I stand here in Marcy's tiny kitchen, pummeled by my own life choices without a cent to my name, relying on my next meal from this widowed mother's refrigerator, the only thing I can think of to be grateful for is that my mother isn't here to witness my downfall. That phrase, never put your eggs in one basket comes to mind. I sure picked the worst basket possible.

My phone vibrates in my pocket, making my spine go rigid. I silenced it after the fifth message from Dallas. I don't even have to look to know it's him again. I have no desire to see where he's at on the rollercoaster of emotions that constitute his shitty apologies. They range from sarcastic to remorseful to demanding.

"Dallas?" Marcy asks, raising a brow.

Shrugging, I mumble, "Don't care. He'll get the hint."

The reassuring smile she flashes me is a reward for courage I don't think I deserve. "So, okay. There is one full-time position, but it's not VRT or O and M work."

"Are you serious?" I practically light up with the news. I don't care if it's not for a vision rehabilitation or orientation and mobility specialist. I will literally do anything at this point if it paves my way of me leaving my past behind. "What is it?"

"It's…for a live-in caregiver, assisted living."

"Lodging?" I chirp, but school my features so as not to offend Marcy. "Why didn't you tell me, then I won't have to commandeer your couch anymore so you can have your living room to yourself again."

"You know I don't care if you use my couch. It's not that. I've had a hard time filling the position."

"Really? We've got plenty of caregivers registered with the agency."

"I know, but it's not finding a suitable caregiver that was the problem, it's more of a…client problem."

"Oh?" Now she has the rest of my attention. I knew this was too good to be true. Apparently, even when you're desperate you can still be a skeptic. "What kind of client problem?"

"It's this guy who recently started losing his vision. He declined any vision rehabilitation or orientation and mobility therapy services."

"Does he not have insurance?"

"He does, and it would cover our program sending someone out to do some in-home visits, but his family caregiver who took the consultation call after the hospital referred him to us said he didn't need it. Then, about a month ago, he called and asked if we could send someone just to help with household chores, but that lasted a week before he sent them packing."

"Okay, so…maybe they weren't a good fit?" I suggest cautiously, knowing how hard Marcy works to place the right people together.

"It was Claire Bocance," Marcy huffs.

"Oh. Shit. Claire is like the nicest person I know."

"Exactly. So, I vetted another worker, one who assured me she could handle any type of client, and well, here we are," she huffs, tossing the dish towel on the counter.

"What was the problem this time? Did she quit or—"

"No. He fired this one too. Said she smelled like his…Aunt Loretta, I believe, and that he could feel her staring at him and didn't like the way she breathed so heavily."

A live-in assisted living caregiver doesn't pay as well as what I'm used to as a certified therapist, but it would be a roof over my head and a bed that I earned on my own rather than charity from someone who's seen me at my worst. I can breathe quietly. I never stare. Dallas taught me how to master both of those things, when I learned it was best to go unnoticed if he was in a foul mood. I don't know what an *Aunt Loretta* smells like, but surely, my scent can't compare to a woman's. Maybe I've got a chance.

I can save up enough money to get my own place until Marcy finds another long-term VRT position for me. I can recuperate enough until I can ride my bike again or buy another one, if Dallas has trashed mine. It's a halfway house that will allow me to reclaim some of my pride. It's my ticket to forgetting about handsome faces that make me forget my sense of good judgement.

Drying my hands, my voice sounds more confident than it has in a long time. "I'll take it."

Chapter 6

HARPER

With the flutter of my heartbeat in my throat, I wrap on the ominous white door on the twelfth floor of the swanky Little Hell neighborhood apartment complex. Clearly, this Mr. Davenport can afford me. I'm about to get the chance to sleep in style when all I was hoping for was a clean twin-size mattress. I can only hope his family isn't around to get a look at my bruised face and ruin this for me before I even get in the door.

Be confident. Be firm, polite, but firm, I school myself as I wait.

Lots of people who lose their vision learn to adapt. Mr. Davenport's complaints to the agency will not deter me. I'm trained and more than capable to do this job. There'll be no misunderstandings, no intimidation, no foul disposition I can't handle. I lived with Dallas for three years. I can do this. I will *not* be Riley Davenport's strike-three. I can't. I need a roof over my head.

The grumbling of curse words on the other side of the door precedes it opening. Straightening up, I hold my breath, and then…I hold it some more. Are you kidding me?

Riley Davenport wasn't supposed to have incredibly handsome golden skin, floppy sun-streaked hair, the most perfectly kissable lips I've ever seen, and captivating green eyes. I swallow a self-pitying groan. Either homelessness and starvation or a perpetual hard on are in my future. The man in front of me is everything I've sworn myself off forever.

"Shit. That was fast!" he says through a mouthful of… cheese crackers?

"Um… Mr. Davenport? Hello, I'm…"

He shifts a baseball bat to the crook of his elbow where he's holding a red box of crackers. His arm extends, bringing his hand toward my chest. Marcy said his file indicated he was on the low vision spectrum when he registered. Maybe his depth perception is off. I raise my hand to shake his, but instead he pats my chest. His hand drops lower, and he pokes his fingers at my middle like he's searching for something, making me wince.

Frowning, he looks up. "You got the goods?"

"The *goods?*"

"Yeah. I asked for three boxes of *Better Cheddars.*"

I blink, reduced to speaking in slow motion. "*Better...Cheddars?*"

His brow creases. He rotates the box in his hand and speaks like I'm the dumbest person on the planet. "The world's most delicious cracker? Tiny circles of cheesy goodness?"

"Uh, no. Sorry. I...don't have any."

His heavy sigh reaches my face. "You know, blind people can leave grocery delivery reviews too. Right? Rita and I have a close relationship, and that woman does not take kindly to delivery mishaps."

Jesus. He's hot and has issues. Just my luck. Am I a magnet for attractive head cases?

"Mr. Davenport, I think there's been a misunderstanding. I'm from Home Reach, the caregiver agency you contacted."

His brow furrows again. He rummages in his cracker box, retrieving what appears to be the last handful of his kryptonite and shoves it in between his sexy lips. "You're not from Fresh Farm?"

"No. My name's Harper Reid. I'm here to..."

"Do you have any snacks?"

"*Snacks?*"

"Yeah. *Snacks.* Chocolate dream cakes. *Funyuns.* Oh! Or maybe those little donut packs, but not the crunchy coconut ones. Those things are an abomination to all things snack related."

I have no clue where my next meal is coming from, and the thing that stands between me and landing this job depends on my ability to produce snacks? Slack-jawed, swallowing air between me and Snacky McSnackers, my single remaining nutrient rich brain cell remembers my mad dash packing to get out of the apartment last week before Dallas returned.

"I...think I might have a granola bar in my backpack."

The entrancing green eyes narrow in my direction as though I've spoken blasphemy. "*Granola?*"

A word has never been uttered with such contempt. I'm doomed. He takes a step back. A second later, the door slams in my face.

My side still aches from Dallas' roughhousing. I'm hungry, my pride having made me forgo Marcy's offer of breakfast. Combined with my injuries, my poor sleep from crashing on Marcy's couch all week is leading to a level of exhaustion I've never known. With that slam of the door, all my hopes go up in flames along with my last shred of fortitude.

I drop my forehead to the wood with a *thunk*, wondering if I even have the energy to make it back to Marcy's place. My resting place gives way, causing me to stagger forward. I blink through bleary eyes at a contemplative Riley Davenport.

We stare. Judging by the way his gaze pings around my head, I wonder if he even knows I'm still here.

And then he asks, curiously, "What kind of granola bar?"

I've never been so relieved to have a questionable snack in my gym bag. Dropping to a knee, I unzip my backpack, trying to remember which pouch I put it in.

"Uh, I think…it's fruit and nut."

Glancing up to see if my token will meet his approval, I'm met with a curled upper lip. "No chocolate chips?"

Shit. Is this really happening?

"No, sorry."

My shoulders sag, feeling every ounce of the weight of his sigh. The door slams shut again. I stare at it stupidly with my inadequate granola bar in my hand. Today is not my day. This week is not my week, but this life—the messy, screwed up life I got myself into—is mine.

Shifting, I ease down onto my ass and use the door that won't open to me as support. At least I can get some benefit from it. My phone vibrates in my pocket. I'd like to think it's Marcy, asking me how my introduction with the *Louisville Snack Smuggler* went, but I somehow doubt my luck is that good today.

I've been working with the vision impaired for five years now. Letting my eyes slip shut, I bask in the darkness that I teach about. Sometimes I wish I could block out all the pain and ugliness I've seen. I know it's not that simple, and that it's a fool's dream to wish for a lack of sight, but I wouldn't mind blotting out a few memories just to drop some of the weight I'm carrying.

There's a creaking noise a second before I tumble backward. Peering up from where I'm sprawled on the floor across Riley Davenport's threshold, I stifle a delirious laugh at the sight above me. A smattering of sandy hair decorates his shapely calf muscles, rising all the way to the shadows inside the legs of his basketball shorts. His broad shoulders cast a shadow over me. Strands of hair, falling over his forehead, he gazes down at me with *those eyes*. Even at this angle he's probably the most handsome man I've ever seen.

"Can you cook?"

"Yeah. Yes, I can cook."

"Well, get your granola in here and let's talk."

I don't even care that manners appear to be out of the question. Scrambling to my feet, I shoulder my duffel bag and backpack, following him into the apartment.

Baseball bat slung across the back of his shoulders, wrists hooked over each end of it, you wouldn't think he has vision issues by the way he sizes me up as he leans against his kitchen counter. The space is an open concept that expands into a generous living room where the hardwood flooring ends and switches to beige carpeting. Beyond the living room, a wide archway opens to a hallway with more wood flooring, extending in either direction. The only door I can see is open, revealing a home gym that looks twice the size of my old bedroom. It's floor to ceiling windows overlook the rooftop, littered with potted trees and an outdoor dining area.

If this goes well, Riley Davenport will be my most well-off client yet to date. If I'd had whatever resources he does when I was a kid, I would have put my mother in a place like this.

"So, how about this? Three days a week, from eight a.m. to eleven a.m. You can make breakfast, clean up afterward, and then do lunch before you take off for the day. That way, I'll get a few home cooked meals and housekeeping help, enough so that my mother doesn't give herself an ulcer."

Wait a minute. Part-time? I can't live off part-time.

"The agency coordinator said this was a full-time position."

"Yeah, but I did some thinking over the weekend and changed my mind. *Louis'* been helping me with my navigation," he elaborates, shifting his bat, "and I managed to scrub my surfaces without asphyxiating myself. I just need help with a few things I can't do as well as before my accident."

Oh, God. No. Who knows how long until another live-in position opens up.

"Mr. Davenport, I really need this job."

"Well, you've got it. For now. My insurance said it'd cover five more months-worth of home care."

"No. I mean, the agency said it was for *live-in* care."

I've already hit rock bottom, so deciding to beg and humiliate myself is actually an easy decision. It's June. Five months would put a roof over my head until November.

"I...I don't have anywhere to go at the moment, actually. So, I'm asking you to please reconsider that part. I promise I won't be a burden."

He's frowning again. That's not a good sign.

"Where did you live before this?"

"In Irving Park with…" I catch myself, realizing he didn't ask for all the details, but judging by his expression, he's waiting for me to finish my slip up. "With…someone."

"Break up?" he ventures with a knowing smirk. If he knew my someone was a man, would he still find it comical? The fewer details the better.

"Yeah."

"Welcome to the club."

"Oh. I…I'm sorry to hear that."

"Why? She could have been a serial killer."

I have no words, although I agree with his logic. This is definitely not first impression conversation though, so I'm at a loss as to how to proceed.

Working his jaw, he keeps his gaze trained in my direction. I don't know why I'm trying to hold his. The effect those observant green eyes are having on me is simply not rational. More than seeing the fading bruises on my face, it feels like he's looking into my soul.

Sighing, he swings his bat down to the floor and leans on it. "Fine, but you'll have to add a few dinners to your schedule."

"Great! That's great. I can do that. Thank you so much. You won't—"

"Guest bedroom is over there," he interrupts, aiming his bat toward the far end of the hallway. "You can use the bathroom in the hallway. I've got one in my room. I get up early to work out. I don't like to be disturbed."

"Sure. I won't disturb you, that is. I'll make myself useful and stay out of your way just please let me know whenever you need anything."

"How'd you get into home care?"

"I didn't, exactly. I'm a VRT, but there weren't any VRT openings with Home Reach at the moment."

"VRT?"

"Vision rehabilitation specialist."

"What is that exactly?"

"I help people learn how to adapt to their low vision."

He lets loose a scoff. "What? Like teaching them how to be blind? Newsflash—I already figured that out the hard way."

"No, it's more like introducing techniques and services, teaching how to read Braille, and I'm not certified in *O and M*, but I know mobility techniques to help get around outdoors and manage seeing eye dogs."

"You can see, but you can read Braille?"

It comes out as such an accusation, instinct tells me to defend myself, but his concerning lack of terminology and methods tugs at my heart. Marcy said he started losing his sight six months ago. Standing before

49

me like a cave man with his baseball bat, I want to ask, how has no one helped this man yet?

"Yeah. It takes a while to learn. Usually, people who lose their vision later in life don't even bother with it but knowing at least elevator buttons is handy."

He considers my input for a moment and then frowns.

"Did my mother request they send you over here?"

The displeasure in his tone hints at defiance. Maybe *that's* why no one's helped him. The stubbornness is rolling off him in waves.

"No. Our coordinator made me aware that you have no interest in learning any adaptation skills. I'm not here to force anything on you. My background is just a coincidence. I swear. I just needed the work, any work."

"Why do you think I have no interest? You think I like running into shit?"

Wow. Maybe I was wrong again. Note to self—stop trying to figure out Riley Davenport because you suck at it.

"Mar— Um, the agency said your family caregiver declined VRT at your consultation. Did you...have someone call on your behalf initially?"

Face reddening, he pinches the bridge of his nose and mutters under his breath, "Fucking Val."

I have no idea who Val is and don't dare impose by asking. I've barely gotten my foot in the door, and his mood doesn't exactly scream forgiving at the moment, so I keep silent, waiting for his cue.

"I'm going to go work out," he blurts, starting toward the hallway.

"O-okay. Would you like breakfast?" I ask feebly.

"I'm not hungry."

"Alright. Should I—" my voice is lost amidst the thumping sounds of his bat against the drywall.

He stomps into the gym, kicking the door shut behind him. Before I can contemplate my next move, my phone buzzes in my pocket.

I forgot I told Marcy I'd check in with her. This didn't go exactly as I planned, but at least I can tell her I'm employed for the moment. How long this moment will last, I have no clue. Except, it's not a message from Marcy.

DALLAS: You're going to fucking regret this.

A stereo kicks on full blast beyond the gym door, the opening chords of "Dirty Deeds Done Dirty Cheap" by AC/DC pulse through the glass, a clear do not disturb message. I'm as wanted here as I am at home.

"Yeah," I huff tiredly to the empty room. "Pretty sure I regret every decision I make."

Chapter 7

RILEY

Scratch worrying about becoming autophobic. Solitude is apparently the only means of finding honesty and avoiding humiliation. How stupid am I for letting Val handle all my affairs after the accident?

"Oh, that Home Reach place? Yeah, I called them. It's like housekeeping services for the elderly. It's nothing I can't do. Why waste your money?"

Now that Rita's explained to me what a VRT is, I can only imagine what this Harper guy thinks of me and my fucking baseball bat. He didn't talk to me like I was stupid or anything, but his patience and reluctance in divulging his specialty made it obvious he was sparing my feelings for being behind the curve.

Learning Braille for elevator buttons? Why didn't I consider that in all these months? It'd be easy to blame Val dragging and pushing me along as my crutch, but I should have been more proactive.

Laughing, I speak into the evening breeze. "And you told him he can be your cook. Nice one, Riley."

On second thought, I might not recant that request. His last two meals were the best I've had in ages. Dude can freaking cook. This throws a wrench in my groveling plans though. How hard will I have to kiss his ass to get him to show me his Yoda skills for the blind *and* keep *cheffing* it up for me? A man can only humble himself so much in one year.

The crunch of pea gravel behind me draws my head instinctively toward the sound. It's strange that I can sense objects and people's presences now. I thought it was some bizarre blind superpower I slowly inherited as a gift when my retinas got fucked beyond repair. Rita says it's called echolocation, the reflection of sound off objects. Right now, the sounds of the city are reflecting off one Harper Reid.

I've avoided him for the last day and a half, absconding with his culinary offerings like a rabid ingrate to the rooftop patio table, where

I sulked over the absolute waste that I've made of the last six months of my situation thanks to an interrogation of Rita about vision rehabilitation therapy. I realize now, I spent half of those months hoping the doctors could salvage my vision and the other half of it, allowing myself to be coddled by people whom I don't want to be here or won't be here the rest of my life. Okay, give or take a few weeks of me being an idiot when I snuck my lack of supervision past Leigh Ann. I am an idiot, an idiot who now has to do the thing I've come to loathe most—ask for help.

"Mr. Davenport?" Harper calls out, a tremor in his voice.

I don't think I've ever met a more soft-spoken man. It's odd though. He's got this low, thick timbre that'd be perfect for radio or cologne commercials if he put a little more confidence behind his words.

"Yeah?"

"Wh-what are you doing?"

"Getting some air."

"Sitting on the roof ledge?"

"It's my thinking spot." Slapping the space beside me, I offer what I hope is a white flag of truce. "Check it out. You can get a great view of the city up here."

"N-no. No, thanks," he clips, gravel crunching under his feet in earnest now. "Um, why…why don't you get down."

It's a statement, not a suggestion. Maybe I don't suck at not seeing as bad as I thought because the evident concern in his tone has me chuckling. Val's monotone made it difficult to decipher sincerity from sarcasm. I've known Harper less than two days, but his expressive voice is already a breath of fresh air. Maybe there still is some honesty outside of solitude.

"What? Are you worried I'll fall? Wait…did you think I was going to jump?"

"No! I mean, no," he adds with more calm, kind of the way you would address someone who you think was about to jump. "Just it's… it's not safe. We're really high up."

"It's fine. I do it all the time." Rocking back, I swing my legs where they're dangling over the side of the building to show off my air of calm.

"That's…that's great, but could you just maybe get down? Please?"

A trembling hand clamps onto my bicep. Strange. There's that sweet sugar cookie scent I caught when I let him in yesterday. No fucking granola bar in the world smells like that. It must be him.

"Are you shaking?" I scoff when I feel a tremor run from his arm to mine.

"You're freaking me out, to be honest," he says on a breathless laugh.

"Why are *you* freaking out? You're not the one on the ledge."

"No one will ever eat my cooking again, if they think it drove you to jump."

Okay. That was pretty good, even though he still sounds like he saw a ghost. Suppressing a laugh, I make a dramatic sigh and swing my legs around over the ledge. No sense in giving the guy a heart attack if he's got skills *and* a sense of humor.

"Fine, throw in a few pizzas, and I'll keep your secret."

He lets out another breathless laugh, still clutching my arm and urging me away from the edge. "Deal."

"Geez, man. Breathe. What? Are you afraid of heights?" I razz, swatting him in the ribs with the back of my hand.

A sharp intake of breath cuts through the cacophony of city noises. He lets out a strangled sound, his arm brushing against mine, telling me he's doubled over.

What the hell? Is he that fragile?

"There's no way that hurt," I tease.

Panting, his reply is strained. "I have some cracked ribs. They're just a little sore still. Sorry. Not trying to be dramatic."

"Oh, shit. Sorry. How'd that happen?"

"My...roommate and I had a disagreement."

The vague explanation takes me aback enough to extinguish my embarrassment over feeling like a bull in a china shop. I don't think Rob and I have scrapped in years, but when we did, it certainly never resulted in serious bodily injury.

"What kind of disagreement leads to cracked ribs?" I laugh, disbelieving this soft-spoken man could engage in a physical altercation.

"Uh, the kind where I asked him why he spent all of our money."

Friends don't steal money behind their friend's back. His roommate sounds like a piece of shit.

Wait a minute. He said *roommate*. I thought he was out of a place to live because of a break-up? Something's not adding up.

My ruminations must increase his anxiety because he adds, "I'm not trouble. I swear. I never get in fights."

That has me snickering, recalling how many fights I've found myself in over the years, mostly in my younger partying days. Whatever his secrets are, he's clearly not comfortable divulging more than the bare minimum to my questions. I don't know what it is, but something tells me he's not a threat. The brush of his arm lets me know he's wearing a damn long sleeve button up. Guys who wear dress shirts at home and talk like it's their first day at a new school sure as hell aren't the antagonizing type.

I don't care about his past or his situation. He's the first tolerable human being this agency has sent. He's not bossy. He left me the hell alone while I sulked the last twenty-four hours, and he can teach me the independence I need. Clapping him gently on the shoulder so as not to cause him more pain, I impart my reassurances.

"Well, he sounds like a right dick. I hope you at least gave it back as good as you got it."

Another nervous laugh, such a defeated sound. "Not hardly. He's an MMA trainer."

Jesus. The lean muscle I felt under my hand a moment ago speaks of a modest build and a height close to my five-foot eleven frame. I don't know if the rest of this guy is shredded like Rob said the rest of me is getting, but I'm no cage fighter. I like my teeth. And who the fuck uses their martial arts training outside of a ring? That seems to violate some honor code if you ask me.

"So, I, uh, made quesadillas for dinner," he hedges, changing the subject. "That's…that's why I came out to get you. I can try to do pizza tomorrow."

The information is enough, a glimpse of who this stranger in my home is. Maybe I'm getting soft now that I can't see, but a sense of kindredness takes root. I'm not the only one who needs help. No place to live, no money, and apparently a recent ass-beating? The guy's having a hell of a week from the sounds of it. I've never wished anyone ill before but knowing he's as down on his luck as me makes me feel less like…*less*.

"Fuck homemade. I have every pizza delivery place's number within a twenty-mile radius saved in my phone," I tell him as we start toward my bedroom's patio doors.

"Alright." He chuckles. The appropriateness of it this time pleases me. Maybe I've lifted his spirits after my unintentional interrogation of his life.

"So," I preface, "A VRT, huh? If I wanted to learn about some things, would I be taking advantage of your knowledge of that stuff since I'm getting you at a caretaker's rate instead?"

"No! No, I don't mind at all. I'd be happy to go over whatever you want. I'm just grateful for the work and…and the lodging. Really. I'm at your disposal."

Disposal? I know that's a common, polite phrase, but given what I know about him, I can't help but see a picture of a guy who'd give anyone the shirt off his back if they needed it.

"Okay, cool." My bat hits the glass of the patio door, letting me know I've reached the entrance. "What do you suggest for starters? Clearly, skydiving is out of the question."

"Yeah, that's, uh, not until the advanced lessons," he jokes.

He walks ahead of me into my room, waiting to slide the door closed behind me. Not once has he grabbed my arm or nudged me from behind the way Val always used to do. Being trusted to roam free is liberating. I'm someone's equal, not their chore. If he's like this all the time, we might get along just fine.

"You said you're familiar with seeing eye dogs. I'd always meant to get a dog, but then I started dating this woman who hated them. Guess that should have been a red flag right there, but she was hot. You know?"

"No judgment here. I've been known to give up dreams for an attractive face myself."

"Right? What the hell is wrong with us?" My bat clips the corner of my desk where it sits opposite my bed, resounding off the metal frame. Continuing through the doorway down the hall toward the kitchen, my stomach growls at the scent of Mexican delicacy.

This guy can never quit on me. Holy shit. That smells amazing.

"So, anyway," I continue. "I think that's what I'd like to do. Do you have special hook-ups being a VRT? Where can I get a trained dog?"

He slides me a plate, the edge of it stopping just as it brushes my knuckles. Clever. I like his non-intrusive style.

"Oh, um. Well, that's great that you're open to the idea, but it's not exactly a quick and simple process."

"What do you mean? Do they do a background check like shelters do to make sure you're not some psychotic abuser or felon? Because I'll pass, if that's what you're worried about. Don't let the baseball bat fool you."

"No, it's more than that. They want to make sure you have a certain amount of mobility on your own first. Do you…not like your walking cane?"

Great. I'm failing at mobility.

"Yeah. If I could find the damn thing. I think my ex might have thrown it out. She said it was embarrassing."

"Oh." He pauses, not commenting on my accusation, his form shifting in the starburst of dim light in my vision that decreases with each passing week. "I found it folded up under the kitchen sink yesterday. I'll just set it here to your left, if you want it," he adds, placing it on the island counter.

Son of a bitch. That's what I get for dumping her at a luncheon in front of other people. Reuniting with my walking cane, I relinquish my bat on the counter, determined to leave the past in the past. It's time to move forward, time to embrace my new life, and this Harper guy is going to be my ticket to doing so.

"Thanks. So, where's the closest place to get an *eye-dog?*"

"The closest training facility is in Michigan, in Kalamazoo, actually, but—"

"Kalamazoo? Cool. That's only two and a half hours away from Chicago. Do you have a car?"

"No. I just use public transit, but—"

"Can you drive though? Do you have a license? I've still got my car in the parking garage."

"Yeah, I do, but I don't think you can just go pick up a guide dog the day of. It can take months."

"Well, we can at least go check it out. Right? Like get me on their waiting list or whatever? Can you set that up?"

"Um, yeah. Sure. I'll call them tomorrow."

"Great."

I haven't been brimming with excitement like this since the last app Rob and I launched. It's a way forward, a step toward independence, a step away from helplessness. I'm suddenly eager to discover every tool available to me, to test my limits and break through them.

"And Braille?" I preface. "How do I go about learning that?"

"You...want to learn Braille?"

"Yeah. Why not? That whole elevator button thing you said— I've been taking the stairs down to get my mail just to get out of the apartment."

I'm not about to admit that the thought of leaving the building by myself since Val moved out has been too terrifying to attempt. Letting Mom and Dad think I had help these past two months was only a bandage over a festering wound to keep them at bay. I didn't do myself any favors. I've got to make the most of the five months I get this guy, or I'll either end up a hermit or holding a ladder in my childhood bedroom while Leigh Ann bleaches the light fixtures.

Moaning around a bite of quesadilla, I explain my rationale. "I mean, I always took the elevator before, so I'd like to be able to do so again. I'll be old and decrepit someday, if I'm lucky. Stairs probably won't be appealing when that happens."

"Yeah. That's good, actually—doing things you used to do. I know it might seem daunting at first, but non-sighted people can do pretty much everything *sighties* can."

"*Sighties?*"

"Oh," he chuckles. "Uh, *sighted people*. That's what non-sighted people call them sometimes."

Snorting, I nod, processing that I'll now have my own lingo. I wonder what Rob will think about being called a *sightie*?

"Alrighty, *Sightie*," I quip. "Bring on the Braille. Let's get this party started."

56

"Mr. Davenport—"

"*Riley*," I correct, licking sauce off my fingers. "You'll sound like a butler if you call me Mr. Davenport."

"Okay. Well, I just want to make sure you're aware that some of this stuff might not come easy. I don't want you to be frustrated if something doesn't work for you right away."

The optimism bubbling inside me quells at the warning, choked by a resurfacing of the desperation that's been creeping in these last few weeks. Leveling my gaze in his direction, I hope my expression conveys my seriousness.

"It's got to. I can't spend the rest of my life depending on other people. I need to stand on my own two feet. Can you understand that?"

I've just laid it all out on the line to a complete stranger. I'm holding my breath like my fate is in his hands. Why? Damned if I know. The agency could probably send another VRT over that might be even more qualified now that I know I can request someone with that background, but something tells me this shy, cookie-scented, homeless man is the one. Maybe it's the even playing field. He's got nothing left to lose, and I've got everything to lose that I have left.

"Yeah," the smooth voice finally says. "I understand."

"Alright." I breathe out. "Cool." It occurs to me I wasn't exactly a gracious host yesterday. Guess I have more damage control to do. "So, did you get settled in okay?"

"Yeah. Thank you."

"You got enough room for your stuff?"

"Oh, I don't have much, just what's in my duffel bag. I set it in the closet for now."

"You can hang your shit up, or are you having second thoughts about the job?"

"No. It's not that. I'm happy to be here. There's…some women's clothing in the closet though, so I didn't want to mess with anybody's stuff."

"What?"

When he doesn't answer, I force myself to relinquish the best quesadilla I've ever eaten. How come Val had to leave shit all over my apartment if she was also occupying my guest room closet like a hoarder? And who moves out and doesn't take all their shit? No wonder she keeps texting me to get together. Was she thinking I'd ask her to come back?

Over my trash panda ass, she is. I'm Leigh Ann Davenport's son. I know how to clean house.

"*Sightie*, hook me up with the box of garbage bags, will you? They should be under the kitchen sink."

Chapter 8

HARPER

So, Riley's mobility is exceptional when it comes to exorcising his ex's clothes and thirty-seven pairs of designer shoes from his guest room closet. He's a force of nature like I've never seen before, all fluid movements, wild sandy hair falling into his eyes. It's plain to see that although he's clearly irritated at the moment, the man has one speed for everything—determined.

"Fool a trash panda once, shame on you," he mutters, stuffing a purse into the final garbage bag. "Fool a trash panda twice, shame on your *Louis Vuitton*."

And my dumb ass just agreed to take him to the guide dog facility in Kalamazoo. I blame my nerves and the lack of sleep my first night in a stranger's home for making me agree to anything the man wants. I blame the lure of a soft bed and a paycheck. Quite possibly, I also blame the way he moans when he eats and how it makes my recently abused body warm inside like it didn't learn it's lesson.

His gung-ho attitude mixed with that sad desperation on his face when he said he wanted to stand on his own were too difficult to say no to. I'm glad he's interested in VRT, but will he bag up my stuff with as much gusto once he learns it's at least a six-month process to get a guide dog?

I was used to disappointing Dallas. I don't even know Riley Davenport, but the thought of disappointing him seems like a failure I'd not recover from. Maybe it's that light I sense inside him, a light I've never known. Some people are just meant to burn bright, and Riley is one of them. I don't think I have the talent to help him reclaim all his illumination at the speed he desires.

"Would you like me to do something with these bags?" I offer, hating my idleness, since he refused to let me help.

"There's a trash chute at the end of the hallway."

Oh. Damn. He's not playing around.

I don't know why someone would think a walking cane is embarrassing but instinct tells me to pity anyone losing their possessions. I can't reunite this woman with her clothes, but it seems like a waste to toss them all.

"I volunteer at a community center sometimes. They have a clothing donation program to help people looking for job interview attire. Instead of throwing all this away, would you consider donating it to the center maybe?"

Straightening up, he frowns. Me and my stupid mouth, constantly over-stepping with my need to help. Dallas always said I can't leave well enough alone.

"Yeah. That's a great idea. Go for it," he says. "Better someone who can use it who needs it. Come to think of it, I've got some polo shirts in my closet we can throw in here too. Polo shirts would be good for interviews. Right?"

And then he smiles. My God, it's the definition of what a smile should be. The fact that it's over something I suggested sparks a tiny ember inside me as though he's spreading his energy.

What the hell am I thinking?

Remember yourself, Harper. Get a grip.

I stifle a sardonic laugh. I've let Dallas beat my self-esteem down so far, I'm treating an approving smile like a gold medal.

"Yeah. For sure. Alright. I'll call the center and arrange for someone to pick this stuff up."

"You want to get started on the Braille now?" he asks.

Fuck.

And there goes all my hopes of keeping this job. Once he finds out that learning Braille isn't a snap of the fingers, will he send me packing like the last two workers?

I'm a VRT.

Way to go, big mouth. It's my luck he went from no interest in VRT to wanting to learn everything in a week.

Twenty minutes later, sitting on his living room couch, I warily hand him my sensory trainer book that I packed.

"What's this?" he asks, running his fingertips over the fabric swatches on the first page.

"Before diving into Braille, most people start with this sensory training. It helps you get used to different textures."

"Fabric? Dude, I just spent the last half hour elbow-deep in fabric. I think I'm good."

"Well, because Braille consists of fine, tiny dots that are difficult to distinguish at first, it's good to train your sense of touch to differentiate

59

between the slightest change in texture, otherwise the Braille might not make any sense."

"What? Like this'll heighten my *spidey* senses?"

"Sort of. Think of it as being a marksman. The more you practice, the better odds you'll have at hitting a small target."

He hums, considering the tedious task and then lets out a sigh. "Alright. Makes sense, I guess."

Okay, he's being rather…accepting. Maybe the last two Home Reach workers just caught him at a bad time.

I guide him through the first two pages, letting him know when he's incorrectly identified a fabric section as the same as the previous. The subtle changes are difficult to detect, but his expression doesn't reveal as much frustration as I anticipated. The furrow in his brow is the same focused look he had each time he stepped out of his gym the last two days, sweat-soaked and wrecked to the point of exhaustion. When has sweat ever been that sexy?

When he asks to practice studying the textures on his own, I pull my phone out and send a text off to Daniel to let him know I'm alright. Bringing up my audiobook app, I pop in my earbuds. It looks like Riley isn't ready to give up yet, and I haven't listened to a story in a week given the chaos my life has been.

While everything about this prospect leaves me uncertain, there's a sense of safety here, an air of peace. I can't put my finger on it, but it probably has something to do with coming to terms with just how on edge I'd become whenever Dallas was due home over the last few months. How did I let myself get used to living like that?

"You can turn the TV on," Riley's raspy voice interrupts my thoughts. "Just because I can't see it doesn't mean you can't watch it."

"Thanks, but I'm good. I don't watch much television."

"Really? Well, you were cool until you said that. If you're just going to sit there in silence staring at me, this might get a little creepy."

"I wasn't staring." I laugh. "I was listening to an audio-book on my phone."

"An audiobook?"

"Yeah, with my earbuds in, so…technically I guess I was ignoring you."

Why did I say that? He's not Daniel who I can razz freely.

"I take it back," he says sternly. "You're not cool at all. Are you?"

What the? Alright. I guess he's asking for razzing, but sadly his guess is accurate.

"No, I'm not, actually. If you were looking for cool, you really struck out."

"I'm fucking with you. I'm rubbing satin squares like Buffalo Bill here, while you're partying it up over there."

"I'd hardly call an audiobook a party, but they're entertaining. I like getting lost in the visuals and tuning everything else out."

He doesn't say anything, his fingers slowly working over the book. Now I *am* staring. There's something way too endearing in the way his brow furrows and his bottom lip presses into the top one when he's thinking.

"I started listening to podcasts," he says softly. "There's some comedy ones I like, but after a while it feels like I'm listening to them just to kill time." His humorless laugh squeezes my heart.

"Maybe you'd like audiobooks. It's nice to shut your brain off and let someone tell you a story."

"I'll look into it." He shrugs. "I work out too. I'm not a total basket case."

"Yeah. You seemed to hit it pretty hard the last two days. It's impressive that you handle the treadmill so well. The balance is good for your mobility."

"I don't go that fast. I used to run a lot faster, but I found out my limits after a few wipe outs," he says with a wry smile.

"Well, I've been known to fall off a non-moving treadmill, so I'm still impressed."

"Are you clumsy or just not athletic?"

"I do better in the water. I was on the swim team in high school."

"Swim team?" He grins, mischievously lopsided. "Wow, the cool points just keep coming off."

"Hey, I warned you."

A pleasant silence settles between us, but I'm reluctant to get back to my book. Maybe it's because of the little smile that hasn't left his lips. It's been so long since I made anyone happy, truly happy. It shouldn't feel this rewarding.

"Okay. Now you *are* staring. I can feel it."

"Sorry. I was just—" *Staring at your mouth?* Yeah, because that's not totally inappropriate. Marcy really could have warned me he was a smoke show. "I wondered what you did for a living, before your accident."

Snickering, his eyes crinkle at the corners. I've never seen laughter literally bubble so much from a person.

"I was an app designer. Go on. Say it."

"Say what?"

"How uncool that is. I'm a secret geek."

61

"I didn't think that. App design is actually pretty complicated, I imagine. Once again, I'm impressed. I'd have guessed Taekwondo instructor or something."

"You want to know something cool? My Rita app that I use? The one that talks to me?"

"Yeah?"

"Me and my buddy Rob designed it with vocal recognition software. If you've got a good thirty-second clip of someone speaking, you can program the app to speak to you in that voice."

"Wait. *You* designed the Rita app? Like *the* Rita app?"

"Yeah." He chuckles, combing his fingers through his hair.

"Well, you were right. I'm nowhere near that cool."

"You did find my walking cane after it went missing for like two months. Don't sell yourself short."

"True," I concede because he seems to relax the more we banter. *I* feel more relaxed the more we banter. I've never done in-home care. Is banter allowed? "So, can I ask? Why *Rita?*"

He turns his head and looks right at me, his grin splitting his face. Jesus. The man is way too attractive. I've never been so grateful that someone couldn't see. I can only imagine my expression would give me away.

"She was this really sassy convenience store clerk near the college campus where Rob and I studied. We were joking around about whose voices we'd like to use for automation apps and hers got a unanimous vote from the both of us, so we drove back to see her and asked to get a recording."

"That's hysterical. She didn't mind knowing she'd be the voice in your daily life?"

"Not after we told her we were giving her ten percent. She just thought it was cool we were naming it after her, but when we told her we wanted to give her a cut, since she was one of the reasons we got the idea, she wanted to adopt us."

"Wow. That was...really generous of you."

"Not really." He shrugs, brushing away any notions of conceit. "It kind of ruined the whole thing, to be honest."

"How so?"

"Because she wasn't sassy anymore after that. She couldn't stop thanking us and hugging us. It totally ruined the image I had of her in my mind."

Shaking my head, I don't know what to make of this man who's laughing at his own nuances. How can he be the same person who fired two Home Reach workers? Underneath that veil of dissatisfaction I've seen glimpses of, he's joy personified, a rambunctious kid in a man's body.

It's sad, so damn sad that a man like that loses his vision, a man who seems to appreciate everything. And somewhere across town is a man who doesn't appreciate anything he sees and leaves the world an uglier place wherever he goes.

Chapter 9

RILEY

The smell of the parking garage reminds me of freedom. What a cruel smell it is. I'm ecstatic to be getting out of the apartment, pumped I'm about to get a dog, but it's still evident that I can only do those two things because Harper is going to drive me. It puts things into perspective. How much will a lifetime of taxis cost me?

Trying to remember Harper's advice from over the past two weeks on a few walks we've taken, I flick my wrist, making an arc with my cane, rather than waving my arm back and forth like I used to as he walks beside me. There's little contrast in the dimly lit garage with its dark pavement, something else he's been teaching me about. It's preventing me from making out vehicular objects, but I remember how close the first parking space is where I keep my bike.

When my cane hits the back tire, I pause. "Motorcycle?" I ask.

"Yeah. Good call," Harper says to my left, my car keys rattling in his hand. Sometimes I think he makes noises just so it's easy for me to locate him.

"Can you do me a favor? We've got a little time. Right?"

"Yeah. We'll be early. The tour isn't until ten-thirty."

"With me not working anymore, I was thinking that I should probably sell my motorcycle. Can you help me uncover it and take some pictures with your phone I can use to post somewhere online later?"

"Oh, um. Sure. Of course. This is yours, huh?"

Peeling off the cover, my hands itch to feel the vibrations of the motor through the handlebars, the warm June wind in my hair. "Yeah. No sense in keeping it though. I'm going to need to make my budget stretch if I want to keep living here unless I buy some little house in the suburbs like where I grew up."

The idea actually is more tempting than not, but I'm grateful he doesn't offer his sympathies about me having to downscale. Plus, it's probably in poor taste to complain about finances to a guy that had no-where to live two weeks ago.

Cover off, I run my hand over the chrome of the fuel tank, down the leather seat. What I'd give for just one more ride. Hell, even just to sit on it.

Hm. Not a bad idea.

"We should probably start it, make sure the battery isn't dead," I tell him absently.

"Oh, uh. S-sure." The keys jangle in his hand, and he adds, "I…will I tip it over?"

"You've never been on a bike?"

"On the back of my friend Daniel's a few times, but I've never driven one."

Zoning in on the rattle of the keys, I snatch them from his hand and throw my leg over the seat. "Hm. That's a shame."

I slip the key into the ignition like it's second nature. Funny how you never lose some abilities, even if they're useless talents now. Turning it over, the motor rumbles to life, charging all the dead spaces inside of me. Amazing how a piece of machinery can make you feel alive. The urge to move, to grasp onto more of that sensation, takes hold. The kick-stand flips up behind my boot through another muscle memory motion.

"Um, Riley?" Harper calls. "What…what are you doing?"

"We should probably drive it around the garage," I tell him mat-ter-of-factly as I walk the bike backward out of the parking space, detecting the apprehension in his voice. "Don't want the tires to get a flat spot from it sitting for so long."

"But I…don't know how to drive a motorcycle."

I have to bite my cheek to fight a smile. He's just too easy. "Well, there's only one way to learn."

"You…you can't be serious."

When I get the bike to where I think it's lined up to clear the driving lane of the garage, I call out, "You coming?"

"No. No, please don't."

The gravity of his tone is too much to hold back my laughter. "Are you scared of everything?"

He takes a moment to consider, before answering solemnly, "Yes, actually."

I can't say I figured the answer would be any different, but I'm sur-prised he admitted it. Harper, Harper, Harper.

Last week, when I got up for a glass of water one night, I heard moaning coming from his room. I figured he was rubbing one out. As tense as he is, the guy needs it, so I didn't bring it up. I'm glad I didn't because pretty much every night that I've gotten up for my midnight snack, what I heard sheds more light on the moaning. There was wailing and whimpering coming from Harper's room. What is he having nightmares about?

"That's no way to live, but suit yourself," I tell him, dying to get some of my audacious streak to rub off on him in the hopes it might help him break through his fears.

Angling my walking cane over the handle grip so I can at least feel if I get too close to the parked cars, I chuckle wondering if I look like a knight with one of those lances extended over their horse. I guess that makes it a riding cane now. Dual-purpose. Who knew?

Revving the motor, I call out, "I'll be back in a minute. Just shout out, if I'm going to hit something. Okay?"

"Wait! Jesus!" He cries, and then I feel those shaky hands of his clamp onto the back of my shoulders. The bike sways under me, but I keep it steady, smirking when I feel him scramble onto the seat behind me.

"I'm not safe. I'm not safe," he mumbles like some discouraging mantra. A little louder and closer to the side of my face, he adds, "Oh my God. I'm going to throw up. Please, Riley. You could kill somebody or hurt yourself."

"Not as long as you be my eyes. Ready?"

"Fuck no!" he barks, but it's cut off when I hit the gas, and we launch forward.

"Good. Here we go." I laugh over his terrified howl.

Arms fasten around my middle, squeezing the breath out of me so hard, I choke out a laugh. We can't even be going fifteen miles per hour. I've barely gotten my foot off the ground.

Harper doesn't seem to think I believe his scared-of-everything comment, because he's chanting, "Oh, Jesus. Oh, Jesus. Holy shit."

"Tell me when to turn," I remind him, starting to worry a bit myself. The guy's face is practically ducked into my neck, paralyzed in fear.

"Turn! Turn!"

The light spilling in from the exterior windows of the garage illuminate a vague tunnel of depth that help me gauge how wide to steer. Slowing down, I creep to a crawl, letting my feet walk us along the edge of the garage wall.

"Don't puke on me," I warn, sternly.

He answers with a moan into my neck. Shit. What if he quits on me? I hadn't even considered that.

Damn it. I guess I've had my fun for the day.

Guiding the bike in an arc, I turn us back around, laughing when he yelps as I give it some gas to clear the turn again. You know what? There really isn't such a thing as too much fun. Gunning it, or rather a sad excuse for gunning it, I break our previous speed limit back toward my parking space just to hear what other kinds of noises Harper can make.

Holy shit, his fingers are strong. I think I'll have indents of the tips embedded into my ribs. It's worth it though. This sensation of having another person cling to me as though *I'm* in control, as though they're depending on me for a change? Maybe I'm a bit of a narcissist, but it sure as hell feels better than being the one dependent on other people.

After his quaking voice guides us back into my parking space, I kill the motor and let out a satisfied sigh. "I don't know. Maybe we should keep it."

"*We?*" He scoffs. "Why?"

"At least until you learn to ride." I shrug.

His tremoring turns to the vibration of soft laughter. "Um, yeah. That's not going to happen. I can't even be a passenger without hyperventilating."

Truth. Not sure what the deal with that is, but maybe that's why life threw us together. It doesn't seem fair for him to help me if I can't help him in return somehow. I have a feeling Harper lives under a mushroom. If anyone can make him crawl out from underneath it, it's me. I've got to be good for something.

"Then you'll need a lot of lessons," I rationalize, dismounting the bike and tossing the keys at him.

Get a dog. Check.

De-scaredy-cat Harper. Check.

Today is full of purpose, and it's still early.

Chapter 10

HARPER

Just when my breakfast finally resettled into my stomach after Riley decided to show off more of his daredevil side this morning, now it's churning again. I tried to warn him that he couldn't just walk out of here with a dog.

That look on his face, the way his bottom lip is pressed into the top one, as the facility's manager explains the process to him is heart sickening. It shouldn't be. He's a grown man. Rules are rules, but the crash from his excitement that's been building over the last two weeks has my empathy meter running high. He's lost his way in life, and I can tell this was a ray of hope for him, even if his notion of guide dogs was a bit misinformed.

Following idly along behind him and the manager as she stops by yet another dog's kennel, I cringe internally. Way to rub it in that he can't get one, lady. Nothing like showing him more of what he can't have yet.

I know he can't see them, but watching him insert his fingers through the chain link panel with a sad smile on his face is more than I can bear. Today can't be over with soon enough. I can't imagine how exciting texture lessons will be after this.

The buzz of my phone in my pocket is a welcome distraction. Pulling it out, I bring up a message from Daniel.

DANIEL: Dickhead's been coming in all week. It's been all I can do not to jump over the bar after him. You're not welcome for that, by the way.

Terrific. Nothing like your friends to help remind you of things you want to forget.

ME: You did the right thing. Thank you for not starting anything with him. It's not worth it.

He doesn't answer, which is unlike Daniel. He's usually pretty chatty before he goes in for a shift at the bar he manages. Just as I'm about to tuck my phone away, however, it buzzes again.

DANIEL: He keeps asking about you.

My heart lodges in my throat. Scolding myself for the millisecond of hope I have that Dallas was asking about me to make sure I'm alright and possibly show remorse, I pinch my eyes shut. It's in my nature to believe there's good inside of everyone. Trying to turn it off is getting easier, but I don't know if I'll ever get used to it. So, I decide to tell Daniel the kind of answer he'd want to hear.

ME: I bet he does.

DANIEL: He wanted to know where you were. I didn't tell him a fucking thing.

Fuck. The familiar panic rises in my chest. I'm scared and angry all at once. Scared he'll find me. Scared he'll hurt me again. Scared I might be dumb enough to believe him if he puts on an apologetic show. And I'm furious that he's bothering Daniel, trying to get to me. They barely tolerated each other the entire time we were dating. I can only imagine how their exchange went.

ME: Daniel, watch your back. Please. Don't provoke him. And thank you for the vow of silence.

DANIEL: He can kiss my ass.

Snorting at the reply, I let out a shaky breath. Typical Daniel. He bows to no one. If I had an ounce of his tenacity, I'd have had a much different life instead of always settling for whatever I get because the thought of speaking up for myself is physically uncomfortable.

Pocketing my phone, I notice I've been left behind and hurry to catch up to Riley and the facility manager. Making my way to the end of the bay of kennels, I pull up short beside them at a smaller set of kennels on the far wall. They look older like they were what was retired when the newer kennels replaced them, but the staff kept them as spares. The manager is grimacing, looking between Riley and the smaller kennels' only occupant, an overweight golden retriever mutt.

His dark brown fur is half fluffy, half naturally shaggy. His tail beats repetitiously against his kennel as though he's impatient with being talked about. Noting Riley's frown as he directs his gaze toward the mutt, hands on his blue jean-clad hips, I catch up to the conversation.

"No, unfortunately there's no room at any of the no-kill shelters at the moment. There hasn't been for some time. We certainly aren't happy about the idea, but if the local no-kill shelter doesn't have an opening within the next week or two, we're going to send him to get put down," the manager explains.

"That's bullshit," Riley huffs. "Just because he failed guide dog training?"

"Well, Mr. Davenport, that is the sole purpose of our mission here—to train and place guide dogs with low vision candidates. We aren't a shelter. We just don't have the resources or the room. Larry didn't even come to us for training anyway. He was a stray that showed up and wouldn't leave. The staff started feeding him since he seemed passive enough, and so we tried to put him through training, but he…he just sort of does what he wants, when he wants."

"Are you hearing this, Harper?" he asks.

"Uh, yeah. Yeah, I'm right here."

Rubbing his palm over his mouth, he squints at Larry. My stomach flips. I should not have this much intuition for a man I've known only two weeks.

"We'll take him," he declares.

"Pardon?" the manager says at the exact moment, I croak, "We will?"

"Yeah. We can't let him be put down just because he's a class drop out. He could be the next dog Einstein."

"Could you excuse us for a moment?" I ask the manager, patting Riley's shoulder to turn toward me.

"I think I've got a towel in my trunk we can put in the backseat of my car. There's a pet store two blocks from my apartment," he rattles on.

"Riley? Are you sure you don't want to think this through a little more?"

"What's to think about? They're going to kill him."

"Ye-ah. I know, but he's not a trained guide dog. He might be more work than you think."

"So what? That's hardly the issue."

"Well, wouldn't you like to wait until you can get a slot at the facility here to train with a real guide dog? I mean, if you can only have one dog, why not get one that'll be of more use to you?"

His lower lip protrudes, pursing into his upper one. Those jade eyes of his laser in on me, commanding all my attention.

"Just because he's not useful like everyone else doesn't mean that he has nothing left to offer," he says, no trace of his effervescence to be found. The rise and fall of his chest, the color in his cheekbones, I know deep inside he's not talking about Larry.

How in hell do I say no to that?

"Yeah. You're right."

I don't know why he lets out a breath like he's relieved. It's not as though he needs my approval.

70

"Awesome. We're getting a dog!" He grins, clapping me on the shoulder. "Now, why don't you go tell Jedidiah the good news, while I work on busting him out of here," he whispers, motioning his head toward the manager.

"*Jedi...diah?*"

"Yeah. We can't call him Larry! That's a terrible name for a dog. This place is awful. They can't even give a dog a proper name. Why'd you bring me here?"

His whisper isn't as whispery as he thinks, so I flash the manager an apologetic smile as Riley turns on his heel and makes his way back over to her. Facing the kennel, I stare at the newest charge under my care, and once again send up thanks that Riley can't see.

Chapter 11

RILEY

Today didn't exactly turn out as I planned, but maybe that was for the best. If Harper hadn't taken me to that affluent dog academy that was holding Jedidiah hostage, poor Jed would still be a dead man walking.

We saved a life. You can't really put a measure of success on something like that.

It was just sheer luck that we stopped for lunch in that little town of Capshaw, and I got a whiff of cheese on the way out. How have I lived an hour away from a cheese factory the past eight years and not known about it? I don't get Harper. He was more ruffled about the number of dairy products I bought than about me adopting a dog I had no intention of getting before today.

"You sure you don't want some more of these?" I offer the plate of cheesy tortellini I bought at the factory and had Harper deep fry when we got back.

"Ugh. No, thank you," he groans. "Uh, I don't think it's a good idea to feed him those," he cautions. "I can still taste his farts from the drive home."

After Jed takes the tortellini from my fingers, I rub his snout. The flesh on his upper lip on one side feels uneven under my touch.

"She warned us he was gassy," I point out. "It's probably just nerves from being around all those other snobby dogs, showing off in front of him all day. Is something wrong with his face? It doesn't feel right on this side."

"Uh, yeah. He kind of has a curled upper lip on one side."

"What? Like a cleft lip?"

"Mm, no. It just sort of looks like he's sneering or permanently disgusted."

Scratching behind the mutt's ears, I smile at the softness of his fur there. "Yeah, but he's cute. Right?"

Harper chuckles. "That…might be stretching it."

"What do you mean? All dogs are cute! What's wrong with him?"

"Nothing. He's…he's perfect. He's perfectly…fine."

Well, someone's beating around the bush. What happened to honesty?

"What? You don't like dogs?" I challenge.

"I do! It's not that. He's just….just—"

"Just what?"

He lets out a flustered sputter and sighs. "I'm sorry, but I think Larry…er, Jedidiah, is possibly the ugliest dog I've ever seen."

"Are you shitting me?"

Harper's subdued laugh is such a surprising sound, I'm not even mad I lost the dog lottery. "Afraid not," he chortles.

"Don't worry, Zeke," I tell the dog, ruffling his ears. "He's just jealous."

"*Zeke?* What happened to Jedidiah?"

"Naming an animal shouldn't be taken lightly. It's a process. You've got to try a few out to see if they fit. He'll let us know which one he likes."

Leaning back into the couch, I kick my feet up on the coffee table and rub my stomach. Maybe I have finally discovered my daily cheese limit.

"I don't think he has a preference," Harper pipes in. "He answered to Larry at the guide dog training facility."

I smell a challenge. Granted I get bored easily these days, so I make challenges out of all sorts of things, but Harper needs his buttons pushed. It's quickly becoming my new favorite past time because he takes it like a champ.

"Really? What about me? Do I look like a Riley?"

"Well, considering that's all I know you as, yeah. Sure."

"No way. I always imagined I should have been Buck or Rocky or something more rambunctious sounding."

"Fair enough," he says on a laugh.

"Smart ass." I give his arm a swat, and he flinches.

What's the deal with that? I didn't go anywhere near his ribs. I've had my share of scuffles, but they never left me gun shy. Granted, none of my scuffles were with an MMA trainer, but I wonder if it runs deeper, considering those nightmares he has.

"What's up with the flinching?" I ask.

"What?"

"No offense, but you seem kind of jittery all the time."

When he doesn't answer, I'm sorry I prodded. I hate not being able to read facial expressions. I've always been blunt, but at least when I could see, it was easy to tell when I'd overstepped.

"You…I just don't know you that well yet," he finally says.

73

"Do I make you nervous?"

"No, but... Well, I guess I'm not sure how to take you yet when you get frustrated or are unhappy with something."

"Really? So, are you saying you're scared of me?" I scoff because the notion is so absurd.

"No," he says unconvincingly. "Just in my experience, anger causes people to be...unpredictable."

I have a feeling that's the most loaded statement I've ever heard. Who was so angry that Harper lived in fear? That he still lives in fear? Did he have a bad childhood?

"I guess the whole baseball bat thing probably didn't help my first impression," I muse, revisiting our introduction.

"Sorry, I didn't mean that I thought you were..."

"I don't have a temper," I offer when he continues to flounder. "Yeah, I've gotten frustrated more in the past few months than I have been in my entire life, but laughter cures everything is my philosophy. I'm not going to go all *Hulk* on you if I don't like something."

"Alright," he lets out on a nervous laugh.

I'm not convinced that he's convinced, but it's a start. It's so odd to even have this conversation. Me, scary? Rob would laugh his ass off.

"So, what about you?" I preface in an effort to steer toward less serious conversation. I don't understand how a guy who hides such a good sense of humor can be so closed up, only talking when I ask questions.

"What about me?"

"Do you think you look like a *Harper?*"

"Again, that's all I've ever known, so I couldn't imagine looking in the mirror and thinking the face looking back at me has a different name."

I've never met a *Harper* and can't piece together a picture of what he might look like. As I stare at him, I wish the fog of blurry lights and shadows would clear just for a few seconds. I've met plenty of people since I lost my sight, mostly at the doctor's office, and I don't really give a damn that I won't be able to see them, but there's something about Harper. He's an enigma.

His presence puts me at ease. I can tell him anything without judgement or being treated like an invalid. He doesn't mind that I use the screen reader app on my phone and impressively can understand the pace at which I listen to it read to me. Val and my parents always said it sounded like an old cassette tape being eaten and couldn't understand how I'd adapted to hearing things at that rate. I've found myself excited to get out of bed in the morning, knowing I get to bullshit with him some more. It'd be nice to know what the face of the person who's brought this breath of fresh air into my life looks like.

"It's not fair, you know?" I mutter absently.

"What?"

"I'll never see the people I know age. I'll never know what anyone new I meet looks like. Just…being blind is like being stuck in the past, if you think about it."

As soon as the words are out, I wish I could pull them back in. I've never been one to wallow in self-pity.

"It was just an observation," I add. "I'm not having a moment or anything."

"No, I get it, but…there's still ways to see, ways to discern people's features."

"How?"

"Well, you're lucky. You weren't born blind, so you have frames of reference to fall back on. Like me for example, I have short dark brown hair and brown eyes. Can you picture that?"

"Why did I think you were blonde?"

"I don't know."

"So, you've got brown Flock of Seagulls hair and shit-colored eyes. Yeah, that helps," I joke just to be difficult.

"Flock of Seagulls? How old are you?"

"Thirty-two. How old are you?"

"Twenty-seven."

"Twenty-seven? Whoa, you've got to be the oldest twenty-seven-year-old I've ever met."

"Why's that?"

Waving my hand in a flourish I digress. "The button ups, the books, the smooth, deep voice. Oh, and the whole cautious grandpa act. Dude, you're an old man trapped in a young man's body. You wear house slippers and smoke a pipe. Don't you?"

"This is really good for my ego," he deadpans.

"That's what you get for letting me pick out an ugly dog."

Laughing, he clears his throat. "Can I…see your hand? I want you to try something."

Curiosity has me holding my hand out, palm up without question. His fingers wrap around my wrist, gently turning it and pulling it toward him. The touch makes my pulse skip in anticipation. My palm connects with warm flesh and…whiskers.

"You've got stubble," I let out, surprised by the discovery.

"Most of us old guys do," he jokes, letting go of my hand.

My heart rate speeds up. It feels like I'm invading his privacy, but I don't want to pull my hand away. He's the one who put it there though, so it gives me the confidence to stay.

"Do…people really do this? Touch people's faces?"

"No. I've heard most people think it's unhygienic, and there's really no proven data that the whole touch to brain activity helps identify facial features."

His jaw flexes under my hand as he speaks. There may be no proven data, but I'm fascinated to feel the facial structure of this secretive person who's come into my life and given me hope and entertainment. Reaching out my other hand, it trembles just before I connect with his cheekbone.

I'm touching another man's face, something I don't recall having ever done to anyone, but circumstances have changed. I don't care what anyone would think. I can only imagine so much. Imagination isn't reality, and Harper's the first new person in my life who I give a damn about enough to want an accurate depiction of him.

"It's probably only unhygienic now that I'm using *this* hand," I jest to deflect the awkwardness of this exploration as I trail my fingertips up until I find his hairline. "This is the one I used to feed Boomer the tortellini."

"Fantastic," he huffs on an amused breath, but it's choppy like maybe this is weird for him too even though he suggested it.

Given that he just admitted he was wary of me and now he's letting me touch him, I don't dare make any sudden moves. I'm aware this exercise is for me, for him to appease my need to see the stranger in my home, but it feels like a bridge of trust. I know I give him shit, but it feels imperative to respect his anxiety and phobias. People should feel safe. It's a basic human need.

His hair is soft, not too long, not too short. Moving over his temple, the curve of his brow bone meets my touch. There's a patch in the delicate hairs where his brow is split by a mar of rough skin. A cut, perhaps? He tenses under my fingertips. I can't help but notice the extra bit of warmth there and a hint of swelling, so I move on without a word. Was it another gift from his roommate to go along with the cracked ribs?

Drawing my fingertips under his eye, I trace them over the bridge of his nose. It's straight with a gradual slope down to the tip. He's definitely not an old man, although when I said that I was just surprised he wasn't in his mid to late thirties.

"You're good-looking, aren't you?" I chuckle, withdrawing my hands.

"Uh, that's debatable," he replies, clearing his throat.

"You're going to give Boomer a complex. Two handsome guys to compete with? That can't be good for his self-esteem."

"And one of them incredibly modest to boot," he adds.

I open my mouth to ask what he thinks of me but shut it when I come to my senses. That's just weird. What do I care if he returns the compliment? Like he said, what does it even matter what people look like? It's not like I've ever been jealous or competitive if a guy was better looking than me. Why I feel like I want his approval, I don't know. It must be the disadvantage of being seen without seeing. Maybe it's because if he thought I was pleasant to look at, he might be more at ease.

Getting up, I pat my leg and call to the dog. "Come on, Boomer. Let me go show you the gym and burn off some of these tortellini."

"You're seriously going to work out after you ate all of that?"

"Why not?"

I need to do something to get rid of this energy inside me. It must have been that stupid energy drink I had on the drive home. My pulse is still skipping along even though the bizarre facial recognition lesson is over.

I wonder if Harper would like to run. No. He said he prefers swimming. Hm. I think my sports club membership is still good. I should take him to the pool there before it expires, get some use out of it. If I could still see, I could teach him how to spar in case his next roommate is another asshole.

Next roommate… I guess he's kind of my roommate now. I'll have to introduce him to Rob. I bet they'd get along well.

I wonder if he'll want to hang out when the five months are up? Or would that be weird?

Chuckling at myself over the abundance of Harper-thoughts as I enter the gym and whip off my t-shirt, I realize the irony of my question.

"Not any weirder than touching his face. Huh, Boomer?"

Chapter 12

HARPER

Fortunately, today didn't include any motorcycle lessons or the adoption of more pets. I'm calling that a win. Riley informed me he wants piz-za…again, so I don't have to cook tonight either.

He and Larry…or Jed, or Boomer, or Zeke—whatever he's calling him—will probably be in the gym for another half an hour for his night-ly ritual. The man is a machine, sometimes working out twice a day.

The glow of the setting sun through the patio doors of my room cas-cades beautiful hues of pinks and oranges onto the beige carpeting as I rifle through the dresser for a pair of pajama pants to get ready for a hot shower. I think it's the first day it doesn't hurt when I lean over.

My strength has been returning by the day. The pain, except for the occasional ache in my ribs, is almost non-existent after two and a half weeks in Riley's sanctuary. How long it'll take to mend the other wounds, the ones I feel deep in my soul, I'm not sure, but I'm grateful. I'm in a much better place.

It's difficult to believe I ever warred with the idea of leaving Dallas. I somehow feared life would be worse without him, without our routine as toxic as it was. It's a jarring contrast to my new routine, one filled with everyday tasks that become an adventure laced with laughter.

I sorted the kitchen cabinets today with Riley, convincing him to stow his snacks alphabetically rather than strewn in a line across the counter. How is this much serenity my life now?

I want to believe it, want to revel in it, but there's that alert part of me that can't. I think that's what I hate most about what happened. I'll never trust anyone again, never trust happiness. Will I constantly be blurting out paranoid observations like I did on Riley's sofa the other night?

I can't believe I implied that he's scary.

Great. Now he thinks I'm afraid of him.

My phone chimes the message alert, revealing Daniel's name.

DANIEL: You up for lunch tomorrow?

I hate messaging. Dallas and I got into so many fights over miscon-strued text messages, they make me anxious, so I hit the call button in lieu of replying.

"Hey. Are you alright?" Daniel asks over the noise of a crowd.

"Yeah. I just figured this'd be easier than texting. I can see if I can get away for lunch tomorrow or maybe a little after lunch. Do you work tomorrow?"

"When am I ever not working?" he sasses. "And what do you mean, you *think* you can get away? You're allowed a lunch break, aren't you?"

"Yeah, but I usually make Riley lunch."

"Well, make him a sandwich, throw it in the fridge, and tell him you have plans with your best friend who's been worried sick about you."

"Guilt much? Thanks a lot." Daniel's dramatics know no bounds when it comes to me. The joys of being a best friend. "Yeah, I can proba-bly do that. It's just that…we just got a dog, and I worry about leaving him if he needs help with it or something."

All I can hear are the voices in the background, so I wait as I head into the bathroom. He probably has a customer at the bar to serve.

"*We* got a dog? Did you just say *we?*"

"Well, yeah. I meant, I went with him to get it and drove them home, so yeah. We went to get the dog."

"*Home*," he emphasizes. "Uh huh."

Rolling my eyes, I put the phone on speaker and kick my pants off. "You know what I meant."

"Uh huh," he repeats.

"Oh, knock it off. So, where are we meeting?"

"Maybe I should come over and see where you're living now, meet this guy. I mean, five months is a long time. I should probably know how to find you."

"No!" I rush out way too cautionary. "I mean, it's not *my* place. It'd be rude to just invite someone over."

"What's the address?"

"Daniel," I whine, pinching my eyes closed. "No."

"Well, now I'm not giving up until I get it out of you."

"Ugh. You're such a pain in the ass."

"And you just got out of a shitty relationship and are super vulnera-ble, so I need to make sure this guy isn't taking advantage."

"Oh, brother. How can he take advantage if he's straight?"

"Please. Straight is just one sexual encounter away from gay."

Shaking my head, I start the water in the shower. Daniel's never made his misplaced resentment of straight guys a secret.

"Really? This coming from you?"

79

"Address," he demands.

"Oh my God. Fine, but don't embarrass me, and don't be rude."

"Whoa!" he cackles. "It's worse than I thought. He's hot. Isn't he?"

"I don't have time for this. I'm hopping in the shower."

"Alone?"

"Yes! Alone! I'll text you the address. Bye."

The hot water is a balm on my tight muscles as I step under the spray. Damn Daniel for it doing little for my agitation though. I can't believe he's coming here tomorrow. He'll find a way to make something out of nothing.

I'm a year older than him, but he treats me like a little brother. Why wouldn't he though? Typical Harper—the jittery scared guy who needs a protector. Riley even called it the other night on his couch.

Along with my skin, my insides warm at the memory. As embarrassing as it was, there's something about being understood that's touching. Just the thought that he gives a damn enough to pay attention to who I really am for better or worse is humbling.

"God, listen to me," I whisper into the spray, rubbing my face, except it does the opposite of washing away Daniel's insinuations.

Maybe because it's been so long since I've been touched with care, I retrace Riley's gentle discovery he made of my face the other night. If only my lover's caresses had remained like that. To be honest, Riley's exploration felt more tender than Dallas' clumsy affections did in the beginning. I can only imagine what that vivacious man in the next room would be like in bed, attentive, playful, laughing.

The thought makes me chuckle and blush all at once. I am so screwed when Daniel shows up tomorrow. I'm not losing my head over a straight man who's been kind to me, but there'll be no way to hide Daniel's assumption about Riley's looks. The man is hotter than anyone has a right to be. As long as I leave the room when he eats, I'll survive the next five months. His food moans should seriously be outlawed for indecency.

O-kay. And that's enough of that. I'm going to need a cold shower if I keep running down the list of *Rileyisms* that are quickly becoming appealing to me.

The steam is so thick I can barely see, the mirror, a clouded sheen. Cracking open the door so I don't asphyxiate from the sauna effect, I towel off. Hanging it up on the wall rod, I survey myself. I've been avoiding doing so, too ashamed to see what I let happen to me, too sickened by the reminder of what occurred.

The bruises on my ribs are a pale shade of yellow now. In a few days, the reminder might be gone entirely. *Good-looking*, Riley said. If he could actually see me and the split still healing in my eyebrow, would he think that?

"Of course not," I chide myself. "Because he's *straight*."

The door swings open, hitting the interior wall with a *thump*, triggering unwanted memories. I jump back on instinct, covering my cock with my hands as my eyes meet Riley's. For a second, my brain flashes the word *danger*, but then I remember it's Riley. Maybe he needs something. It's then that I notice he's bare-chested and...holding his hand over his gym shorts like he's cupping his cock too. What the...

"Harper? Is the toilet free?" he pants from his workout like he just came from an orgy. "I'm about to piss myself from those damn energy drinks." Wincing, he reaches out toward the toilet.

Right. He can't see me. Easier to think than to believe though.

"Y-yeah," I get out, carefully reaching to my left and lifting the toilet seat for him, making sure it *thunks* against the reservoir tank to give him a point of reference.

When he positions himself and starts to drop the waistband of his gym shorts, I realize in my shock, I'm staring.

Oh my God. Don't look at his dick. Don't look at his dick.

Turning my head toward the shower when he frees himself, I tense at his audible sigh of relief and the following stream he produces.

"Oh, thank God," he moans, even throatier than his food-appreciation noises. "Sorry, I didn't want to have to fumble all the way to my bathroom."

"No problem. It's your apartment," I choke out, contemplating if I should step back into the shower. No, that would be totally obvious.

Thank you, Daniel, for distracting me so much I forgot my clothes in my room.

The four feet between me and the towel rack might as well be a continent for how my ass is shoved up against the wall in between the toilet and the shower, practically facing Riley. I'm so close, if I step forward, any one of my naked parts might brush against him.

And speaking of naked parts, my peripheral vision is giving me an eyeful. If I thought his food moans were illegal, they've got nothing on his bare, sweat-drenched chest. Holy shit.

This is a test, standing here naked next to my employer who's only wearing perspiration and a pair of thin gym shorts. It's a test I'm going to fail because after reliving the innocent face touching in the shower like a pervert, now I'm standing here cupping my junk with no hope of my hands being able to hide what's happening behind them if he doesn't get his enticing body out of here in the next ten seconds. I'm going to VRT hell, buck naked with a hard on.

The jostle of his arms tells me he's tucked himself away. When he flushes the toilet, I spare a glance.

Fuck. Wrong move.

He has a happy trail, a sexy, sandy-colored happy trail. Of course, he does. He's always happy.

Uhn. Make it stop. Take my eyes instead.

Turning his back to wash his hands in the sink doesn't improve my situation. The sinewy cords of muscle stretched across his back are an entrancing pattern. I can't tear my gaze away.

My phone pings. My phone, where I left it on the counter next to Riley.

"You need to get that?" he asks, shifting his hips to the side. No way am I walking over there even if I could get myself to move.

"No, it's…probably just my friend asking about getting lunch tomorrow."

"Oh. Well, you should go. Don't think you have to sit here and babysit me."

"Alright. Thanks."

"I was thinking of having some of my buddies over tomorrow night actually. You're welcome to invite your friend, if you want."

Why is it taking him so long to wash his hands?

They're clean! They're clean! Leave. For the love of baby Jesus, please leave.

"He…he, uh, works nights at a bar, but thanks though."

"Oh, okay. You ready for pizza?" he asks. Just my luck that he's feeling extra chatty right now.

"Huh? Uh, y-yeah. Sure."

When he reaches to his right, I cringe, watching him dry his hands on the towel I just used. Turning around, he leans against the sink and narrows his eyes at me.

"What's with the nervous Nelly talk again? I thought we were cool. Are you still scared of me?"

"N-no," I try not to stutter, but fail miserably, a fine sheen of sweat forming on my skin. "I'm…we're…we're cool. I…you just surprised me. That's all."

His brow furrows at my verbal diarrhea. Just kill me now. "So, pizza. Right?" I force out enthusiastically.

"Yeah," he replies suspiciously.

My heart stops as his eyes canvas down the length of my body from head to toe. His eyes might as well be lasers the way the slow perusal burns me up from head to toe.

Frowning, he glances toward the shower stall. "Did you…just get out of the shower?"

"Um, y-yeah." As if that wasn't a dead giveaway, I quickly follow-up with, "All done. I'm…done now."

More brow furrowing. More frowning, and then he gives a single nod and pushes off the counter.

"Alright. I'm going to call for the pizza," he rushes, bursting out the door as quickly as he entered.

"Fuck," I finally breathe, my head thumping back against the wall.

How can I be hard when that entire event should have been terrifying? Squeezing the head of my cock to chase away the sensations, I know exactly why.

Note to self—lock the door next time.

Note to Daniel that I will not admit to Daniel—yeah, he's hot.

Note to Riley—I am absolutely scared, scared of how irresistible you are inside and out.

Chapter 13

HARPER

I've answered other people's doors a few times, mostly elderly clients with mobility limitations I've met for in-home sessions. Walking to the door to let Daniel in shouldn't feel like I'm breaking the law.

His eager knocking isn't helping. It's fitting really. It sounds as bossy as him. I need a new best friend. Either that or I need Riley to stop hovering in the kitchen as though he's curious to meet Daniel. Doesn't he have one of his seven workouts a day to do or look up ridiculous names for Eisenhower? Yeah, I doubt that latest one will stick either. That poor dog is going to be as confused as he is ugly.

Grabbing my jacket off the coat peg in the entryway, I yank the door open and find Daniel in his classic jeans and black leather jacket look, hair slicked and parted to the side in the only style he knows. His megawatt smile makes it difficult to hold onto my annoyance.

"Hey!" I greet cheerfully because it is good to see his obnoxious face. "Ready to go," I declare, making to hustle out the door.

Except, he claps me on the shoulder, shoving past me into the apartment. Dick.

"So, this is your new gig, huh? Shit, the ride up was worth it. Nice digs," he says way too loud.

Shutting the door, I scramble after him. Riley pushes off the island counter, his playful smirk ever in place. He throws a chin nod toward us.

"Hey. Daniel, right? I'm Riley."

"Yeah. Good to meet you," Daniel returns, stepping forward when Riley offers his hand.

Why does this feel like a kid bringing home their first date to meet their parents' approval? Shit. Why do I feel like Riley is the date and Daniel is the parent?

This is Daniel's fault. He planted that seed in my head last night.

To make matters worse, he glances over his shoulder at me after taking in Riley. The hike of his brow and that smug look he levels at me tells me how this lunch conversation is going to go. I glare back, the message something along the lines of it's-not-my-fault-he's-that-fucking-hot.

Daniel snickers and shakes his head at me like I'm a lost cause.

Thank you for the faith, ex-best friend.

"So, how do you know Harper?" Riley asks.

"We roomed together in college."

"Oh," Riley coos, smile widening as he glances to me. "He's your Rob then. Huh? That's cool."

"Rob?" Daniel inquires, appropriately puzzled by Riley-speak.

Right. Pay attention, Harper.

"Uh, yeah. That's your old college buddy. Right?" I babble to fill in the blanks.

"Yeah," Riley concurs. "You'll get to meet him tonight. He's stopping over with a few of my friends."

Great. I nearly forgot. What are Riley's friends like? I imagine one throws knives, another rides motorcycles in those round cages at carnivals. I'm sure I'll fit right in. Can't wait.

"Well, you kids have fun. Take your time. Don't hurry back," Riley imparts cheekily.

I think that's his way of telling me to let loose and relax. What a thrilling image I've given him of myself.

Ugh. Listen to me. I'm starting to sound like a smitten teenager who wants to impress a crush.

Blathering out my thanks and our goodbyes, Daniel and I make it to the elevator before I realize he hasn't said a word. He's never this quiet. Hitting the ground floor button, I glance over at him.

"What?" I ask, finding him staring at me with mirth in his eyes.

"You are so fucked."

"What?" I scoff.

"No, it's fine," he backpedals, raising his palms. "I was worried maybe you were secretly still pining over Dallas, so…this is better. Totally fucked up, but better."

"I have no idea what you're talking about," I grump, folding my arms over my chest and staring at the elevator floor countdown. "So, he's a nice, good-looking guy—a *straight*, nice, good-looking guy whom I'm grateful to work for and get to stay with until I find a place of my own. That's all you saw."

"Right," he drawls. "And you *don't* want his nice, straight dick in your mouth."

Pinching my eyes closed doesn't do a damn thing to blot out that inappropriate image. "Daniel," I heave in frustration. "No. I've sworn off men for a while. Okay?"

I don't trust his silence. And this is possibly the slowest elevator ride ever.

"Because I'd totally let him put his dick in my mouth," he adds.

That's it. Now he's just trying to provoke me. Scoffing, I turn and give his shoulder a shove. "You're such a ho," I snap, but it comes out chopped with laughter.

Cackling, he gives me a playful shove in return as the elevator doors open. "Takes one to know one."

Maybe I needed this, a sense of normalcy. Despite the discomfort of the topic of his razzing, it's good to be myself again. It's good to be the Harper from three years ago, the one who wasn't swept up by a handsome face and pretty words that eventually oxidized into harsh ones. Maybe I actually am free.

Daniel doesn't let up his teasing throughout lunch, but I fall into our old playful bickering I haven't lost myself in since dating Dallas. I never realized what a rift it caused in our friendship. It feels like coming home, understanding just how much I missed this openness with Daniel.

"So, Dallas and the guys are going out of town tomorrow for a week for the Mitchell fight," he says, his tone and expression going serious.

My stomach drops at the change in subject. Now I get why he went out of his way to make me laugh for the last hour. I wish he'd just lead with this bit of information.

"I know you said you wanted to go get some of your stuff from your apartment, so that's why I brought it up. I'm off next Thursday. I can meet you at Riley's, and we can take a cab over there."

I hate that my life has reduced me to needing a guardian. I'm a nervous, jumpy, "old man", who needs a babysitter.

"No, thanks. I can do it. I should just call him and tell him I want to pick up my stuff."

"You are not fucking calling that prick, Harper. No way! He asks about you every time he comes in and smirks at me like he thinks it's just a matter of time until he gets what he wants."

"What? Why didn't you tell me?" Bile rises in the back of my throat, but I don't want to show Daniel my fear. "I'm sorry. I…I'm so sorry that you—"

"Stop! Do not apologize for him. I didn't want you to think about him. That's why I didn't say anything, but if you've seriously lost your mind enough to think he'll be pleasant and just let you waltz in and get your stuff, you're delusional." Sighing, he wads up his napkin and throws it down on his plate. Clasping his hands together under his chin, he focuses on a smudge mark on the table, adding, "Marcy said he stopped by Home Reach and wanted to know where you were working."

A panic bubble expands in my chest. Dallas hasn't been the flower-buying type for the past year, having foregone the gesture after our third or fourth blowout. Given the angry messages he's been texting me, and my lack of responses, I don't imagine he came looking for me to share romantic overtures.

"It's alright," Daniel adds, his gaze scanning my slack jaw. "She didn't tell him anything. Company policy, client confidentiality, and all that. Sent him packing. She didn't want to worry you, but she thought I should know to keep an eye out for you."

Sputtering, my face heats. I'm grateful I set up a new bank account during my stay at Marcy's to have my paychecks deposited into. I'd like to think Dallas had a change of heart, that he remembered how good it was in the beginning, but my newfound common sense tells me his search mission was likely motivated by bitterness.

I'm still receiving messages from him every few days. The ones that appear to be declarations of love and remorse, carry a sentiment of blame that deplete any hint of empathy. The last one said something along the lines of how I abandoned him. I doubt he meant emotionally. I was his cash cow, supporting his careless hard living because I thought that's what a supportive partner would do, support without asking what the support was for.

Forcing myself to meet Daniel's concerned gaze, I swallow against the sour taste of self-disgust. Daniel, Marcy, and if Dallas is successful, Riley too could be brought into my mess.

"Thanks for the warning."

"So, don't go there alone. Okay? Promise me?"

Nodding, I wonder just how pathetic rock bottom is supposed to feel. Someone please tell me that it doesn't get worse than this.

"I promise."

Chapter 14

RILEY

When Harper left for lunch with his friend, I imagined he'd come back a changed man. I was starting to wonder if he even had any friends, since he never talks about anything personal, whereas I spend half the day babbling on about my life like it's a household sitcom.

As Rob passes me another beer where we're sitting on my couch, watching the football game, I don't think I can begrudge Harper for returning changed for the worse. He was even more quiet than usual when he came back like something was weighing on him that wasn't when he left.

Sitting here, sandwiched between Rob and Marco, while our other buddy, Jasper shouts at the TV from my recliner, I can see how friend-time doesn't always hold appeal. Tonight certainly won't change me for the better. I was worried the guys wouldn't enjoy hanging out with me like they used to now that I can't see, but from the sounds of it, they're having a grand old time. I can't say the same for myself.

"Oh, fuck yeah! Look at that pass!" Marco shouts, slapping his knee, shaking the couch.

"Holy shit. That was beautiful," Jasper chimes in. "He's going to break his pass record from last year. I swear."

To my left, Rob leans in and mumbles, "McCutchin just made a forty-yard pass to Treemont."

Good old Rob, always thinking about everyone but himself. Smiling, I give his thigh a fist bump in thanks for trying to keep me out of the dark.

The soft thump of footsteps against the hardwood flooring in the hallway snares my attention over the noise of the game. I don't even have to get a hit of his sugar cookie scent to know it's Harper. I know the sound of his walk now. He excused himself for a phone call earlier, shortly after the guys arrived, and never resurfaced.

"Hey, Harper. You want a beer?" Rob asks.

"No. No, I'm good. Thanks. Just came to grab my left-overs from lunch."

"Leftovers?" I balk. "Grab some pizza. There's plenty to go around."

That subdued chuckle of his floats over the back of the couch as I track him entering the kitchen. "Pizza…again. How tempting."

"What?" I squawk, detecting that dry humor of his that cracks me up. "Are you disparaging my food choices?"

"Riley, I don't know if anyone ever told you, but pizza's not a food group."

Rob snickers beside me. I can't fight the grin on my face, hearing Harper's snarky side make a reappearance. It feels like I earned a badge, getting him to open up in front of other people.

"Yeah, it is," I protest. "It's *all* the food groups. I'm probably the most well-balanced person nutrition-wise in this apartment right now."

"The fifty pounds of cheese in your fridge might say otherwise," he replies, his footsteps heading back down the hallway.

"Hey, you can stay and hang out," I call, my heart growing heavy at the thought of him disappearing again.

He's certainly better company than Marco and Jasper. Come to think of it, he's actually better company than Rob too, and that's tough to beat. I don't know why I thought inviting them all over was going to be fun. I feel like all I've accomplished is squander Harper-time. Weird. It's not like I'm not around the guy all day long already.

"Nah, that's okay. I appreciate the offer, but I wanted to catch up on some things, and…I thought I'd take Larry for a walk around the rooftop to stargaze while you visit with your friends."

"You mean, Copernicus?" I correct, throwing out the latest Lar-ry-name that Harper disapproved of.

Chuckling, he comes back with, "Yeah. That's the one."

"Fine. Suit yourself, old man."

Note to self—Harper likes stargazing. When his footsteps disappear down the hallway, I'm reminded of bursting in on him when I went to take a leak yesterday. Pretty sure he was naked and was just too kind to mention my folly.

How did I not figure that out the second I barged in there when the cookie-scented steam hit me? Oops. Awkward. Well, probably more awkward for him judging by the way he was stammering. Being blind for the win for me. I saw nothing, and that's my story.

Okay, so I saw a warbled, skin-colored outline once I focused on him. Not the same thing as seeing him naked. Whatever. It's not like either of us have never been in a locker room.

"Well, that was adorable," Jasper says.

When Marco and Rob chuckle, I'm at a loss as to what I missed. Stupid fucking idea to invite them over to watch TV that I can't see. Was there a funny commercial?

"What?" I query. I've tried limiting my interrogatives, accepting that there's some things I'll miss, but it's difficult to keep quiet when I'm the only one who missed a joke.

"*You two,*" Jasper clarifies. "You sound like an old married couple."

"What? Me and Harper?" I laugh. "He's cool. I'm glad they finally sent someone decent over."

"Uh huh," Marco pipes in. "Geez, Val's barely been gone three months, and you're already shacking up with a guy and finishing each other's sentences. When's the wedding?"

The guys laugh along with my own disbelieving mirth. Being ribbed again feels good like I'm still the same old Riley, but something twinges inside me knowing the joke is in part at poor unsuspecting Harper's expense.

"Come on," I scold. "Leave him alone. He's a good dude."

"Oh my God. You're sticking up for him. It *is* serious," Jasper barks.

"What? I'm just following proper bro-code since he's not here to defend himself against you ass wipes."

"*Ass wipes?*" This from Marco. "Whoa ho! I know things proba-bly change when you lose your vision, but I didn't think it meant you couldn't tell the difference between a cock and a woman."

These fuckers. At least Rob isn't in on it. I can take it as good as I give it, which is why they're doling out this level of harassment, but my face burns. It's burning because for that brief moment yesterday, I didn't realize there was likely a naked cock just a foot away from me.

"Laugh it up, picking on a blind guy," I grouse to shut it down.

Marco thwaps me in the bicep. "Ah, come on. We're just fucking with you." He laughs, but then adds, "I won't mention it to Jill though because she'll get Val on speed-dial and tell her she's been replaced."

"Damn right," I joke because, if you can't beat them, join them.

And if I had to spend the rest of my life on a deserted island with either Val or Harper, I'd choose Harper. Cock or no cock.

Jasper finds my comeback amusing enough, he belts out another peal of laughter. "Just make sure you treat him better than his last boyfriend. Unless you're the one who did that to his face."

Marco snickers at the comment, but my smile fades. Harper's been here almost three weeks. If his face still looks messed up, that must have been some beating he took. That's not the thing that hangs me up though, rather Jasper's choice of words, particularly *boyfriend.*

Harper did say he was homeless due to a break-up. His ambiguous replies when I mentioned my thoughts on Val shift into a different perspective now. Was his *roommate* a boyfriend rather than a roommate?

"What?" I say in a daze, aware I've fallen out of the conversation.

"It looks like somebody jacked up his face not too long ago," Rob explains in a more candid volume.

I hope to hell Harper can't hear these idiots. If he values his privacy so much that he intended to keep his sexuality to himself, it's none of my business. Actually, maybe it is my business. The guy lives here now or for the time being anyway, and these guys are crossing the line. So what if he likes men?

"Oh, yeah," I agree casually, prepping to shut down the shit talk. "A buddy of his screwed him over for some money and that's how he paid his debt when Harper asked him to pay up."

"Shit," Rob curses.

"Oh, that's fucked up," Marco concurs.

"Right?" I agree, to conceal the way my brain is reliving every conversation I've had with Harper, hoping I didn't say anything that made him uncomfortable.

Why do I feel so shitty that he didn't think he could tell me? Maybe I'm reading too much into it. He might not be into guys.

It's weird though, now that the possibility that he is has taken root in my head, I can't really think of him as straight. Why does that make me…happy?

I've never had a bi or gay friend. Am I proud of myself for getting one? Maybe it's the privilege of knowing his secret or figuring one of them out like I'm some expert sleuth. Either way, I need to pay better attention if I'm going to be living with the guy. What kind of roommate doesn't know shit about the guy he's living with? I need to pay more attention to him and make sure he feels welcome.

Chapter 15

RILEY

"What the hell is detasseling?" I ask as we stand in line at the coffee shop down the street from my apartment.

I've picked up on the fact that Harper's suggestions to run tiny errands are actually a subtle excuse to get me to either use my cane outside or walk with Larry. The man has style the way he lets me keep my dignity. Plus, I kind of don't mind going anywhere with him. It's like being at summer camp and making a new friend, but a summer camp that doesn't suck.

Since the guys came over a few days ago, I've upped my roommate trivia knowledge, slowly garnering more information from Harper. Right now, he's telling me about the little town of Spring Valley he grew up in and the various jobs he had as a kid. He had a lot. I get the impression he's been working since he learned to walk.

"It's what they do to seed corn, corn that seed companies use to sell to farmers to plant in their fields. They hire kids to pull the tassels off the corn during the summers to help pollinate the corn a certain way. It's almost like a rite of passage for kids in rural communities doing this job."

"Huh. That's cool."

"Not really. It sucks. It's damp and muddy in the morning. The dew from the corn soaks your clothes, and then in the afternoon it's hot as hell. The corn leaves and pollen itch your skin. There's bugs, and the pay is pretty crappy."

"And here I was thinking of buying a little house in the country. You're really selling me on the idea."

"The countryside is nice, just…don't get a job detasseling," he jokes, his palm lightly touching in between my shoulder blades to let me know the line is moving.

Funny. Mom latches onto my arm like I'm a leaf that's going to blow away. Dad puts his vice grip sausage fingers at the back of my neck like he's getting ready to have a talk with me like he used to when I was a kid. Harper's just suave about everything, neither dragging me nor shoving me along like a bulldozer the way Val used to do. He's always at my side like we're just two buddies hanging out, not a guy leading a blind guy.

When it's our turn to order, Harper orders his boring old man coffee, and then the barista guy asks me what I want. "I'll have a mocha-Frodo-baklavachino-frappe with two pumps of kryptonite and an extra shot of I-don't-want-to-take-a-nap-later."

The anticipated silence follows, making me proud, but Harper ruins it with, "He'll have an iced cappuccino with an extra shot of espresso and two sugars."

"Spoil sport," I mutter, but am silently impressed he remembers what I like to drink.

"They have granola parfaits," he whispers teasingly.

"You're fired," I deadpan, getting a laugh out of him.

"You two work together," the barista asks. Nosey bastard.

"Uh, yeah," Harper answers. "Can we get an order of those toasted cheddar bites?"

"They have cheddar bites?" I ask, perking up. Why is he just telling me this now? "Dude, give me an order too," I tell barista guy.

"No," Harper corrects. I'm about to throat punch him and tell him both his employment and our new friendship is over, but he adds, "Just one please. The ones I ordered are for him."

Oh. He ordered me cheesiness of his own accord. Ten points to Harper.

"You're hired again," I inform him.

"Glad to hear it."

Larry helps me find a seat by locating crumbs under a table. When Harper joins us and sets our cups down, he leaves to retrieve my cheddar bites. The first cup I grab is warm. Definitely Harper's old man coffee. Sliding it to his side of the table, I can feel where the barista wrote on it. My texture lessons are paying off. Not that it'd be difficult to tell the cup is marked. The writing is…gritty. Did he fucking use a glitter pen?

Damn it. That shit's going to be everywhere.

"Son of a bitch," I mutter, dusting off my hands.

"What is it?" Harper asks, taking his seat, bringing the scent of warm cheese with him.

"I think our barista glitter bombed us. Did he use a freaking glitter pen on your cup or something?"

"Yeah," he says chuckling.

"Laugh it up. That shit's everywhere. Your name isn't that long. What the hell did he write on there? *Have a nice day picking this shit off your clothes?*"

"Uh," Harper hums, turning the cup.

"What? What's it say?"

Clearing his throat he says quietly, "Looks like…he gave me his phone number."

"What? Get out of here!"

"What? You've never had anyone give you a phone number?"

The statement is such a downplay and certainly not the typical response a straight guy would give. It further confirms my suspicions from the other night, but that's not what takes me aback. I'm annoyed with the glitter barista. Why am I annoyed with the glitter barista?

The more I think on it, all I can come up with is this is *my Harper*. He can go get his own.

"Yeah, but he's got some balls," I mutter.

"Why's that?"

Harper's nervous laugh makes me regret my tone. Does he think I'm working up to saying something homophobic? Has he had to deal with that before?

"Because we walked in here together," I explain. "Two guys walk in together and he hits on one of them? I mean, what the fuck? We could be a couple for all he knows."

"Oh," he lets out on a laugh. "Uh, yeah. Pretty bold, I guess."

These cheese bites are terrible. They're lukewarm. How do you ruin cheese bites?

"So, are you going to call him?"

"What?"

"The glitter barista. Are you going to call him?"

"Um, not likely."

Good. He's smart. I knew I liked him for a reason.

"That's probably for the best. If he's got glitter pens, I bet he's also got a *BeDazzler*. I mean, I suppose it'd be a bonus to be reflective in nighttime traffic, but in the daytime you'd be like a prism, blinding people left and right."

Fuck. That would give Harper job security. Why am I talking?

"That wouldn't exactly be good for my professional reputation."

"Exactly!" Integrity. He's got integrity too. Yeah, glitter barista can go hit on someone else's roommate.

On our way out, the disturbing incident is all but forgotten after we settled into an amusing argument over Larry's newest name. When I toss my cup in the trashcan, however, I hear the distinct sound of glitter barista's voice.

"You have a nice day. Come back soon!"

"Thank you," Harper calls out politely.

Come back soon? Ugh. Who is this guy? What if Harper ever comes here for coffee without me? I need to shut this shit down. I mean, the poor guy doesn't need to be harassed by unwanted admirers.

Reaching for him, I catch his arm, smiling at the way he instantly stops for me. That's right, glitter man. *I'm* priority number-one. Roommate El-Supremo. Slinking my arm around his shoulders, I angle my head toward the counter.

"Yeah. Thanks. The cheese bites were cold though. They better not make my boyfriend sick."

Harper's intake of breath has me wondering if maybe I got it all wrong, but he makes no claims of denial once we get outside, and I drop my arm. Adjusting Marlon's harness before we start our walk back, I shrug.

"So, he shouldn't bother you anymore," I venture.

"Yeah. I was terrified. Thanks for the help."

Smart ass. It occurs to me though, if Harper isn't into guys, he sure as shit is probably wondering if I am now.

Whatever. I'm way cooler than glitter man. I wonder if Harper thinks so?

Chapter 16

HARPER

"Are you sure you don't need me to come in with you?" I ask Riley as we approach the reception desk at his ophthalmology appointment.

"Nah, I'm good," he says, rubbing Larry's ear. "I've got Bruce to keep me company. Go run your errand."

"Alright," I let out on a nervous breath.

If I sweat anymore, it's going to soak through my shirt. I'm a terrible friend and a terrible employee. Daniel's going to kill me when he finds out what I'm doing, but I'm not waiting until tomorrow to go over to my old apartment with him. I've been worrying myself sick about it with each passing day since he told me about Dallas going out of town.

Dallas' trips have gotten cut short before, and who knows how reliable Daniel's eavesdropping was. I need to do this on my own anyway. I shouldn't have to drag my best friend with me as a lookout just to grab some clothes out of an apartment I paid for on the regular. I'll just get Riley checked in, and then I'll zip over there, fill my duffel bag, and be back before he's even finished. Everyone knows you have to wait at least an hour to get in to see any kind of doctor, appointment or not.

"Yes, Mr. Davenport," the receptionist concurs. "We have you down for one o'clock, but I'm glad you're early. The doctor's had a cancellation, so you can go right on back."

Fuck.

A half an hour later, I rise from my chair in the waiting room when Riley and Larry emerge from the exam rooms' hallway. The melancholy expression on his face is enough to make me forget my dilemma and enough to make me forget about him possibly guessing yesterday that I'm gay.

"Everything go okay?"

The bright smile he flashes me doesn't quite meet his eyes. "Yup. Still blind. Follow-up in three months."

How could I have sat here worrying about my own drama when he was in there dealing with the reminder of what he lost? Was he hoping for good news? I know he's told me all he can see is blurs of light in good lighting and that he has no chance of recovering his sight, but I also know plenty about false hope. I know how it fools you into believing that better days are ahead.

"I'm sorry, Riley."

"Don't be." He shrugs. "So, ready to go run your errands? What's on the agenda?"

"Oh, it's okay. I…I can do it some other time. You don't need me dragging you all over for my obligations."

"Nonsense. You uprooted your life to come live with me. I know you've got shit to do, so let's just go do it. I could use a distraction anyway. There's plenty of time to sit around my apartment."

"Well, my…roommate is out of town, so I thought I'd go grab some more of my clothes while he's gone, but I don't think that's a good idea. Seriously, I can just go with Daniel tomorrow."

"He's gone, you said?"

"Yeah, until Saturday, supposedly."

"Well, let's go get your shit then."

When I don't budge outside the door of the doctor's office, fumbling for a polite way to decline, he elbows me in the arm. "Come on. Time's a wasting."

I know him well enough that there's no point in arguing. He's talked me into ordering pizza three times this week already. I never want to see another pizza again. Plus, the knowledge that I have his car at my disposal today is tempting, in case there's time to grab larger items.

By the time we pull into the parking lot of my old apartment, I'm on the verge of having a heart attack. My palms have saturated the steering wheel with so much sweat that my hands slipped off it the last two turns.

Daniel's intel better be right. Why did I think I could do this?

The red brick building that once looked like home, now looms ahead of me like the return to a crime scene. The window flower boxes of my old neighbors are fool's gold, a gift bow on a bear trap.

"I'll just be like ten minutes tops," I inform Riley, grabbing my duffel bag out of the back seat.

When I round the other side of the car and step onto the sidewalk, the car door opens behind me. I turn around just as Riley's cane taps on the pavement.

"What…what are doing?"

"Coming with you," he says, opening the back door to let Larry hop out harness-free.

"Uh, Riley, I don't think that's a good idea," I caution, scanning every darkened shadow of the apartment complex in my paranoia.

"I won't break anything," he rebuts. "I can carry a bag or something. Come on."

He starts tracking his way down the sidewalk in the wrong direction. Great. Just what I need, to get my patient killed.

Rushing after him, I loop my arm around his shoulders and steer him back in the other direction. Larry looks on at us, relieving himself on the row of mailboxes in front of the building, tongue lolling out, oblivious, but curious. I slow when we near the car, but Riley keeps moving down the sidewalk. I've been around him long enough to know he excels at echolocation and probably knows he just passed by his car. Is every man in my life a stubborn ass?

"Riley, please. I'd feel more comfortable if you waited in the car," I plead, hurrying to catch up to him. "I don't want anything to happen to you."

"What's going to happen to me? I throw my back out? I never said I volunteered to carry your big screen TV."

Hilarious. He chooses now to dispense his jokes?

"Look, Daniel said he thinks Dallas is out of town, but what if he's wrong? Sometimes he comes back early."

Frowning, he draws his cane in an arc when we come to a T in the sidewalk. "So, we just knock and tell him you're here for your shit."

Scoffing at the mental image of that scenario, I cringe, imaging Dallas' fist slamming into Riley's face. I'm flattered he's being all protective like he was over the barista the other day, but glitter barista is an entirely different story than Dallas.

"It's not that simple. Okay. He's…he's…." Floundering, I feel like a hyper Chihuahua zipping back and forth in front of Riley. I had meant to bar his path, but inadvertently led him to my doorstep. The way his cane taps against the doorframe, I can tell he's figured it out, since he stopped moving when I did. The man is an evil genius.

"He's what?" he hedges.

"He's mean. Okay?"

"Like he's an asshole? Yeah, I picked up on that already."

"No. Like…he's violent."

Frowning, his gaze moves from the door to me. When he gets all serious like this, I swear it feels like he can see me. Reaching out, he cups the side of my jaw and rubs his thumb across my cheek. The simple touch cuts the anchor on the tension coiled around my spine, and I finally remember to breathe.

"Harper, you have stuff in there that's yours. Right?"

"Yeah." I gulp, my pulse downshifting from the soothing tone of his voice.

"You bought this place or paid rent. Right?"

"I paid the rent."

"Then we have every right to be here and to get your stuff. Okay?"

Exhaling, I nod, forgetting he can't see me, and then remembering his hand is on my cheek, so he can feel my motion of agreement. Turning, I insert the key and push the door open.

For some reason, I imagined being met with broken glass from the coffee table still littering the floor, overturned dining table chairs, the dinner I made on the floor amid the broken plates. Just like my affections, it's all swept up and gone though.

Lights off, the shadows create an eerie freeze frame in my mind. Dallas' gym shoes strewn about that I used to pick up and put on the rack. Newspapers and his stupid MMA magazines littering the dining table. An endless line of beer and liquor bottles lining the kitchen counter. Throw pillows haphazardly squished in locations that defy feng shui. And the coffee table...its glass top, now replaced with a piece of particle board, topped with a bong and a dozen beer bottles, a sorry memorial to the death of my naiveté. It's like viewing a grade-B version of my former life.

"He here?" Riley asks.

"No. No, I don't think so."

Shutting the door and locking it in the hopes it'll give me a few seconds notice, should Dallas show up, I place my hand on Riley's shoulder. I don't want to let him out of my sight, even if it's only a room away.

Instinct tells me to offer him a drink, to give him a tour, but this isn't my home anymore, and there's too many hazards now. It can't compare with his high-dollar penthouse, but it's certainly in a much sadder state than how I used to maintain it. It tells me I was the glue, holding everything together, cementing the illusion I wanted to see. I couldn't bear Riley assuming this is how I lived. How many times am I going to be grateful that the poor man can't see?

"I just need to grab some clothes. This way," I urge, gently guiding him along with me toward the bedroom.

My face burns, taking in more of the chaos that's ensued since I left. A vomit stain on the carpet in the hallway. Women's underwear hanging off the end table, confirming my suspicions of Dallas cheating on me when he was on the road with his straight, horny goons, ever surrounded by adoring women. He never let on to his friends that he was bisexual. I was always just his "roommate", so what I told Riley wasn't a complete lie.

Stupid. How stupid was I to put up with that for so long?

There's no sign of my bike anywhere. I can only venture that he destroyed it in a rage or pawned it for money to party.

In my bedroom, as soon as I relinquish Riley to go for my closet, a sense of urgency hits me again. I never belonged here, not in this apartment with Dallas, not in the life I thought we were making. Wrenching clothes off the hangers, I can't stuff them in my bag fast enough, my hands quaking.

I didn't belong here then, and I sure as hell don't belong here now, towing my client along to a viper's nest. Have I ever made a wise decision in my adult life?

Please, God. Just let me finish this. Don't let him come home.

Chapter 17

RILEY

I don't have to see to know that Harper's face probably looks distraught right now. The sounds of hangers screeching across the closet railing and the successive rustle of clothes being stuffed into his bag are a solid indicator of his trepidation over being here. I'd give anything to help him get through this right now, but my specialty is making light of things, and there's no making light of this disturbing misery he's in.

Moving deeper into the room, my cane brushes the edge of a mattress and then comes to an open space. I can hear the dead air in front of me, telling me there's more furniture ahead. A dresser.

Trailing my fingers across the surface, I make out the edge of a picture frame, and then another. Picking one up, I wonder if it's a photo of Harper, of his family, or Daniel.

"Do you want these?" I offer, holding up a frame.

"Those aren't mine," he says distractedly before returning to his wardrobe.

He's definitely got clothes in that closet from the sounds of his hasty packing. Maybe his roommate decided to claim his bedroom after Harper left.

There's a latent hint of sugar cookie scent in the room, but there's something else too, something distinctly not sugar cookie, something distinctly not Harper. It smells like Harper mixed with sweaty gym socks and cheese, but not good cheese, rather old stale cheese. It smells like abusive asshole cheese. Frowning, I set the picture down. This guy is an abomination to cheese. Now I really hate him.

The way Harper grew more anxious since he went out to lunch with Daniel last week makes more sense now. He knew this was coming, planned it in silence, fretted about it in solitude. Nobody gets that bent out of shape over a roommate. The absence of any denials yesterday at the coffee shop tells me glitter barista may have called it right. I'm just starting to wonder why I'm so bent out of shape over my roommate.

It's a shot in the dark, but all my shots are in the dark. Facing the closet, I ask the question I've been wondering all week, the one that's making a pain twist in my chest that feels a lot like jealousy.

"Did you love him?"

Chapter 18

HARPER

The quiet words pack a powerful force both cornering me into the spotlight of the truth and setting me free by knowing he may have an inkling of what Dallas was to me. Daniel says I'm terrible at hiding my emotions. Riley may not be able to see with his eyes, but he knows how to see other ways. I had a moment of panic yesterday when I thought he figured it out, but like everything, he took it in stride if he did catch on. He's been honest with me since day one, wearing his humiliations on his sleeve with much more dignity than I have.

The mortifying words tumble out, an offering of honesty in return for his kindness. "I thought I did. Once."

"Harper," he calls out when I don't elaborate further.

I can't. I can't tell this man who was smart enough to boot a woman after a few months who prevented him from becoming independent that I was a smitten fool through a year of bashful flirting and then a hopelessly optimistic romantic for another two. He's so much braver than I am.

"Harper?"

"I'm almost done," I force out with as much control as I can, wiping the tear cascading down my cheek.

I don't want to know what he thinks about me being gay now that it's officially been confirmed or me being stupid and gay. It's probably too much to hope that he'll forget all about this, and that we can go back to that delightful ease of teasing.

"You said he was violent," he hedges. "Violent how?"

Of course. Of course, the universe has to rip me open even further until there isn't a shred of dignity left to my name.

"In every way. Okay?" I mutter, hoping the clipped response downplays the importance of the topic to him.

His hands are warm, grasping onto my shoulders. My spine is stiff as a board, but I realize it's the first time I haven't flinched from his contact. It's a touch I welcome because it's Riley. When an arm snakes across my chest, tugging me back against his, my body gives up all defenses, settling into the comfort with a shaky breath. The whiskers on his chin tickle the skin on my neck. His hot breath steady and strong against my pulse as he just holds me like he's keeping me together.

I can't remember the last time I felt this safe in this room. It's ironic, Riley lives in the Little Hell neighborhood, but my time with him there has been nothing short of heaven.

His throaty voice is low and thoughtful. "Did he fuck with any of your shit?"

"No," I let out on a scoff at his solidarity, not caring anymore that I can't hide the sound of my sniffle. "He probably thought I was dumb enough to come back."

The prophecy reminds me of how foolish it is for me to be here right now, dragging Riley along with me, and also the contrast in the images I have of the two of us in my mind. Standing in this room is a sickening reminder of how I'm used goods, garbage, tainted, so very abstract from the beautiful, perpetual ray of sunshine with his youthfully innocent sense of humor who's standing behind me. I pull away to get back to my packing, feeling the enormous loss of the comfort of his arm around me.

"Does he sleep in here?"

"Yeah. Still looks that way."

"Do you need to sit down for a minute?"

"No. I just really want to get out of here."

"Sure." He pats me on the back, but it's more of a rub, more understanding comfort. Why is he always so amazing?

"Um, where's the bathroom?"

"Behind you, then to the right."

The sound of his cane tapping against the bathroom doorframe, brings more reality into focus. This was *my* apartment. Riley's in *my* apartment, in *my* bathroom.

Maybe in another life, where men don't have to cry, he'd be bursting in on me every morning like he did the other day. I wouldn't cover up, but rather open my arms, expecting the intrusion as part of our daily ritual. There wouldn't be broken ribs and broken coffee tables, only ugly dogs named Larry, the sound of laughter, and mischievous green eyes that soothe my aching soul. Maybe in another life, there's a gay Riley for a guy who's gotten everything wrong in this one.

Chapter 19

RILEY

I didn't expect that learning Braille would be enthralling. My suggestion to Harper that we finally dive into it after he unpacked the stuff that he rescued from his old place was an attempt to distract him from his shitty afternoon. He was right about learning the fabric swatch differences thing. This shit is like running my fingers over a bunch of cupcake sprinkles someone dumped on the counter. I can't believe he knows how to read it.

When I figured out how daunting it would be, I asked him to give me a page of numbers instead of letters. I started this because I wanted to know elevator buttons, so why shoot for the moon? The alphabet can wait.

I've been running my fingers over numbers one through ten for the last half an hour. I think I'm getting it or could get it, but to say I'm distracted is an understatement.

Harper.

Harper, Harper, Harper.

That's the only message I can focus on right now after this afternoon in his apartment.

Violent in every way.

The recall of his words makes me shudder. I don't want them to mean what they probably mean. Who could do that to a person? I've never understood how a human being could intimately violate another person.

I had to hold him after that. The flinching, the anxiety—he needs to know there's kindness left in the world. He needs to feel safe. What the hell kind of life is it if you're afraid of your own shadow? And I thought I had problems. My frustrations are child's play compared to what I imagine he's been through. I only wish I could have thought of something more than missing the toilet accidentally-on-purpose to pay that asshole back who hurt him.

His warmth is soaking into my skin from where he's sitting next to me on the couch. It's pacifying a protectiveness inside me, knowing he's close by where no one can hurt him, knowing he can be free from worry here.

I want to toss this stupid Braille book and put my arm around him again, so I can feel the proof in his body that he's actually relaxing the way he slumped into me earlier. I've never been into guys, but for some reason I have this urge to reassure him that a man can be physically tender, to show him he deserves nothing less than that. I keep thinking of that day he got out of the shower, revisiting the way my pulse rocketed. It's crazy…absolutely crazy, but I keep wondering if the droplets on his skin would have tasted like sugar cookies.

Holding and kissing? That'd be awkward though coming from me. Right? He'd know it was just sympathy since I'm straight, and I know how much I hate sympathy. So, why do I still want to hold him and… taste him? I think it might actually make *me* feel better, so I guess it's more selfish than sympathetic.

"If you get me a Braille phone, don't expect me to be able to call 9-1-1," I joke, eager to disrupt the silence.

He doesn't answer.

Shit. Was that a bad joke? Did he ever have to call 9-1-1?

Very maturely, without a thought of deflection, I add, "I'm sorry. Am I boring you?"

Again, no answer.

Holy fuck. Is he dead?

Reaching over, I graze the side of his face with my fingers, trying to ignore the way the contact makes my breath catch. "Harper?"

Something hard and plastic tumbles down. An earbud. He lets out a little grunt, followed by an audible suction of breath.

Oh. He's asleep.

Duh. He's still warm dumbass.

I'm an idiot. This whole day has me acting all Mother Hen for the guy. He's probably just drained after what he dealt with today, and watching me learn Braille is about as exciting as listening to Larry lick his nuts. That dog has issues.

Feeling the couch cushion, I recover the earbud. Must be an exciting book if it made him pass out. It's probably a how-to on matching your old man pipe with your slippers.

Popping it in my ear the smooth baritone of a man's voice is narrating. Harper could totally do that job. This guy's voice is clearly stage quality, but I like Harper's better.

Holy shit…did he just say…

"Dustin's hands travel down my abs like a potter, smoothing clay. His fingers, cresting the curves of my hip junctures send a shudder up my spine. He's here. He's touching me. This is real, I chant as my mind unfolds all the layers of pent-up lust. He's not marrying that woman his family wants him to marry. He's not ashamed to have his hands on another man's body. He's free. We're free, even if it's a lie, even if it's only for tonight."

Oh! Um…oh.

Damn.

I turn my head to reassess the shy, quiet guy I know as Harper, but of course, I can't see him. Who'd have thought this sensitive, unassuming man would be into…

Whoa! Dustin's hand just made contact. Aaand…Jesus!

Are narrators supposed to make the moan sounds of the characters? It feels like I'm in the bedroom with these two guys.

Naugh-ty Harper. I'd have never guessed. Maybe he would be into shower droplet tasting. Fuck, the thought makes my cock stir. What is the deal? Were the guys right? Do my senses not care now whether it's a man or a woman because I'm blind? I call bullshit on that because I guarantee you Val does nothing for me now, and the thought of Marco or Jasper? If I went gay, it sure as shit wouldn't be for either of those idiots.

Face burning, feeling like a perv, I crack up at the spicy story. Well, good for Harper.

Everybody's got to have a hobby, a source of enjoyment, a way to relax and unwind. I so have to give him shit about this sometime though. Wait, that might be a bit immature.

I mean, it's not like I've never had a sexual fantasy in my head. Clearly, I just had a bizarre one now.

You know what? I'm still going to give him shit though because this is bullshit now that I think about it. I've been sitting here feeling up fabric swatches the last three weeks while he's been having someone talk dirty to him. That's so not fair. I mean, he could've put it on speaker. I can still feel shit and listen at the same time.

Did he think I'd be weirded out? What's the big deal? It's kisses and hands and sex talk. It's all the same in the end. Right? The goal is always the same. Two people figure their shit out and then get off.

I've never listened to romance. Can't say I thought my first exposure to it would be about two guys, but hearing someone narrate about touching a guy's cock and how it feels is a memory I can relate to fondly. I mean, it'd be nice if someone besides me touched my cock again someday—preferably someone who doesn't insist I wear polo shirts—so a romance book is a passable substitute for now. Plus, it's a peek into Harper's world. I wanted to know more about him.

Is this what glitter barista wanted to do to him? I don't like that idea. We're never fucking going there again. I have no idea what the guy looked like but he's not right for Harper. Harper deserves clever flirting and someone who uses normal pens.

Smirking, I wonder if he has a favorite book character. Does he go all gaga for cover models the way women used to do over that guy, Fabio?

Oh, shit! Dusty's going down…downtown to P-town.

Holy fuck. Is he still going to go through with the wedding?

Chapter 20

HARPER

Oh my gosh. What time is it?

The blurry numbers on the cable box under the TV come into focus. Eleven p.m.?

Whipping my head to the right, I give a start. Riley's still sitting here on the couch with me. Crap. I'm employee of the year. I hope he didn't need anything.

He's staring at the floor, arms folded across his chest with one hand up to his mouth. His teeth are biting into his thumb in concentration. I've never seen him so deep in thought.

"Riley? Are you okay?"

He must be really zoned out because he makes no indication that he heard me. Wait a minute. Is that…one of my earbuds?

Locating my phone in my lap, my screen shows the Eagan Brannigan novel I was listening to is still playing…the very *graphic* Eagan Brannigan, king of male/male romance novels.

Oh, my sweet baby Jesus.

Fumbling for the stop-button, I hit it before I can even think of an explanation to fill the following silence. Hyperventilating, my gaze connects with Riley's.

He looks like he just came out of a fog, a thick, heady sex fog, pupils blown, sexy lips parted like an addict begging for more. I blink and shake my head, getting snared on the memory of his *boyfriend* comment the other day at the coffee shop that made my heart flip. Could he be… No way. It must be the lighting and my grogginess.

"Harper?"

"Hey, I…sorry, I fell asleep."

"Yeah." He chuckles, popping my earbud out and handing it to me. "You were zonked out. I thought you were dead."

Taking the earbud from him feels like being handed a scarlet letter. How much did he hear? He's been cool so far about me being gay, but hearing an explicit account of two men pleasuring each other might put things a little too much into perspective. No way am I diving into an awkward book club conversation right now.

Deflect. Yes, deflect.

"Sorry. Did...how did the Braille go?"

"Oh, um, it might take me a little while before I've got it down, and...I got distracted." He gestures with his chin toward me, a playful smirk on his face. "I kind of listened to your book."

Awkward book club it is. What do I say to that? Seriously, what is the appropriate response?

"Real deep stuff, I know," I joke nervously.

Chuckling he grins. "No. It was...it's a good story. I mean...I wasn't expecting a story, but...there's really a story."

I can't take it anymore. Now he's humoring me over my infatuation with gay romance novels. I'm just going to go find a place to die.

"Uh, ye-ah. Glad...glad you liked it. Okay, well, um...I'm going to head to bed."

"Oh, alright."

Why does he sound disappointed? "I'm sorry. I didn't ask if you needed anything."

"No. No, I'm good. Goodnight."

Halfway to the hallway, I grow a spine. Stopping, I turn back. "Riley?"

"Yeah?"

"I just, um, thanks...for earlier today."

"Nothing to thank me for."

Right. It was nothing, or maybe he wants to forget about that half-hug now that he's heard my man-porn. Fucking kill me now.

Stripping down to my boxers in my room, I plug my slutty-talking phone in on the nightstand, and then burrow my head under my blankets. This was just a dream, a very bad, awkward dream. Everything will be fine in the morning.

We're in my apartment. Riley's arm is wrapped around me, his warm breath on my neck. I'm melting into him, trembling as my hand grasps over top of his, holding his palm to my beating heart.

It's a beautiful apartment. We've made a beautiful life here. I'm so happy waking up to the sound of his laughter every morning that it terrifies me it's not real.

That noise...

That stomping sound of heavy, angry footsteps. I know that sound.

Oh, no. It's *him*. It's Dallas.

"This isn't your life," he snarls, ripping Riley away from me. "You don't get to have nice things. You only get me. I'm what you chose. Did you forget that?"

His voice gets louder with each ugly taunt, each cruel verdict that can't be true.

He's got Riley by the lapels of his leather jacket, swinging him around like a rag doll.

He can't do this. He can't take him away from me. This is *my* dream. Not his. He's not supposed to be here, but he is. Will I ever escape him?

I scream, watching him throw Riley's body into the wall, but nothing comes out. The harder I try, the more my lungs burn, I can't produce a sound to stop it.

"Harper?" Riley calls, low and smoky.

"No!" Finally, my vocal cords work. "No, stop! Please stop!"

I can't shake the hands off me. He's got me. He won't let go.

"Harper! Harper, it's Riley. You're okay. It was just a nightmare. You're alright."

"Riley?" I pant, blinking up at him, looming over me in my bed.

In *my* bed. In *his* apartment.

A wet sneeze draws my eyes to a lump of fur curled up on the floor. Larry glances up at us, his tail thumping against the carpet.

I was dreaming. Oh, geez, Riley heard me.

"Yeah. You're fine," he soothes, rubbing my arm, his biceps flexing in his white tank top.

God, he's sitting on the bed. I can smell his spicy scent, feel his body heat.

"Well, at least I hope you're fine," he adds. "Are you...fine?"

Sitting up, I wipe the sweat from my brow. "Yeah. Yeah, sorry. I...I don't know why I think about the shit I think about in my sleep."

Settling back against the headboard, he lets out a puff of breath and shrugs. The way his hair falls in his face is too reminiscent of the good parts of my nightmare, loved-up looking. Brushing it from his eyes, he smirks, but even in the shadows cast by the hallway light, I can tell it's one of his sad, self-deprecating smirks. I know the difference now.

"Sometimes I dream that I'm falling again," he says softly, staring into the darkness. "I'm on the side of the rock face. I can see Rob a few feet away from me. I can see the sunlight glinting off his helmet, off his caribiners, and then my line gives out just like it did, but I don't hit the ground. Just before I get there, I wake up, and for a few seconds, I'm in this daze where I think that I can see, that I *should* be able to see, because I didn't hit the ground this time." Chuckling he continues, "But I can't. It's like finding out all over again that I'm blind." Picking at the comforter, he hums contemplatively. "I don't know why I have that dream."

I know he's not telling me out of self-pity, but I want to comfort him. How can there be so much I want to tell him and yet he always finds a way to leave me speechless?

"So...nightmares are a thing," he adds with a shrug. "I think everybody probably has them sooner or later."

Could he stop being so perfect? It's like any one of the conversations I wish my father had with me when I was little that never happened before he left us. Riley would be a great dad. I wonder if he knows that?

"I met Dallas three years ago," I blurt out to stop the images of little Rileys running around the kitchen. "We were roommates, him, me, and another guy, one of the trainers at his gym. I had answered an ad for a roommate after college. The other guy moved out after I'd been there for six months, so...it was just me and Dallas then. That's...well, things changed, obviously. I hadn't even known he was bi before that. He was...really sweet at first, affectionate, just as vulnerable about a new relationship as me."

"I wish people came with warning labels," he offers when I trail off. "Or like a character trait menu on a video game." Holding his hand up like air brackets, he accentuates, "Likes cheese. Has ugly dog. Weaknesses: pizza. Strengths: insatiable modesty."

I sputter along with him. Fucking Riley.

Sighing, he rests his head against the headboard. "We take chances on people, the same way they take chances on us. If we didn't, everybody'd be alone."

Maybe that's what we are, what the basis of this growing bond I feel between us is. We're both two lonely people who were alone.

"You got your phone?" he asks.

"Yeah. You need something?"

"Well, if you can't sleep, we could listen to that story of yours."

Is he serious? Okay, I appreciated the concern, but now he's going overboard. I know he knows it's a gay romance.

"Riley, you don't have to humor me. I'll just fall back asleep. I'm fine."

"Yeah, but..." he huffs, sounding agitated.

"But what?"

His frustrated breath ghosts across the distance. Turning toward me, eyes wild, he gesticulates. "Does Dustin go get his man, or does he marry that chick his family's trying to force on him? It's fucking killing me not knowing! I swear, my brain's going to explode!"

Holy crap. He's...actually serious. I've created a gay porn monster.

When I'm finished picking my jaw up off the mattress, a laugh bubbles out of my throat. "Um, I'm not sure. I didn't get that far yet."

Grabbing my phone and pulling up my audiobook app for him, I hesitate before handing it over. Yes, I'm giving my straight patient, who's sitting in my bed after calming me from a nightmare, a gay romance book. Just a totally normal day that I'm sure violates not a single Home Reach policy.

"Yes," he whisper-cheers, looking down at the glow of my screen like it's a box of *Better Cheddars*.

Disbelieving, I shake my head and tap the play button for him where he left off earlier. And then I wait. I wait for him to get off the bed and go back to his room.

He does neither. Instead, he leans back against the headboard, crosses his ankles, and folds his arms across his stomach, a disturbingly serene smile on his face.

"Oh, you meant...like right now? *Here*?" I clarify, realizing he's settling in.

"Oh." He frowns, straightening up. "Don't you want to know what happens?"

The evident shock on his face that I might not is probably the most bizarre and yet adorable reaction of his to date by far. After everything he did for me today, he can listen to all the gay smut that he wants.

"Sure, but don't be mad if I fall asleep."

"How can you sleep through this shit? It's too intense!"

Yawning through a laugh, I roll onto my side and tug the covers up to my chin. "Long day," I rationalize, my eyelids growing heavy already, and if my back is to him, I can pretend this isn't happening.

"Yeah," he concurs, his hand fumbling to pat my head like he does to Larry.

Smiling at the darkness, the sound of the narrator telling the sordid affair of Dustin and Jacob piercing the silence, I realize this should be awkward, but it doesn't feel awkward. I don't detect a hint of self-consciousness. It just feels...normal. It's Riley. He makes everything okay.

I'm not afraid that someone touched me. I'm not afraid that there's a man in my bed. It has nothing to do with the growing ideas of attraction to him. I think I've made a new friend, one that provides some-thing Daniel can't.

Maybe that's what I really needed all along, someone kind and alone just like me because together, we're not alone.

Chapter 21

RILEY

"Well, it's official. Leigh Ann's going to adopt you," I tell Harper as we fold clothes in my laundry room.

"I'm sure you're more than enough to handle. Why would she want a do-over?"

"You have no idea. Pretty sure she tried to give me away a few times. Once a year, she'd dress me up and tell me to go knock on doors for candy."

"Halloween?" he asks, sounding confused.

"No, just a random day of the year. She said to tell whoever gave me candy that they had to let me live with them or I'd call the cops on them for giving candy to kids."

A t-shirt hits me in the face. "Shut up. Your mother is the most normal person I've ever met."

"Are you sure we're talking about the same person?"

Folding the shirt he chucked at me, I realize what a good mood I'm in. This is the first time since my accident that I haven't gotten antsy when Mom stopped by. I know she loves me and worries about me, but since my fall her visits have felt more obligatory than social. My penthouse became a time machine where I've been perpetually fourteen again in her eyes, and she has to ask if I'm taking care of myself. Today was…different.

"Hey, I'm sorry she asked you so many questions," I tell him. "About your family."

"It's okay. She was just making conversation that anyone would."

Harper, always gracious. I didn't want to find out by forced interrogation that his father left when he was a kid and his mother passed away the year he went to college. Mom and I both gave him our condolences, but it feels like we stole something from him. The way his pitch dropped when he answered her question, I can tell it resurfaced a sensitive wound. Still, it was a welcome change, having Mom's focus on some-one besides me.

For the first time in months, her visit felt like a visit instead of a wellness check. She didn't clean a single thing while she was here. I've been promoted from invalid back to son.

Smoothing the ripples out of the shirt, I realize it's a dark fabric against the stainless-steel laundry room counter. Harper helped me organize my dresser drawers into two sections, lights and darks. He's been teaching me about contrast since I can detect a modicum of shades in well-lit areas.

We ordered white plates because he said they'd be easier to spot on my black countertops than the stupid black stoneware ones Val got when she started playing homemaker. He threw a white throw blanket over the back of my beige couch, and now the piece of furniture is an easily spotted beacon, rather than a blur I have to fumble to locate. He acts like it's nothing. I don't think he has any idea how much he's literally changed my world. He's a compass that's made it possible for me to navigate again.

Running my hand over the shirt, I know I should be grateful for what I've learned to distinguish, but the former me, the sighted me, makes me greedy. Is it navy or black? Hunter green? Dark gray?

I'm not the only blind person this has to frustrate. It's human nature to desire free will, to be able to make simple choices.

"If I could still see, I'd come up with a way for non-sighted people to be able to figure out which clothes of theirs were which," I complain. "Like old black t-shirt with mustard stain from the Superbowl on it, end quote."

"Hm," Harper hums thoughtfully. I've noticed he never refutes my musings, making me believe anything is possible. "Too bad they don't have an app for that."

A charge of adrenaline shoots through my bloodstream, the sensation I used to get when I was finishing up an app, I knew would be a hit. He really is my compass.

Reaching out, I clutch onto his shoulder. The need to brace myself so I don't float away with excitement, overpowering. "That's brilliant. Don't they have anything like that already?"

"Well, there's clothing with specific texture designs to make it more appealing to the non-sighted, and there's apps where you can video call an assistant to review your wardrobe for the day."

"No. Who wants to have to have a fashion consultant on speed-dial? This is the twenty-first century. I'm talking about something that you can use and point at your clothes like…like a QR code. You scan it like with your phone, and it'll read off what the piece of clothing is."

"Oh, yeah. Yeah, you could use fabric labels, or I think they make adhesive ones that you can stick permanently to clothing now. I guess, you could print those labels or codes or whatever on those tags if…if they were programmed somehow. I don't know if that's even possible. Is that stupid?"

"No!" I laugh. "It's fucking genius! And I know how to do it. That's what I do…or what I did. Holy shit, Harper!"

After an hour of searching possible existing technology, we learned that two talented tech college students designed an app that will read manufacturer labels with special QR codes. While I'm overjoyed someone thought of people like me, I still want to take it one step further on a DIY level, something that doesn't make the visually impaired have to rely on whether or not a clothing manufacturer used specific labels.

"Maybe you could safety-pin QR tags to the clothing that you just take off before you wear them and then reattach them in the wash, if people don't want to get or can't afford a fabric labeler," Harper suggests, making me want to squeeze the crap out of him.

Grabbing him by the arm, I start walking. "Come on."

"What…where are we going?"

"To my computer. I need your help."

"With what?"

"Designing our clothes-reader app."

"*Our*…Riley, I don't know how to design apps. I barely know anything about computers except how to check my email."

Catching the light flooding through the opening of my room, I get behind him and urge him by the shoulders. "Yeah, but I do!" I counter. "I was an app designer. Remember? I'll walk you through it."

"Wh-what if I screw it up, and it doesn't work."

"You won't. I'll tell you what to type and how to use my design programs."

Finding the back of my office chair, I pull it out and pat the seat for him to sit down. This will be the most exciting project I've ever worked on. I've designed useful apps before, ones that made things convenient for people, but this…this could change lives.

"But," he huffs, sounding pained, "what if I do something wrong, some minor mistake that prevents it from working and we can't find it because I don't even know what to look for. I…I don't want to disappoint you."

"Is that code for you're still scared of me, and you think I'll go all *Hulk* on you if it doesn't work?"

"No. Yes." I can just picture him with his face in his hands, sighing.

"Harper," I say sagely, guiding him by the shoulders to sit down. "I'm an app design guru. If it doesn't work, it'll be because I failed you. I can do this. Trust me, and if it doesn't work, but it will, I won't get mad."

It's quiet for a moment. He exhales. The chair swivels, brushing against my knee. "How do I even turn this thing on? It's like something from NASA."

The smile on my face is so big it hurts. I can work again. I can make something.

In the morning, after keeping Harper up way past his bedtime, I blink at the sunlight coming through the patio doors. Why is it so bright today? Am I dreaming again?

Holy shit…

Blinking, it's like looking through a straw, but I can see my patio table on the rooftop walkout. It's happening again. How long do I have?

Scrambling out of bed, instinct tells me to grab my phone and search the internet for something. Wait. Our app. I could check on our app. That'd be more useful than me looking up some world wonder.

My toe bashes into something soft and warm. A groan rises up from the floor.

Blinking, I see fur, wild dark chestnut fur. Holy shit. It's Larry. He's…he's…

Damn.

Laughter erupts from my belly. I can't stop it. I'm shaking, it's pouring out of me so hard. Eyes watering, Larry blurs in front of me. It's not just the tears though. I can tell. The tunnel vision is narrowing, but I don't even care as I wipe my eyes. I got to see my dog.

Squatting down, the picture fogs entirely back to nonsensical starbursts. My reliable sense of sight by touch returns with ease, allowing me to find and scratch under his chin and behind his ears.

"He was right," I tell him affectionately. "You *are* the ugliest dog I've ever seen."

Chapter 22

HARPER

I never imagined I'd be designing an app, entering code into a computer program, and enjoying it. When Riley is happy, it's difficult not to also be happy. He's set the standard for happy extremely high this past week that we've been working on his project. He's like a little kid in a candy shop. If I thought he was charismatic and confident before, I don't know what to call him now, but that light burning inside of him has grown brighter with each piece of code he's dictated to me. He already had a screen reader app installed on his computer, but it only serves him to a degree considering the complexity of the programs he has to use to design his apps and the need for someone to relate a description of how the visuals are appearing as intended. There's quite a bit he could do on his own, but he seems to enjoy having me be involved in the process. Watching him come more alive has been a gift, but it's not the only one I received this week.

I've heard nothing from Dallas. By now, he's home and would have realized my clothes are missing from our closet. Yet, it's been silent. No harassment. Not even feigned messages of remorse or ugly love. I want to believe that means it's over, that chapter of my life, but I don't trust the silence. I don't trust my luck. I don't trust how good I feel. Maybe Daniel scolding me when he found out I went without him reinforced the danger.

It's July already. I've been at Riley's for almost five weeks now. That means there's a little less than four months left on his service contract. I should be looking for a new apartment, something modest I can slowly furnish. How good I feel has nothing to do with me not having looked yet. At least, that's what I've been telling myself. Failing to believe my inner monologue about thinking of Riley as a new friend has nothing to do with it either. Just a friend, nothing more.

His body heat is a new article of clothing I've worn this past week at the desk in his bedroom. He's perched on a footstool next to me, invading the shit out of my personal space while I try in vain to concentrate on typing and reading back the code rather than concentrating on his scent or how close his mouth is to my face.

"Do you mind if we call it quits for the day? I just made like five typos. I think my eyes are getting tired," I plead, a desperate cop-out to create some distance from his ever-growing magnetism.

"Oh, yeah. Sure. Sorry. What time is it anyway?"

"Mm. Five o'clock."

Groaning, he rises up, stretching until his happy trail peeks out from under the hem of his shirt above his jeans. "Uh! No wonder my stomach is eating itself."

Tearing my eyes away, I deflect from the thought of placing kisses there. "Your stomach is always eating itself."

"Come on," he says, patting me on the shoulder. "Let's take Russell and go out to eat. You pick."

"I get to pick? Does that mean I get to pick which toppings on tonight's pizza?"

"No, smart ass. Whatever you want. I've been working you over-time all week. Wherever you want to go. My treat."

Working me over…that's as far as my brain got before I filled in words like working me over *the couch, the bed, the kitchen counter.* Why did I have to get a job for a guy who's hotter than the sun and makes my world a brighter place than it's ever been?

Fantasizing and doing are two different things though. Even if he was bi, I don't know if I'd be ready to…to be intimate with anyone again. The possibility of kisses and touching though…with Riley? I could handle that, more than handle that. And now I'm getting hard.

Food. Right. I'll just eat my feelings, all my so-not-thinking-of-him-like-a-friend feelings.

An hour later, we're sitting in Madame Sue's Garden eating the number-five and the number-seven. Okay, Riley also got the number-two and the number-twelve.

I'm starting to bulk up, living with him. I hadn't realized how the past few months of fights with Dallas had affected my appetite. I look… healthy, vigorous even.

Right now though, I probably look like I'm going to be sick. Groaning, I tug at the belt on my khakis.

"I don't know where you put it all," I tell Riley, watching him stuff another shred of Mongolian beef in his mouth.

Moaning around a bite, he forks another piece of meat and tosses it over the side of the table to Larry. Cringing, I catch my breath when it bounces off Larry's head and lands on the floor next to the last six pieces that he threw him.

I could say something. Five weeks ago, I might have, but telling him his folly would be like telling a kid that unicorns aren't real.

"I have magic places inside of me that can harbor reserve calories for emergency situations," he explains through his chewing.

Magic places? Yeah, I'm well aware of his magic places. Damn it. I'm doing it again.

"What? Like an energy boost for superhero tasks?"

"Mm. No, but that sounds cooler than the bullshit I was going to say." He cackles.

Laughing, I give a start when the waitress catches me by surprise at the side of the table.

"Excuse me," she whispers. "Can you please tell your friend to stop throwing food on the floor?"

Crap.

Riley's brow furrows. Could this waitress be ruder, assuming he's deaf as well as blind, but that's not why he's frowning. He glances down at Larry and inches his boot around on the floor, stopping when he connects with his rejected offerings.

"Damn it, Russell," he mutters. "That's like four seventy-five worth of Mongolian beef. What's wrong with you?"

"I was going to pick them up," I explain to the waitress.

Returning her sour expression, I'm interrupted by a bark of laughter from across the table. It doesn't end there though. Riley roars until he's wiping tears from his eyes. It's then I finally realize that my silence over his dog treat mishap is the source of his comic relief.

"Harper, you kill me," he chokes out, panting. "You're alright. You know that?"

I don't think it'll ever be such a privilege to pick food up off a floor with someone again.

When we get back home, he does what he does every minute of the day, surprises me again.

"You want to listen to an audiobook?" he asks, dropping down on the couch and removing Larry's harness.

"What kind of book?" I ask, hurrying to pull up the trending menu on my audiobook app, since all I have in my library are books about things I'd really not mind if we did to each other.

"Whatever you've got."

"You probably don't want to hear what I've got. If you tell me a genre though, we can search what they have."

"How many, Harper?"

"Huh?"

121

"How many romance novels do you have in your library?" He grins.

"Why does it matter?" I laugh nervously.

"Because I want to know."

Scoffing at this uncomfortable game of chicken, I huff. "A lot. Okay?"

"What's a lot? Thirty? Forty?"

"Um, more than that. I like the stories. Okay? They're…the happily-ever-afters give me hope."

And as usual, my big mouth killed the mood. His expression is somber as he nods. "Play one."

Right, idiot. Remind him that you didn't get a happily-ever-after. Let's add *mopey whiner* to the list of redeeming qualities I've shown him.

"Riley, you don't have to humor me. Honestly, it's alright if we—"

"No, I'm serious. That one you played a couple weeks ago felt like TV for me. I could see it in my head. They're more descriptive than movies on TV. Just…they're not all as sad as that one was, are they? I don't want to be depressed."

"It wasn't sad. It had a happy ending."

"Yeah, but they had to go through hell first! Thank fuck, you fell asleep, or you'd have heard me sniveling like a baby!"

"Wait, you cried?"

"It was sad and…and emotional!" Fidgeting, he cards his fingers through his hair. "Are you going to play one or what?"

I really shouldn't let anything he says or does at this point surprise me, but pouting over the possibility of being denied another romance book takes the cake. Plus, I can't measure how sweet it is knowing he can cry when he gets emotional and over the story of a gay couple to boot. If he could stop being so damn wonderful that would really help out with the butterflies he gives me.

"Yeah…sure," I concede.

Smiling triumphantly, he settles back into the couch and kicks his feet up on the coffee table. "Do you have any funny ones?"

Sputtering, now it's my turn to tease. "You want a romcom?"

"Yeah, unless you want to be my therapist afterward. We need to *decode* after all the app work. Find something that'll make us laugh."

"I actually thought about becoming an audiobook narrator," I ramble to fill the silence.

"Heck, yeah, you should!" he exudes. "You have the voice for it. I'd totally listen to you all day."

He would? I threw that out there to hear him tease me. I didn't expect support for a pipe dream I've never admitted to anyone.

Once I find the least steamy romcom I have in my library, I put my phone on speaker and hit *play*. How did we get here? What does it mean? Does it mean *something*...that something is changing?

I can't say I ever get fully comfortable on the couch because it's gay romance...with an audience...with Riley as the audience. I mean, I know what's eventually coming in the story. The first hour is actually quite entertaining, listening to his amusement and ad lib commentary of the story. By the end of the second hour though, it's all I can do to sit still and regulate my breathing.

We've reached the initial sexual attraction, the flirting, the innuendos. This book has become a diary of my thoughts about Riley, and now it's being read aloud.

Pinching my eyes shut, I practice my mantra. *He's your friend. He's your friend.*

My mantra is broken, watching him with his knees tucked up to his chest beside me, lips parted, gaze far away as though he's fully immersed in my addiction now too. How am I supposed to think of him as a friend when he's rewritten my definition of perfect boyfriend material?

Pausing the book, I get up. "Hey, it's getting late. I think I'm going to turn in."

"Oh. Okay."

"Did you...want to use my phone?" I offer.

"No," he lets out on a laugh, face flushed. Maybe he's reached his limit of romance novels. "I'm going to head to bed too."

"Alright. Goodnight."

"Night."

Stopping to give Larry a pet, I chide myself. I'm becoming so attached to the both of them, to the entire package of Riley's life. The knowledge that I'll have to say goodbye to them some day is a dark cloud over me.

"Hey, Harper?"

Stopping in the hallway, I turn back. "Yeah?"

"I just...wanted to say thanks...for everything." The words leave me dumbstruck, but then he fills the silence with more. "You make me useful again."

Is it pride or longing that swells in my chest? He makes *me* feel useful too, but it's more than that. He makes me feel appreciated and seen, a lot like what I imagined love is supposed to feel like.

"I'm glad, Riley."

Chapter 23

RILEY

"I can *feel* you staring," I warn to the darkness. "Not cool, man! I don't watch you lick your nuts. Go in the other room. Daddy needs privacy."

Russell finally gets the hint and snorts. His doggie paws brush against the carpeting as I track him waddling out my bedroom doorway.

Dropping my head back to the pillow, my exhale is both from relief and frustration. My semi is still thick in my hand underneath the blankets and that gnawing arousal festering beneath the surface is the kind I know that's not going to go away until I take care of some business.

Stupid bromance books. I suggested it because I wanted to do something Harper would enjoy. Why did the story turn me on? Thank goodness Harper went to bed. I don't know how much longer I could have sat there like a pretzel to hide my hard on.

That first book didn't get me this hot and bothered, granted it was deeper material and my first exposure to bromance. I was stuck between shock and rampant curiosity.

This romcom we started tonight though? I was more invested. The banter, the teasing—it reminded me of…me and Harper. It felt… more believable.

Man, I still can't believe he never said anything about all that food on the floor at the restaurant. Mom and Dad, Val, any one of my friends, including Rob, would have warned me to keep us from being scandalized.

Harper.

Harper, Harper, Harper.

He kept his mouth shut to save me from being embarrassed. It's the little things that make the biggest impact sometimes.

Was he that gracious with that jerk-off he dated? Did they go out to dinner and laugh like we do? I want to believe he had that, but somehow doubt that was the story he was living. He *should* have that though. Nobody's more deserving of having one of his romance novel happy endings than him. How could anybody squander a guy like Harper? He's...he's just so...

Remembering the feel of his back pressed against me when we went to his apartment, the way he sagged into me, I can't find the words to describe our connection. It's so strong. There's a pull whenever he's around. It's not energy drinks that has my heart fluttering lately. I haven't had one in weeks. It's...it's him. It's the way he makes me feel.

My hand squeezes away the painful urge of lust in my cock. How can I be hard when all I'm focusing on is the memory of Harper's potent cookie scent in the crook of his neck when I held him in his apartment?

A vision flashes in my mind, a split-second picture, and then it's gone. Skin. Soft skin at the nape of a neck, a man's neck. My lips pressed to it. My lips...Harper's neck.

My eyelids spring open, my pulse rocketing out of control as my cock kicks like a mule in my grip. Oh, my word.

Harper.

Harper...Harper...Harper.

My disbelieving laugh breaches the air above me. I release my grip on my cock. Physical attraction is the least of my focus right now. Staring into the blackness, I can't see a damn thing, but I see more clearly than I possibly have my entire life.

The way I still want to ban him from visiting all coffee shops in the Chicago area isn't friendly protectiveness. The way we laugh and tease, it's not the same as with Rob. With Rob, it's entertainment. With Harper, it's like I'm addicted to trying to win a prize—his happiness. The way I feel whole whenever he's near, the way I spring out of bed now each morning, eager to meet the day, knowing it'll be spent with him, teasing him, him teasing me back—they're all messages I've been trying to conceal with the label of *friend*. He's so much more than any friend I've ever had...any girlfriend too for that matter.

I know the problem I'm having with his stories now. I want him and me to be in those stories. *I* want to be the hero, his happily ever after, not some asshole MMA trainer or barista with offensive pens.

I'm thirty-two. It doesn't make any sense, but part of me thinks maybe I don't know shit about sense. Testing myself, I imagine Harper on a date with glitter barista.

My teeth clench, pain erupts in my chest. Fuck that. I'd cover myself in glitter, if that's what it took for him to choose me over that guy.

Okay, what about Rob? If Harper and Rob dated, if Rob kissed Harper, I'd...I'd...ah, fuck. I'd totally cut my best friend. Sorry, Rob.

Holy shit, I've got it bad.

Wow. I...fell for a man?

Try as I might to focus on my thoughts, the physical responses haven't diminished. The thought of wrenching Rob away from Harper, so I can be the one to claim a kiss sends a rush of warmth all the way to my toes. My cock thickens to the point of being painful, imagining Harper's voice in my ear, his careful hands on my body.

I feel like a thief, fantasizing something I know I have no right to, but I want to know. Because he'd want to do those things with a boyfriend, wouldn't he? He said his romance books give him hope. The tightening of my balls, the tingle growing there, the aching need making me draw my knees up as I pump into my fist, make me grateful that so far it feels like I could give him that hope, that my body is on board with my heart. Fuck, it's crazy how on board it is.

Panting, I zone every brain cell in on making this feel as real as I can. Harper pressed behind me, his hands running down the front of my chest like Dustin's did in that first book we listened to. This time, Harper is the potter and I'm the clay. Fuck, I will be his clay whenever he wants if it feels like this in real life.

Those hands…those hands that have guided me so many times grip around my cock, making me release a strangled moan into the room. "Yeah," I pant. "Guide my cock too."

My face heats, hearing the sound of my needy commands. I've talked dirty before plenty, but it was always for my partner. It never turned *me* on this much. My dick tells my brain to shut up, and I gladly oblige.

Bucking into my hand, nothing could stop me. The thought of my hand being Harper's instead is full-blown erotica overload. I come so hard and so long, I have no idea how the hell I'm going to find all the mess. My pulse is like a jack rabbit's, my body a spent noodle, sinking into the mattress.

Damn.

Through my self-induced sex fog, I have my answer clear as day. Remembering Harper's novels, I realize this is the part where the "straight" guy is supposed to freak out and try to reject his "strange" new feelings.

Covered in my warm release like I was drunk while basting a damn turkey, the idea of rejecting what I just experienced is about as appealing as wearing polo shirts for the rest of my life. That rejection part of Harper's books really sucked. I mean, that would be incredibly hurtful to Harper, if I did that. Wouldn't it? The thought of trying to convince myself what I feel isn't real, that I can't give him these feelings because we're both men, makes me ill.

Fuck that. I've never been good at letting anyone tell me what to do. I'm going to write my own damn book.

Okay. Next chapter—am I supposed to care what my friends and family would think? I honestly have no clue because people always surprise us. I mean, you think you know someone. You think they're normal, and the next thing you know, they're dressing you in a pink polo or bleaching your light fixtures. I don't get that part of Harper's books either.

Why does it matter what other people think? They're not the one with the feelings. These are *my* feelings, and…they're making me smile. Tiny bombs of giddiness go off in little explosions from the center of my chest to every nerve ending, basking in this sensation of bliss. I really, really like what I'm feeling.

Laughing, I'm too overwhelmed by the wonderful possibilities to analyze it any further, too grateful for the joy bursting around my heart, but a panicked thought derails everything.

Holy shit. Thank goodness Harper's attracted to guys or this would be the most depressing romance novel plot ever.

Wait a minute…it still could be.

Shit. I'm an idiot. It takes two, dumb ass.

How does Harper feel? Is a blind, baseball bat-wielding, motorcycle-riding, cheese-addicted, pain in the ass appealing to him?

Fuck.

Okay. This novel officially sucks.

Chapter 24

HARPER

"Are you sure you don't want to try this? I'm telling you, it's better than any pizza in the world," Riley instigates across the table at the ice cream parlor we stopped at on our way to the grocery store.

"That comparison is supposed to sell it to me? No thanks. I still can't believe they keep *Captain Crunch* in stock just for you."

"Because I'm a genius. It tastes like an ice cream cone when you mix it in with the ice cream. I bet it's their bestseller. They should probably just comp me every time I come in."

Shaking my head, I focus on my boring chocolate cone to avoid watching what his tongue is doing and the goosebumps it's giving me. It's blistering outside, almost August. I shouldn't have goosebumps.

"Why don't you just eat a cone then?"

"It's not the same. This tastes like a cone but better. It's like cone two-point-oh. Come on. Try it."

Before I can protest, the cold wet tip of his double-scoop cone connects with my cheek. "Did I miss your mouth?" he asks innocently.

"You did that on purpose," I crack up, reaching for the napkins.

"I'm so sorry," he laments in his signature deadpan, but then another wet kiss of ice cream grazes my earlobe.

"Riley! Come on!"

"What's the matter? Did I miss again?" he asks, running his fingers from my ear to my cheek, smearing the mess.

Grabbing his wrist, I hold him at bay and bop his nose with my own cone, unable to stop my laughter. He gasps and stretches that tongue of his up to the tip of his nose, eyes crinkled at the corner with laughter.

"Huh. And I was just going to say, I didn't think you could get any sweeter, but I take it back."

What is he saying? Does he know how much that sounds like flirting? He's been acting strange the last two weeks. Sitting closer to me on the couch, giving me friendly little rubs between my shoulders, asking my likes and dislikes—I swear I'm not imagining the extra attention. Plus, not only have audiobooks become our nightly ritual, he's…been asking questions. Last night's was the most uncomfortable.

"So…prostate stimulation? That's…that's really a thing? Like…what does it feel like?"

Trying to describe a prostate orgasm to your straight boss-slash-patient should not be among anyone's job experiences. Going to bed, stabbing your mattress with an erection after listening to racy books with your boss-slash-patient shouldn't be either.

Now I'm sweet and getting ice cream kisses. He's blowing the few courtships I've had out of the water, and he's not even courting me. He can't be. It's just got to be his curious brain, lack of filter, and…I don't know, but I'm not going to make it three more months if this keeps up. At least this rollercoaster of foolish attraction is better than what I'd been dwelling on.

Chapter 25

RILEY

I have no idea what I'm doing. Is this like a date?

Of course not. He doesn't know it's a date. I guess, it's a wooing.

Wait. Scratch that. I don't even know if he wants to be wooed. I need to listen to more of his damn books.

Canvassing the sidewalk with my cane the way Harper taught me, I'm a bit out of my element without the aid of daylight and Russell as we walk toward a bar a few blocks from my apartment. The occasional streetlight provides enough illumination to help me re-center every few paces, but much like my knowledge of Harper's feelings, I'm in the dark for the most part with my night blindness in full effect. Wobbling through an unlit patch, a hand reaches across my back and clasps onto my shoulder.

"You good?" Harper asks.

Why is it when you realize you're attracted to someone, every touch of theirs becomes more significant?

"Yeah." I let out, breathlessly. "Guess I'd better not drink too much, or it'll be an interesting walk home."

Chuckling, he squeezes my shoulder. "I've got you. Drink as much as you want, just…no motorcycle lessons tonight. Okay?"

"Promise." I laugh, fighting a grimace over my past transgressions. Do I even have a chance in hell with this guy? "Tonight's for you anyway," I remind him. "You've been pulling double-duty being a VRT and an app designer. I'll behave, as long as you make sure you have fun."

"Riley, it's impossible not to have fun with you," he says in that serious tone he gets like it's an insult, but it has me smiling.

Good. He thinks I'm fun. That's got to count for something. It makes me realize the goal of tonight—it's an exploratory mission. I'm going to read his every word, his every move like Braille. I know people. I won't suck at this kind of Braille.

Inside Joe's Tap, the incredibly elegant dive bar my suave ass chose for this romantic exploration, Harper guides me by the shoulder to the bar. Does he know how much I appreciate not being shoved or lead along?

I haven't been in a bar since my accident. The trepidation of crowded public places hits me as soon as I sit on the stool and absorb the full effect of the background noise. Pool table balls clacking, the hum of bar chatter coming at me from every angle, the thumping beat of a crappy speaker system—it's a bit much. As soon as the warm skin of Harper's forearm brushes against mine as he takes the stool beside me, the roar of the noise quells. That peaceful connection is there again like we're tethered together by an invisible cable.

After we order our drinks, I'm left with the decision of how to dive in. Do guys flirt the same way men and women do? It sounded like it in his romance novels, but what does Harper like? Maybe that's where I should start.

"You're good at it. You know?" I preface.

"Good at what?"

"VRT. How did you get into it?" I ask. "I mean, what made you say this is what I want to do with my life?"

"Well, it was an easy decision, really. It kind of chose me," he explains on a self-deprecating laugh. "My mother was blind, so I kind of grew up knowing a lot of what I ended up studying in school. I guess, if you think about it, I took the easy way out. No chance of failure."

His mother was blind? What was it like growing up like that? He's literally been helping blind people his entire life.

"You…you told my mom your dad wasn't around. Was it just you and your mom then?"

"Yeah. He left when I was eight, or well, that's the last time I saw him. He was a truck driver. He was on the road a lot, so he wasn't there much before he took off for good anyway."

Shit. Who does that? Who leaves a little kid and their blind wife to fend for themselves?

"That…had to be hard for you and your mom," I flounder for something to contribute. So much for me showing him a good time tonight.

"No, not really. I…it's all I knew. She had retinitis pigmentosa. It's a hereditary disease, so she knew for a while that she'd eventually lose all her sight. I mean, we were prepared. We knew it was coming. That and she was diabetic, so complications with that kind of sped her vision loss along. She had me tested for RP when I was little, but I didn't have the markers. I was more afraid of developing diabetes actually. To be honest, the diabetes was the worst of her battles, since she liked to eat whatever

and whenever she wanted without regard to her sugar level. It's what
ended up killing her in the end."

Can I hold him again? Geez. Would he hold me? Because I think my
heart just cracked in two.

"What did you do?"

"I…she wanted me to go to college, but I didn't want to leave her, especially when her health got worse. We…I needed to save up more money anyway. I worked a few jobs in our hometown, and when she passed,
I just…I guess I was kind of lost for a little while. I took her guide dog
to a training facility, sold our house, and went to college. I was already
two years behind, so VRT seemed like it'd be the thing I had the most
leg up on. I wasn't big on the idea of staying in a dorm, and I'd taken a
few basic classes at the local community college, so I was able to live off
campus. I had some money saved, but I didn't want to burn through it,
so I answered an add for a roommate. That's how I met Daniel."

"Is he a VRT too?"

"No," he laughs. "Business major. He wants to run his own bar someday or a nightclub. I don't know. Something loud with lots of people
and flashy lights where he's the center of attention. The opposite of me.
That's Daniel."

Smiling, I'm grateful he had that spitfire persona around to help chip
away at his sheltered, small-town shell. But look where it got him? I
know the rest of his biography.

"What about you?" he asks. "Did you always want to be
an app designer?"

"No. I wanted to play video games, be an Olympic soccer player, and
race motorcycles. Not in any particular order."

I can just picture him shaking his head as he laughs.
"Your poor mother."

We get to talking about our project, which leaves me grateful for
getting my foot out of my mouth by asking about his family past. I sense
he's getting as excited as me about our app because he pulls his phone
out and rattles off search results of fabric label printers that he must have
looked up on his own.

I could see us doing this on the regular, spitballing ideas, shooting
the breeze, laughing. Doing anything…together. The idea of anything
sounds better with him.

"You want another one?" he asks, tapping my pint glass, making me
realize I've felt like just a normal guy at a bar for the last two hours.

"Yeah, sure."

After he calls the bartender over, he excuses himself to go the restroom. I could so take a piss right now, but I don't want to dampen the

evening by making him help me find the bathroom. That's not romantic. I can hold it.

The bartender sets our new round down in front of me and asks which pile of cash to take the charge from. I tap on the stack of bills I set in front of me when we got here but decide to use the solitude to my advantage.

"Hey, can I ask you something?"

"Sure."

"My buddy," I begin, nodding my chin toward Harper's empty stool, "What does he look like?" Tapping my cane where it's folded up on the bar, in case she hasn't figured out the obvious, I elaborate, "Can you describe him for me?"

"Hm." She hums. "About six-foot, nice skin, fair complexion, dark-brown hair, dreamy, soulful brown eyes like melted chocolate, a good nose."

"A good nose? What does that mean?"

"Okay, how about this. He's a cross between Zac Efron and Josh Hutcherson."

Who the fuck is Josh Hutcherson? She's terrible at this.

"Is that good?"

"Well, I wouldn't kick him out of my bed."

Damn. Mental image. Thank you TMI bartender.

"Noted. Thanks." I chuckle, trying to humor her humoring me, while my stomach flips at the idea of what would happen if I were in a bed with Harper again.

"No problem, sweetie."

"Um, hold up. Do I...look alright?"

Chuckling, she pats my hand. "Good enough to eat. You two would make a cute couple."

Guess I wasn't very subtle. "Oh. Heh. Thanks."

"He's coming. Look sharp," she warns.

"Hey, I thought you said I already look sharp," I snark.

"You'll be fine." She laughs. "He hasn't taken his eyes off you all night."

Well, well. Exploration complete. Harper likes to look at me.

Ouch. What the fuck?

My stool rocks under my weight, jarring me enough my beer spills over the top of my pint glass. Setting it down on the bar, I barely shake the liquid off from where it spilled on my hand when a body slams into the back of my stool again.

"You wanna go man! Let's go!" someone yells behind me.

The sound of a glass breaks. There's more shouting. I can't even get out of my stool, the chair back caging me in. Every time I try to stand up, it's jostled by someone bashing into it, forcing me to stay pressed up against the bar. Fumbling, I reach for my cane, my pulse skittering out of control.

"Harper?" I call out but can barely hear my own voice over the ruckus that's ensuing.

The bartender is screeching for whoever's fighting to stop. I sense so much movement around me, pockets of air shifting in quick succession, that I don't even have my bearings anymore. A cold sweat breaks out on my skin.

"Harper!" I yell again. If someone hurt him, I'll never forgive myself for bringing him to this shithole.

A hand clamps onto my arm, making me flinch. Great. I'm going to get jacked in the face, and I can't even defend myself. Wrenching my arm away, the hand doesn't give.

"Riley! Riley, I'm here!"

Thank fuck. It's Harper. Reaching for him, his fingers clamp around mine, settling my breathing.

"Let's get out of here," I plead.

"Yeah. Come on."

His grip is tight, his elbow locked at the joint to keep me close as we shift through bodies. I can feel the balmy August evening air coming in through the doorway and the sounds of people with the same idea as us bailing outside. We're jostled a few times, but still connected, reassuring me.

When we reach the sidewalk out front, the tension in my shoulders relaxes. I've got his hand gripped in mine across my stomach like a lifeline. Just as I'm about to relinquish it, I change my mind, instead lowering it to our sides.

As we walk farther away from the chaos, I feel his grip go lax in mine, so I hold firm, eyes ahead. Yeah, I'm being sneaky as fuck, or... well, maybe not all that sneaky, but I don't want to let him go yet.

"We're outside now," he says. "It's okay."

"This is easier," I tell him, squeezing his hand. "Then I don't feel like I'm in front of you or going to smack you with my cane."

"Oh."

Was that a good *oh* or a bad *oh?* What the fuck am I doing?

"Do you mind?" I venture.

"No. No, it's fine," he says pleasantly enough that I believe him.

Fighting the smile on my face, I tuck my cane in my back jeans' pocket. I might have grabbed his hand because I was terrified to get out of that bar unscathed, but I'm holding it now because it feels right. His hand was meant to be in mine. It makes sense there. I don't want it to ever stop making sense.

Chapter 26

HARPER

Does he realize what he's doing? I mean, really realize? He's holding another man's hand, a gay man's hand, a gay man who is stupidly, utterly, hopelessly smitten with him. I knew he was a lot of things, but I didn't think he was cruel.

"So…that was a bust," he says as we make our way down the street.

"Yeah, I'm just glad we got out of there intact."

"I know how to show a guy a good time. What can I say?" He laughs.

Is that flirting or just typical no-filter Riley humor? My face heats at the idea of him contemplating showing me a good time. Yeah, right. Not in the way I hope it to mean.

"So, what did you do for fun growing up? You and your mom? I imagine it was…different than what I knew."

"Oh, uh, well, I used to read her books."

"Really?" He beams. "Now why does that not surprise me?"

Laughing, I kick at a rock on the sidewalk, my hip accidentally bumping against his. "Because I'm boring?"

"Are not. You are the least boring person I know."

"And you're the best liar I know," I challenge.

"Ouch!" He winces, putting his free hand over his heart. "So, what did you guys read? Wait a minute," he enthuses, stopping us in front of a restaurant just down from his apartment. "Is that where the whole romance book obsession came from?"

Ah, kill me now. How do I walk myself into these mortifying confessions?

"It's not an obsession," I mutter.

Cackling, he squeezes my hand and…his thumb grazes over my knuckles. "Keep telling yourself that."

My breath catches in my throat. A zip of current runs from my hair follicles to my toes. I can't even handle his thumb grazing over my skin.

135

"She...she wanted me to learn all the things she couldn't teach me," I babble. "Even...sex education." Laughing uncomfortably as my palm sweats. "Or at least that was her justification maybe, so she'd have someone to read to her."

The way he's smiling at me like I just told him something adorable rather than humiliating is messing with my already foggy head. Do I always see what I want to see?

"Wait...did she know...that you're..."

"That I'm gay?" I spit out the label we've never named, hoping it'll tear his tempting hand away while also hoping at the same time it won't. "Yeah. I told her when I was fifteen. I kind of wish I hadn't though."

"Why?" He frowns, and there he goes again, rubbing that thumb. "Was she not supportive?"

"No. She was. I just...I think she felt bad she'd been making me read her all these straight romance books for a few years, so she figured out how to get audiobooks from the library after that. When she did that...I guess I kind of missed our tradition, this thing we used to do together."

Chuckling, he gives me a smile that could cure any hurt. "She sounds like she was pretty cool."

"Yeah. Yeah, she was."

"Riley? Oh my gosh. Is that you?" A nasally feminine voice calls out, jolting me out of the entrancing picture in front of me.

"Val?" Riley calls out, letting go of my hand.

Val? As in...*the Val?*

A leggy blonde approaches from the front of the restaurant, leaving behind a gaggle of female friends who stay huddled near the entrance like curious meerkats. Riley starts toward the clip of her high heels against the pavement, his warm hand now stuffed in his jeans pocket, our moment a forgotten blip in time.

Val slips her hands up his biceps, reaches up on her toes, and plants a peck on his cheek. "Hey, how have you been?"

My throat closes, watching his hand find her waist, his face angling to accept the kiss on the side of his face. I can't watch. I don't want to watch. Maybe she won't hide his cane this time. Maybe they'll make up and get back together, and she'll be the one treated to that Riley light that burns inside of him instead of me, but I don't have to watch it happening.

Giving her a polite smile, I turn my back to offer them privacy and pretend to check my phone. I still haven't looked for an apartment. What's wrong with me? This thing between us felt like something. It felt like more than just his playful sense of humor, but then again, I thought what Dallas offered felt like love once, didn't I? Am I ever going to learn?

"Well, it was good to see you," Val says as I hear Riley's feet scrape the pavement closer to me.

"Yeah. Take care."

Turning around, my stomach twists seeing the wistfulness in her eyes as Val returns to her friends. They pile into a taxi and it pulls away.

"Harper?" Riley asks, his hand outstretched to me.

He wants to hold hands again? Really?

Don't be stupid, Harper. You just got your heart back. Don't give it away again.

Extending my elbow, I move in close enough for him to reach it. "I'm here," I reassure him.

His hand slides down my arm, but I shove mine in my pocket before he can get to it.

He is *not* frowning because he can't hold my hand. There's no way that's why he's frowning. Get a grip, Harper.

I start us walking. Maybe it's my pity party, but the silence gnaws at me. Curiosity over what happened with Val gnaws at me.

"That was your ex?" I venture.

"Yeah."

"You could have gone with her."

"Why would I do that?" His laughter feels like mockery now rather than a special sound shared by the two of us.

"I don't know. You just still seem friendly, so…I meant you could have gone with her if you wanted to catch up."

"We've got nothing to catch up on."

"Right," I mumble.

Who needs words? He even admitted once that he tolerated her because she was hot.

"Sorry I flaked out in the bar," he says. "Do you want to go anywhere else?"

"No. I'm good." I'm hung up on unfounded jealousy, while he just went through his first public shake-up as a non-sighted person. Now, I feel even worse. "Uh, we're at the street," I inform him, stopping us at the curb.

His hand slinks down my forearm again. His fingertips wait at my wrist, making it clear he's expecting a hand to cross the street.

I'm supposed to help him. It's my job to help him, even though I don't think he needs it. He's grown more capable each day. He could pull out his cane, but it's dark out, which means his night blindness is in full force, and I selfishly want him to touch me again.

Reluctantly slipping my hand in his, it doesn't feel the same as before. The act, no longer meaningful. When we reach the other side of the street and he steps onto the sidewalk, I attempt to pull my hand free, but he hangs on.

"What if someone sees you again," I huff, managing to slip my hand from his, and offer him my elbow instead.

The beat of silence scorches me in shame. Am I taking out Dallas' rejection on him? Did I really just say that about a straight guy who deserves any chance at happiness with someone he can get, even if it's his ex and I don't approve of her?

There's a wrinkle in his forehead as he slowly cups my elbow. I wish the ground would open up and swallow me.

The remaining two blocks to his apartment are swathed in miserable silence. My stomach is in so many knots over my petulance, I don't think I'll eat for a week.

By the time we make it up to his apartment door, I almost wish he'd chide me, tell me how foolish I acted, warn me I got the wrong impression. Anything would be better than Riley not speaking to me. I just ruined the one good thing in my life, probably because I'm sulking over the delightful text message from Dallas this morning.

DALLAS: You forgot some of your shit when you snuck in. Get over here and get it.

I barely left anything there, other than furniture and appliances I know he's still using. My paranoia tells me his demand is a trap, a way to get me in his presence, so I ignored it just like all his other messages. And then...Riley held my hand, and I didn't feel like garbage anymore.

After I let us in and lock the door, I find him still standing a few feet away. This is it. This is the part where he lets me down gently or kicks me to the curb.

I'm going to be sick. I don't want to hear either. Shuffling past him, I set his keys on the island counter.

"Do you need anything before I go to bed?" I rush out, anything to hurry extinguishing this petty jealousy I feel over my straight employer.

That's right, Harper. *Straight. Employer.*

"I need you to tell me what happened," he says, a furrow in his brow, gaze fixed on my chest.

"At the bar?"

His jaw is set as he shakes his head. "No. After the bar."

Shit. Just because he's blind doesn't mean he'd miss when someone pouts like a school girl with a crush. Way to go, hormones.

"Just...a few people spilled out. The fight stayed inside. I didn't see anything."

"No. After that." His calm, patient tone amps up my humiliation when it usually does the opposite.

"What? What do you mean?"

"You went all quiet."

"Oh. I...I'm just tired."

"You don't sound tired. You sound...different."

"*Different?*" I squirm, avoiding his gaze.

"Yeah, like we were laughing, having fun, then you just closed up."

I let loose a nervous laugh because I haven't given myself away enough already. Why did he have to hold my hand? Why does he have to be so magnetic? Why am I so weak?

"Sorry. No. I'm fine."

"Harper? Did somebody say or do something that upset you?"

"No. It's nothing. Everything's...fine. It's...I'm fine."

Hands on his hips, that sexy mouth of his that I've stared at more than I care to admit quirks up at the corner, one brow arching. "Say *fine* one more time."

Face aflame, I sigh in defeat, then murmur pathetically, "Fine."

Snickering, he does that sexy hair sweep thing he does, then as though someone flipped a switch, his expression turns somber. "Are you...mad that I held your hand?"

"No. I told you. I didn't mind."

He steps forward, taking more of the precious air I can't get into my lungs whenever he's this close. "Then what's up?"

"Nothing. I'm..."

"*Fine?*" he ventures.

"Yeah."

God, his heat. It's radiating off him like a woodstove, warming every frozen tendril of my soul. I want to burrow into his arms and let it swallow me whole, let it incinerate me into a pile of ashes, because that's what I'd be if he touched me...really touched me, the way a man touches a man. The way I want to touch him and be touched by him. The weak part of me is grateful my back is to the island, leaving no option to retreat from the threat of combustion.

"I...liked holding your hand," he murmurs, his eyes scanning my face in a way that tells me that lick of his lips might actually mean what I want it to mean.

I can count every thunderous heartbeat, pounding in my head as I stare slack-jawed. Am I hearing what I want to hear? Finally, my voice croaks out, "Yeah?"

"Yeah." Another step. Another lick of those fucking illegal lips. "But you let go."

What is he even saying? He *liked* holding my hand?

"Well, your ex was there, and you let go so..."

"So she wouldn't think I'm as helpless as she likes to think I am."

Another step. How am I not in flames? Following his gaze, I glance down at the brush of his fingers against mine. He's holding my hand. A touch so innocent shouldn't make your heart do somersaults.

"She...you're...you're not helpless, Riley."

My chest is a bellows, seeing the same rapid rise and fall in his. All my senses are drowning in that spicy Riley Davenport scent as he reaches up and strokes my cheek.

"Were you mad I let go?"

I want to laugh deliriously. He doesn't need to be more alluring by whispering like that. I'm already dead.

"Maybe," I whisper back.

"I didn't want to let go," he murmurs, stroking his thumb over my jaw.

"No?" I practically choke on the question, amazed anything is coming out of my mouth.

"No." He shakes his head. "Did you...want me to let go?"

I should lie. I should absolutely lie because whatever this is, it's foolish and dangerous and irresponsible. But whatever this is, it's so damn intoxicating that I can't.

"No."

"I'm sorry," he breathes, not kissing, but letting his lips brush mine with his words for a beautiful almost-kiss. "I won't let go next time."

I could live off that almost-kiss for the rest of my life, but he stays, his breath battling against mine. Closing my eyes, I want to live in this moment of interlaced fingers, chest to chest, his nose brushing against my face, that thumb, tracing my jaw. I can taste possibility, but I swear this is enough. I don't need anything more than this perfect, frozen moment in time.

"Harper." The way he whispers my name, it's half-plea, half-prayer.

I break the shortest-lived oath ever made, dusting my lips over his. An almost-kiss is not enough when Riley Davenport is breathing my breath and calling my name like he's begging me to save him with my mouth.

Brush. Brush. Hold.

The tip of a sweet wet tongue, seeking permission, tracing the surface of my lower lip. Delicately, savoring. Whimpers—both his and mine. He's telling me a secret—his lips were made for kissing. I'll never tell a soul as long as he doesn't stop.

I *should* stop. I know this, but the mantra in my head is loud and insistent.

I deserve this. I deserve this.

I am dying on that hill right now, even if it's a lie. They'll have to drag my lifeless body off it, have to pry my fingers from the soil and watch them dredge channels in the dirt as they pull me away. Because this is the kind of kiss you still fight for even after you die.

I've held onto all the wrong feelings, all the wrong moments, gripping them like the reins of a runaway horse. That's just the way I grip Riley's scruffy jaw as his head slants and his tongue sweeps over the top of mine.

For some reason, I assumed he'd taste like *Better Cheddars*, but his nectar is more addictive than his love of those little orange crackers. Sweet with an after burst of hops, my taste buds salivate for more as he closes the final inch between us, pressing my ass against the counter.

His lips drag over mine and suckle in slow motion. For a guy who's perpetually impatient, the man makes kissing an art form. And then I hear it, amidst my own panting whimpers.

"Mm. Mm."

Christ, he's moaning like he does when he eats. The vibrating sounds act like a charming flute's melody, stirring my cock to life. I want to lay down on this counter and be his next meal, but an inconvenient sense of duty tells me I'm taking liberties.

My senses are lit up like Christmas. I can only imagine what he's feeling in the dark after being locked away without touch or companionship for two months before I came along. That's all this is for him. Sensory overload. He's straight, and I'm a freaking *Better Cheddar*. More importantly, I'm homeless, and I have my tongue in my paycheck's mouth.

"Shit," I gasp, when I manage to tear my mouth away from his. "I...goodnight!"

My body shouts that it's a crime how I peel it away from his, but what does my body know? I'm saving the both of us from an epic mistake.

"Goodnight," he calls.

Don't look back, Harper. Don't look back.

Ignoring myself, I steal a glance on my mad dash to my room and stop in my tracks. He's...touching his lips, the lips that just kissed me, the lips that I just kissed. He's touching *our* kiss, and he's...smiling.

Chapter 27

RILEY

What comes after a feelings exploration mission that ends in a kiss? An abruptly ended kiss followed by no mention of said-kiss this morning? Do I move onto the wooing? Should I reassess the feelings exploration? Why are men so complicated?

We're talking. That's not the problem, but it's our same old back and forth of ribbing each other. Yesterday, I'd have welcomed it. Today, it just makes me wonder if I've been set in the friend-zone, yet I can't find the words to broach the subject.

So...what'd you think of that thing I did with my mouth last night?

Nope. Not happening.

He guided me through making breakfast this morning, working on helping me orient the stove top. If he wants to clean up egg yolks, that's his choice. At least, it made for a good distraction until we got back to working on our app.

Being stuck a foot away from his cookie-scent all day while he input our data has been torture. I need to get away from him and get him away from anything that feels like work.

What does Harper like to do? Well, besides listen to romance novels? That would be a little too obvious after last night. I also don't think I could withstand the torture after discovering the feel of his lips on mine.

The chair creaks as he stretches. "I think my ass fell asleep a half hour ago," he groans. "I can't imagine you sitting still in an office all day long."

"I didn't. Rob and I had a basketball hoop on the wall, and there was a ping pong table in the break room."

Chuckling he asks, "Where was your office located? At a fun park?"

"Okay, so the ping pong table may not have been in the break room. More like in a supply closet that no one was using."

"Why am I not surprised?"

"Hey, you said you like to swim. Right?"

"Ye-ah," he drawls suspiciously.

"Why did you answer like that?"

"I…why do you ask? Is there a water rugby game you want to go to or something?"

Fucking Harper. Snorting, I ruffle his hair. "No, but if I find out that's actually a thing, we're so doing it." Getting up, I make my way to my dresser. "I've still got a few months left on my sports club membership. They have an Olympic-size pool. You got any trunks?"

"Yeah. You want to go swimming…now?"

"Why not?"

"Did you doctor say if it was alright for your eyes?"

I like that he worries about my well-being, but what do I have to do to get him to turn off his caretaker mentality for a few hours? "Yeah. It'll be fine. I won't get my face wet."

After taking José out to do his business, we walk the five blocks to my sports club. The cane practice on the street is good for me, although I'd prefer a certain hand to hold. I'm getting pretty good at it in the daylight and might even trust myself to go somewhere alone if I really needed to.

Once we stow our stuff in the locker room and get in the pool, it takes about ten minutes to convince Harper I'm not going to drown if he doesn't stick by my side. "I'm fine. Go do your thing," I assure, splashing him.

"Alright. I'm just going to do a few laps."

Treading water at the side of the pool, I listen to the methodical swish of his arms cutting through the water, his steady inhales and exhales, dedicated lap after lap as he passes me. I can tell he's in his element. Quiet, unassuming Harper, so talented. I'd give anything to see it. Did he win swim meets in high school? Was there no parent there to see him do so?

A voice in my head keeps telling me that people who know me might balk at this sudden attraction I have for a man, but I can't find a reason to question it. Every time I try to be analytical about it, to cover all my bases and make sure I'm not just swept up in something, I come up with the same answer. I'm happy.

I'm happier than I've ever been in my life, and that's saying a lot since I lost my sight this year. I'm happy because of him. How does he think he's boring when he can make me laugh harder than anyone I know? The only thing that would make me happier than how he makes me feel is if I could make him as happy as I am. And that's the allure, the siren's call that tells me not to try extinguishing whatever this is.

143

Stripping out of my wet trunks a half an hour later, this isn't the first time I've been naked in a locker room in front of a man. It is, however, the first time I've been naked and can't see who's watching me, the first time I've been naked in front of Harper.

Is he watching me? Just the thought of his eyes canvassing my body sends my head spinning, my pulse spiraling. The thought of me being in one of his books, of him picturing me in one of his steamy love stories, turns me on. I'm still not sure how all of that works, but no vision has ever felt more right. Reaching out, the damp steel of the lockers under my palm steadies me, my body swaying from lightheadedness.

"Riley? Are you okay?"

"No." I laugh breathlessly. "I can't breathe, and my heart is beating fast."

His warm palm covers the clammy skin over my left pec, turning my skin to gooseflesh and searing me all at once. "Do you have heart problems?"

"No." Of course, his assumption is clinical. I hate the reminder that he sees me as a patient, but warm at the concern in his voice.

"Does anyone in your family?" he asks, holding my pulse point on my wrist, which makes my heart kick like a mule.

"No."

"When did this start?"

The second I smelled sugar cookies and heard your nervous voice when I opened my door two months ago?

Licking my chlorinated lips, I swallow, unsure why I shoot for honesty. "A few weeks ago."

"*A few weeks ago?* And you didn't tell me?"

"I thought…maybe it'd go away."

"Riley, you should have said something! How often does it happen?"

I want to laugh at the irony. He was worried about me drowning. The only thing I'm in danger of drowning in is him. Catching my breath, I confess, "Whenever I'm near you. Whenever you touch me."

His hand goes slack on my wrist, blasting the fear of rejection through me. Grabbing his hand, I give it a squeeze. "Does that… happen to you?"

"Riley," he says so softly, I can barely hear him. "You're straight. This isn't…attraction, what you're feeling. You just think it is because… you think you need me."

Because I *need* him…

Because I'm fucking blind.

I'm *mistakenly* attracted to a man for the first time in my life because I'm so pathetically helpless that I can't tell the difference between want and need. What the fuck did I expect him to think?

Staggering back, I scour the bench with my hand, locating my jeans. Shoving them on without even bothering with my underwear, I stuff my bare feet into my sneakers.

"Right," I mutter. "Right."

"Riley," he pleads.

I hate how it's dripping with sympathy. I've had enough sympathy to last me a lifetime.

Fumbling for my cane, I telescope it and smack the fronts of the lockers, scrambling toward the doorway. If I could run, I would.

"Riley, wait. Please. I didn't mean—"

"Save it. I know what you meant."

"Riley!"

Somehow, I make it across the lobby and out the entrance doors of the building. The sounds of the city engulf me, the hum of car engines in the street. Holding my arm up, I pray an eager cabbie sees me and sweeps me away. My cane finds the edge of the curb, but I'm walking so damn fast I don't stop in time and step onto the street.

A car's brakes screech to a halt. The heat of its grill warming my leg through my jeans.

"Jesus! Riley!" Harper calls out behind me.

Feeling the side of the car, I make out the familiar shape of taxi numbers and feel my way to the passenger door. "Shit, man. I'm sorry!" the cabbie calls through the open window.

"Don't worry about it. You free?"

"Yeah. Where you need to go?"

Wrenching open the door, I drop inside on the passenger seat just as Harper's feet pound the pavement behind me. He calls my name again, panting, and then asking for the driver to wait. The backdoor opens and then closes as he settles inside.

I've been rejected before. It's not cool to go postal when someone doesn't return your affections. Being seen as a needy invalid who doesn't know what his dick or his heart wants is something entirely different though.

Tossing money at the cabbie when we arrive at my apartment, I don't even know how much I gave him, but judging by how appreciative he sounds, it's too much. Shoving out of the cab, I know I'm being stupid, but I can't bring myself to wait for Harper.

I make it through the lobby doors of my building and to the elevator, surprised to discover how easily I can discern the up from the down button by reading the Braille. What a nice fucking reminder that he's just here to do a job. I'm a job, not a man. How stupid was I to think it was anything else to him?

145

"Riley, please. Wait," Harper pants, shuffling into the elevator behind me.

When the doors close and the stifled air makes the silence thicker, I can't hold back anymore. "I don't *need* you around. I *want* you around. There's a difference. All you had to do was say you didn't…" I huff in frustration. "I'm a grown man. I can take it."

I brace myself for his reply, but it never comes. The elevator shuttles us up and dings at my floor without him uttering a syllable.

Fuck.

I've never been cross with him before. Is he scared of me again? I told him I'd never lose my patience. After what he's been through, why the hell would he want to take a chance on any man let alone a "straight" one who can't see. I'm a fucking sure bet, aren't I?

By the time we make it down the hallway to my door, my guilt and his silence is eating me alive. I did need him…at first, but can't you need someone and want them at the same time?

When he gets the door open, I step inside and hover nearby, waiting for him to lock up. My ire has settled enough, I can think with a clearer head. I don't care if he thinks the basis for my attraction is that I depend upon him. I don't care if the feelings aren't reciprocated. I'll get over it somehow. I don't want him to go.

"I'm sorry," I tell him, setting my cane down on the counter so I at least look that less blind for my delivery. "I was an ass. I get it. I'm your paycheck, and I made it weird. You never asked for me to…put the moves on you. I just…I thought—"

I don't get to finish. Hands cup my face, and then warm lips press against mine. His stubble brushes against my chin. His thumbs stroke gentle motions against my jaw as his mouth tenderly captures my lower lip, and then my upper one. I'm holding my breath, my mind scrambling to remember what part of his love stories this is, what it means. His mouth breaks away, and his forehead rests against mine.

"Was that…a pity kiss?" I manage, wondering if I've just been treated to more sympathy.

The breath from his scoff ghosts my skin. "Did it feel like pity?"

"I'm not sure. Maybe you should show me again."

"That was a you're-my-boss-but-I-can't-help-it-any-longer-kiss. I'm sorry. I know you don't need me. I was…trying to be a good employee."

His confession makes me shudder in relief. "I think I like being the boss."

His laughter vibrates in his chest against mine, making me smile. Hesitantly, I find his cheek with my palm.

"Can I…be the boss again?" I whisper, nudging my nose against his, thirsty for more of his surrender.

"Why not?" He chuckles, mocking one of my signature phrases before he seals his lips to mine again.

A fog clouds my brain, drunk on how he tastes as sweet as he smells. I don't know why I imagined men kissing men would be rough and mechanical. We're writing a song, a soft, tender song with our mouths, with our tongues, our heady breaths.

His hand clutches my bicep, lighting me up that he's dropped his modesty for once. My fingers locate his hip. I'm gripping his belt loop like I'm afraid if I let go, he'll disappear. My bare cock is growing thick behind my jeans, the rough fabric brushing against my sensitive skin. I don't even know what he wants me to do, but I don't care. I think I'd do anything, if he asked.

When I'm on the verge of passing out from lack of breath, I draw back, delighted to hear he's panting as heavily as I am. His fingers tremble against my neck, my arm. I'm shaking with nerves right along with him.

His breathy chuckle ghosts my lips. I can hear his smile and brush my thumb across his mouth just to make sure I'm not mistaken. It grows wider underneath my touch, filling my heart to bursting.

Like a kid with a new toy, the fear that I'll break it by smothering it reins in my arousal. "How about we finish listening to that movie we started the other day?" I suggest.

"You mean that romcom book?"

"Yeah." I chuckle, kissing the tip of his nose just because I can.

"Are you…living one of my romance novels vicariously through me?" he asks, playfully, but I sense it's a veil for more of his doubts.

"Maybe that's what you're doing to me," I tease in return.

"No, Riley," he whispers. "Nobody could write you."

I may have lost the dog lottery, but I think that comment means I just won the man lottery. I'll take it and count my blessings. Patting his hip, it's hard to hold back my proud grin.

"Alright, you want popcorn? I think I've got some…somewhere."

"I'll get it." He laughs, pecking me on the cheek.

Settling into the couch, I rethink my position as I wait for Harper. Scooting over to the middle, I pat my side for José to hop his chubby butt up into my usual spot. Might as well make this a three-way. No man left behind.

When Harper comes over bringing the scent of warm, buttery popcorn with him, I swallow, wondering what he'll think of my invasion of his half of the couch. To my delight, he drops down just a few inches away from me and hands me the bowl.

As he brings up the audiobook on his phone, I fish through the bowl for a handful of popcorn to keep my fingers busy. I think I'm going to need a distraction from touching him. Rifling through the fluffy kernels, something round, flat, and crisp brushes my fingertips. There's another one. Fishing one out, I bring it to my nose and sniff.

Cheese. Cheddar cheese. Taking a bite, the familiar taste of my favorite cracker explodes on my tongue.

"Did you…put *Better Cheddars* in the popcorn?" I ask.

Laughing, he hits play and leans back into the couch. "Um, yeah. Any good?"

Grinning, I don't give a shit about occupying my free hand anymore. I know right where I want it. Wrapping my around the back of his shoulders, I hug him to me, erasing the few inches between us. "Yeah. It's perfect."

He's fucking perfect.

Chapter 28

HARPER

"You're fucking him. Aren't you?" Daniel says at full volume across the café booth from me.

It's been three weeks since I stuck my foot in my mouth at the pool locker room and then…stuck my tongue in Riley's mouth. When Daniel asked to meet for breakfast, it didn't seem right to burst the dreamy, delicate bubble of kisses and laughter and couch snuggles Riley and I have been lost in since then, so I invited him along.

I've been waiting for Riley to have a gay freak out, but it hasn't come. I've been waiting to discover a scary, hidden personality flaw, but I have yet to find one. Each day is better than the previous, drawing my heart further and further away into Riley Land.

"Daniel!" I gasp, locating Riley coming out of the restroom. "No!"

"Bullshit. Something's going on."

"It's…complicated."

"Why? Because you work for him or because he's straight?"

Sighing, I drop my face in my hands and rub. "Yes. I'm aware of both. He's just…hard to resist."

"I'd do him." He shrugs, sipping his coffee and glancing over his shoulder at Riley's approaching form.

"Of course, you would. Quit gawking at him. Will you? It's rude."

"Holy shit. You're jealous."

"Don't be ridiculous," I seethe, scooting over as Riley sidles up to the table.

"What did I miss?" Riley asks, slipping in next to me.

"Just me checking you out and Harper trying to deny he was jealous," Daniel says casually, earning him a kick to the shin under the table, since I've admitted absolutely nothing to him.

"Oh, yeah?" Riley smirks, completely unphased by being outed. He rolls up the sleeves of his Henley and sighs. "Well, fair's fair."

149

I'm as confused as Daniel when Riley reaches for my friend's face, but then I snicker when I realize he's reliving our facial touch experiment, but much more dramatically, as though he knows he's poking Daniel in the eye. Watching Daniel flinch and quirk a confused brow at me, it's all I can do not to bust up laughing.

"Hm. Just as I thought," Riley says, withdrawing his hands.

"What?" Daniel asks.

"Hideous," Riley murmurs over the lip of his coffee cup.

"Fuck off." Daniel cracks up.

The grin Riley flashes me and the way he bumps my shoulder with his like he's seeking a pat on the back for effectively ribbing and winning over my friend makes my heart flip. Is this what a boyfriend is supposed to be like? This fun, this simple, this wonderful? Squeezing his kneecap underneath the table to reassure him that I approve of his shenanigans, I feel my cheeks blush when he leans over and plants a kiss on the side of my face.

"Oh my God," Daniel groans. "You two are disgusting."

Later that evening, as Riley invades my space on the couch, Daniel's words come back to haunt me. My face is nearly raw from stubble burn after almost an hour of kissing, but I don't want to push Riley's weight off me. I don't want the anxious stroking his hand is doing to my side to stop. I know what it means, that he wants more. Does he know how much more? Is he sure he wants that with me? We *are* quickly becoming disgusting and as much as it has me on cloud-nine, it scares me for so many reasons.

Am I a temporary itch? I'll never repeat the words I said to him a few weeks ago about him needing me, but they're still lingering in my doubts. He may not need me. Hell, he doesn't need me at all, but is he just lonely? Is it just this bond of loneliness we've shared that's made his head turn?

And what the hell am I doing? I'm damaged goods. It's only been a little over three months since I left Dallas. Responsibility tells me I should still be emotionally healing, maybe even seeking therapy, not running my fingers through my employer's hair and moaning around his tongue.

I can feel his arousal pressing against my thigh again. Groaning into his mouth, I clench every muscle in my body, willing my lust to go away. Larry gave up on us a half an hour ago and waddled into Riley's room. I have no idea what this audiobook is about, the narration a vague background noise to our panting and little moans.

The flesh on my stomach prickles with gooseflesh. His thumb just breached the hem of my t-shirt, grazing across the skin above my waistline. We haven't ever ventured beyond our clothing, not that the thought hasn't crossed my mind at least a hundred times a day. He makes me want to drown in the joy that exudes from him any way I can.

Whimpering from that innocent touch, my heart hammers in my chest when he moans in response, burying his face in my neck. Fuck. I want him to devour me, and I thought I'd never want to be touched again. I thought I'd never want to touch another person again, but it's been all I can do to keep my hands to myself these past weeks since that first kiss.

This is so irresponsible. Am I corrupting him? Does he think he needs to do this because I'm gay?

"Sugar," he murmurs.

"What?"

"You smell like sugar cookies," he says, his lips trailing up my neck. "Drives me crazy."

My toes tingle at the odd but intimate confession. It also helps me slam on the brakes. Of course, he's trying to devour my neck. The man loves his snacks.

I'm a snack.

I want to be a snack, but it doesn't help convince me he'd still want me if he could see that I'm a *man snack* rather than a *woman snack*. If I lay here any longer, I'll give him the entire snack, regardless of my doubts.

I make for a hasty exit, pushing against his shoulders. Pressing a chaste kiss to his lips, I blurt out, "Goodnight!"

And then, I run like a coward to my room and will my erection to go away. Too bad I can't will away all his sweetness, kindness, humor, brilliance, and charm.

I'm totally fucked. Aren't I?

Chapter 29

RILEY

Am I the worst wooer in the history of wooers? It's been almost four months since he moved in and one since he kissed me after our walk home from the pool. What are the bases with men and how long are you supposed to wait before rounding them?

One thing I do know is that your partner shouldn't want to run to his room like you have the plague every time your couch make out sessions get heated. My balls are ready to explode along with my heart. I am a Harper addict both physically and emotionally. If I don't get a substantial fix of him tonight, I might die. Apparently, infatuation not only makes me horny, but also dramatic.

I know he wants me. I can feel it. I can hear it. So, why does he always stop and run away? Am I doing something wrong? Am I taking things too fast? It's not my fault he's so damn irresistible. Mom's told me plenty of times I can be a bit over-the-top.

Maybe I've read him all wrong. Maybe my Harper addiction is making me imagine things I want to be real.

Drawing back, I glance down at the blur panting beneath me on the couch. Swallowing, I wonder if I could see, would I see what I hope to see in his eyes right now?

"What?" he whispers, stroking my jaw.

"You're going to have to help me out here. Either I touch your face the entire time to gauge your expression, or you tell me how you feel."

"What…what do you mean?"

"I mean, am I…taking advantage?"

"Why would you think that?"

"You…I feel like I do all the touching. Are you…not into it? Am I taking things too fast?"

"No. I am…into it. It's just…"

Sensing his discomfort, I joke, "What? Is it my ass?"

"What?" He barks out a laugh, rubbing my arms. "No."

"It's my hair then. Isn't it?

Fingers reach up and card against my scalp, making me want to purr like a cat. "No," he whispers, pecking me on the lips. "I like your crazy hair."

"Freak," I mutter, silencing his chuckle with a kiss. "So, what then? Is it because I'm a virgin?"

Scoffing, he lets out a thick breath. "Um, not entirely, but… that's part of it."

"Hm," I hum, kissing his neck to give me time to figure out how to ease his concerns. "Well, you're the one who said I'm highly trainable."

"I *never* said that." He laughs.

"Oh, you must have been talking about Kevin," I reference Larry's newest trial name. "That's right. You didn't. You never compliment me," I pout with a sigh. "I'm convinced now. You're straight. Right?

Cracking up at my goofy deflection, he cups my jaw in between his thumb and forefinger. "It's just that…I work for you. You pay me to be here. It still feels wrong…like I'm breaking a law or something."

"Nooo. My insurance company pays you to be here." I smile, hoping that solves that bit of nonsense, but his ever-worrisome brain comes back with a quick rebuttal.

"*You* pay for your insurance. It's the same thing."

"Not at all. So, the way I see it, you have five weeks left to violate me before I have to hire you out of pocket to keep you around, at which time *apparently* your morals may be scrupled, *but*…not until then. For now, I'm free game. You're free to wrestle me, but not your conscience." I grin, nuzzling his nose.

"You should have been a lawyer," he grumbles.

"Do you have a thing for guys in suits? Because I can go dig one out of my closet."

I make to get up, but he laughs, tugging me back down to him, back to where I want to be—within breathing distance of a happy Harper. Drawing my head to his, he kisses me sweetly, but sweet doesn't last long. His tongue laps my lip, cresting my mouth, tangling with mine.

My breath hitches when I feel fingers working up my back underneath my t-shirt. Moaning shamelessly is probably a dead giveaway for how hungry I've been for his touch. He whimpers like my noises turn him on. When his hand skirts around my ribcage, all the blood rushes to my head as his fingertips circle my nipple. Tingling static explodes from the point of his touch through my body all the way to my toes, making me shudder.

Pulling back, I pant breathlessly. Since when have my nipples had that power?

"What the hell did you do to my nipples," I demand.

"Sorry, I—" he starts and goes to withdraw his hand, but I cut him off, capturing his lower lip.

"Do it again," I plead.

I can feel his smile against my mouth. His hand caresses over my skin again and traces a tortuous circle, drawing my nipple to a bud.

Fuck…me. I've never been this turned on by someone in my life.

Groaning, my hips grind into his of their own accord. My face heats at my own wantonness, wondering if it's too much for him, if he's going to spring up off the couch like so many nights before, but his body answers mine. Hips rising into me, he undulates, the outline of his cock gyrating against mine. If I thought his nipple play set off fireworks in my body, this ignited the entire damn light show.

"Yes," I hiss into his neck.

His hand moves down my torso. I'm holding my breath, wondering where it's going to go. When he traces the outline of my cock through my pajama pants, I whine like I'm dying and dive for his mouth, pressing my hips into his hand so he knows he's welcome there, more than welcome. I've imagined this, dreamt of it, but neither has anything on reality.

His grip lightly squeezes, so shy it's a tease. Running my hand down his side, I can't take it anymore. I need. I need. I need *him*.

Running my palm across his stomach, I reach for him in the same way. His hardness, his girth, it's a prize in my hand, knowing I'm the cause of it. Leaning up on my elbow, I gaze down at him like someone who could see. I want the sentiment there, the sense that I'm looking in his eyes, even though I can't. I want him to know this isn't just lust. I want him to know that whatever emotion is on his face, whichever expression is on mine, I want to see it and want him to see mine.

"Harper," I whisper my favorite word.

"Riley," he whispers back.

Gliding up his length, so warm through the fabric under my touch, I tug at the tie on his sleep pants. When his fingertip dips inside the front waistband of mine, I answer his question with a passionate kiss. Trembling, I lift my hips in approval and sigh when the air touches the bare flesh of my ass as he slides my pants down my hips. Flooding his face with my panting, the sound of breathing has never been so erotic. I'm leaking. I know I am. Will he care? Will it gross him out?

When his hand wraps around my length, I practically choke from the jolt the sensation sends through me. If he cares, he doesn't say anything, his thumb grazing over my tip and smearing the liquid across the domed head of my cock.

The stifled cry that leaves my lips is a noise I desperately want to hear him make too. Reaching under his waistband, my hand trembles, hoping I can make him feel the way he's making me feel. Svelte and warm, slick with arousal and veiny, I never knew I could love having a cock in my hand this much. The way he whimpers in my ear and his hips jerk, stretch a smile across my face.

"Yeah, baby," I pant, lapping at his earlobe, producing a full-body shudder in him that makes me feel like a king.

When his hand starts sliding up and down my length, it's all I can do to hold it together. Panting, I press my forehead to his and close my eyes, hoping for control.

"You okay?" he whispers, slowing his ministrations.

"Perfect," I reply, pressing my lips to his and trying to copy that swirl of my fingertip over his cockhead the way he did to mine. "You?"

His reply is a moan as his tongue delves into my mouth. After that it's a frenzied blur of eager movements, a race to see who drives the other crazy first.

I let him win, let him guide this dance. His hand wraps around the both of us, slickening us together, mixing our arousal with each slide. The heat of him against me, the delicate skin against sensitized delicate skin, as I rut into his grip like an animal, lets me know I do need him. I need him more than I ever needed anything in my life. Sex has never been so emotionally all-consuming, and this is just a hand job of sorts. It's *him*. It's always him that pulls these wondrous new discoveries from me.

"Harper!" I gasp, spilling over the top of his hand, burying my face in his neck.

He moans, his grip flying faster as my cock twitches, happy to be locked in his clutches. The *schick, schick* sounds of my release as he seeks his own fills me with possessiveness, knowing he's using my pleasure as an aid to give him what he needs.

Take it, I want to growl. Take whatever you want from me.

Squeezing my hand over top of his, I follow along for the ride with his movements, carving out his mouth with my tongue, eating his whimpers. His cry is stifled by our kiss. His body spasms beneath me as another flood of liquid heat spills over our hands.

Fuck. How can you be dizzy when you can't see? Resting my head in the crook of his neck, I absorb the sounds of us both catching our breath.

I just made my man come. *My man.* Huffing on a laugh, I nuzzle his pulse, delighting in its speed against my lips.

"What's so funny?" he asks.

"At least I made you come this time before you ran off to bed," I tease.

"Is that part of your fringe benefits package?"

"Yeah. Get used to it."

Using his shirt to clean us up, he must have taken my teasing to heart. Neither of us make it to our beds. The sound of spicy romance narrating in the background along with Kevin's nasally snoring after he resurfaced, we lay tangled up on the couch. His breathing evens out against my chest, and my eyes grow heavy at a sense of wholeness I've never known.

Going blind might have been the best thing that ever happened to me. It brought me Harper.

Chapter 30

HARPER

"Come on," Riley prods. "*You* say it. Your voice is way sexier than mine anyway."

"*Sexy?*"

"Yeah, it makes me all…tingly and shit." He laughs, shoving his phone toward me with the QR code for his next shirt pulled up on the screen of our clothes-reader app beta model.

"Tingly, huh? Maybe you should see a doctor."

"Just do it. Don't get a big head."

"Fine." I laugh, shaking my head. "This is still ridiculous though. I mean, I get why *you* want it narrated like this, but how are you going to market these prototypes to…"

"To what? *Normal* people?" he accuses, pinching my nipple.

"Ouch! I didn't say that!"

"You were thinking it! Now, come on. Are you going to say it so I can take you out, or what?"

Sighing, I bring his phone up to my mouth and narrate the description he requested for the next article of clothing. "*Riley's funny as fuck blind as a bat man t-shirt.*"

"Yeah!" he cheers. "Nice. Send it to the printer, and then let's get this show on the road."

"You want to wear that out?"

"Yeah. Why?"

"Nothing. I just wanted to make sure I wasn't overdressed."

I'm not sure why he grins at me like he needs my approval for his clothing. The man would make a burlap sack look attractive.

Donning a tan blazer over his bat-shirt, he is a nerdy-bad boy image in jeans and his black boots. And me? I look like the boring guy that never stands out in a crowd just as I always do in my faded jeans and best navy blue pocketed Henley. I'd wear a button up, since I think he's

157

treating this like a date, but I don't want to get made fun of the second he catches on.

Seeing to Larry's needs, we bid him good evening and decide on taking a cab to the bar district downtown. I'd love to go see Daniel at work, especially since he seems surprisingly accepting of me dating my straight client, but don't dare risk running into Dallas and his crew.

Note to self—don't introduce your next boyfriend to your friends until you know he's the one.

The thought catches me off-guard as Riley suggests we play a game of darts at the sports bar we decided on. I already introduced him to Daniel. Is he...my boyfriend? I guess he's not...*not* my boyfriend. Introducing him to Daniel was a much easier decision than I thought, or maybe I didn't give it any thought. My heart patters at the last bit of my prophecy I haven't analyzed yet.

The one. Every fiber in my body shouts I absolutely want to be deserving enough for him to be *the one.*

In typical Harper-fashion though, I start running down the mental list of why he can't be. What will Leigh Ann think of me when she realizes I'm giving her son, who I'm supposed to be caring for, hand jobs? Will Riley grow bored of me? I'm not the most exciting person in the world, and there's only so many audiobooks you can listen to.

As though he can hear my thoughts, he tugs at my hand. "Come on. Are we doing this or what?"

Darts. He fucking wants to play darts in a public place. I guess it doesn't matter how boring I am. Riley will always supply the entertainment.

Twenty minutes into the most terrifying game of darts I've ever played, we've attracted several onlookers who, like me, have probably never seen a blind man throw darts. Like everything else he does, he excels at it though, only hitting the wall beyond the board a few times. And the question on my mind about him growing bored with me, certainly isn't happening tonight.

The man can't keep his hands to himself. They're either in my back pocket, squeezing my ass, rubbing my shoulder or my back. I'm all for being touched anywhere by Riley, but I know he doesn't realize how much of a show he's putting on. Inching away from his latest caress, he squeezes my arm.

"Hey, everything alright? You seem kind of tense."

"Yeah. I just...people are staring at us," I inform him under my breath.

Considering my admission, his eyes scan the room. "At our dart playing or...at us."

Wincing, I rub my forehead, ashamed to have even brought it up to him. I don't want to ruin the evening by making him self-conscious. I don't give a damn what people think of me, but it's not fair to Riley to not know when he's being gawked at.

"Both, I think. Mostly us, I guess," I confess. "Sorry, I just thought maybe you'd want to know. I don't mind, but—"

"No. It's cool. Why would I mind?" he replies effortlessly. Running his hand up my arm, I drink in just one more reason why I appreciate him as he smiles at me. "Are you okay though? Do you want to go somewhere else?"

"No, it's fine. I'm fine."

Sputtering, he snakes his arm around my neck, tugging me into a light headlock. "*Fine* in Harper language is not fine. Hang on," he says, pulling his phone out of his pocket. "Rita, search for gay bars near me."

I have sorely underestimated the internet and Riley's app building capabilities, because he does in fact find us a gay bar just a block over. It's definitely not the fanciest place I've ever been in, but it eases my nerves for him as soon as we step inside.

A streamer of Pride flag pendants hangs behind the bar that's packed with same-sex couples. A jukebox is playing, serenading couples on a small dancefloor. The vibe is chill, and not a soul inside gawks at my date like he shouldn't have his arm around my waist. I still can't believe he brought me here, but then again, everything about Riley since day one has taken me by surprise.

After two rounds of drinks and chatting with a nice older gay couple at one of the pub tables, they leave us to go dance to a folky-pop song by Niall Horan. Riley rubs the back of my neck, a sweet massaging motion that makes me long to curl up on the couch with him again. Sooner or later, I wonder if we'll make it to a bed, but I don't want to be the one who pushes that ticket. I've been doing the best I can to avoid it and take things slow.

"Are you going to dance with me?" he asks.

"You want to dance?"

"You think I can't?" he challenges, standing up.

"I don't think there's anything you can't do, Riley."

I'm not about to tell him that I can't dance. Daniel says I move like I'm trying to get a bug out of my pant leg, but I guess Riley won't know that. Blind boyfriend for the win.

Out on the floor, I nod to the couple we visited with, flashing them a nervous smile. They look as curious as I am to see Riley's moves. And... oh my word. I guess...you *could* call that dancing?

He's swinging his slender hips off-beat to the music, arms to and fro like an Irish jig, which somewhat fits the spunky song. Grinning like a fool, he sticks one finger in the air and wriggles his hips, spinning himself in a circle on one leg in…what appears to be a Riley version of the dance move the sprinkler.

My laughter is interrupted by his complaint, "Are you leaving me hanging? Your ass better be dancing!"

"I'm here," I tell him, capturing his hand.

He pulls me into him, settling his hand on my hip. Now we're two horrible dancers dancing together instead of alone. I don't think I've ever had this much fun. Staring at the mirth in his eyes, a feeling chokes my throat, a feeling a lot like love. He spins me, laughing and guiding me back to him with an astounding amount of ease like we fit, like I'm a missing piece he's bringing back to him.

Leaning in, his lips whisper to my ear. "Why didn't you tell me about this?"

"About what?" I ask, rightly confused.

"This," he whispers, reaching between us and grazing his fingertip over the hardening length in my jeans.

"That I have a cock?" I sputter, blushing that he's caught me.

"No. That it's hard," he murmurs, dusting his lips below my ear.

"Why would I tell you that?" I ask innocently, swallowing against the rising fire he ignited in my belly.

His hips shift, pressing into mine. The clear outline of his hardness presses into my hip. "So, I could tell you about mine."

How have I fallen for a straight man who's a gay Don Juan? Whatever liquid he wants me to be, I'm a puddle on the floor.

"I…I work for you," I manage, the responsibility to slow this intoxicating allure between us rearing its dutifulness.

"Not really. You just make sure I don't hurt myself."

"Well, you're still how I get my paychecks."

Nuzzling my neck, he adds, "If I fire you, will it go away?"

"Doubtful," I practically sigh, telling responsibility to go fuck itself as I lay my head on his shoulder and melt into him.

"Well, *this* explains everything," a deep voice accentuates each word, sending my spine rigid.

I know that voice. Flinching, I grip Riley's shoulders, visions of my nightmare flashing in my mind.

Dallas. Fucking Dallas. No.

"Dallas," I stammer, drawing away from Riley even as he tries to cling to me with confusion all over his face. "What…what are you doing here?"

"Harper?" Riley asks turning around to face my ex in all his towering, dark-eyed, gym-rat, slickened hair glory. "Who is it?"

Folding his arms over his chest, Dallas' muscles flex, sending a chilling reminder of how much strength they hold. "Oh, just the boyfriend," he sneers. "Who the fuck are you?"

I'm paralyzed in fear, while my mind is racing a thousand miles an hour, trying to figure out how to get out of this situation. Mouth agape, the only part of my body that will move is my gaze. Riley's laugh lines smooth out in realization.

"Boyfriend?" he parrots. *"Oh! Is this the abuser with the tiny dick?"*

"What the fuck?" Dallas barks, shoving Riley's shoulder so hard he sways backward.

That's enough to snap me out of my coma. Jumping forward, I hold my arm out between them to keep Dallas at bay. "Dallas, don't! We were just dancing. Leave him alone."

Riley's hand pats my side, working its way around my front. He draws my arm down, stepping in front of me. Does he have a death wish? He's going to get killed.

Reaching out, his fingertips connect with Dallas' chest. I blink. Even Dallas looks at me as if to say, what the fuck is he doing?

"How tall are you?" Riley asks him.

"What the fuck? Get your hands off me, prick," Dallas snaps, batting his hand away.

"How tall are you?" Riley prods, his brow furrowing.

"What?" Dallas sputters in amusement. "Are you fucking blind?"

"Yeah," Riley concurs, holding his jacket lapels open to expose his bat shirt. "Can't you read, moron?"

I've never seen Dallas so befuddled. His black soulless eyes canvas Riley up and down and then he looks to me, bursting with bitter laughter. "Oh my God. This is fucking rich. You left me for a fucking blind guy?" More taunting laughter to go along with his ableism, making my skin crawl. I remember that laughter and can barely fight the vomit at the back of my throat. "Can't find anyone who can stand what you look like? Can he even find your fucking hole?" he adds, making my face burn that Riley is hearing this disgusting dialogue that used to be my life.

"Six-three? Right?" Riley asks, feeling for Dallas' collarbone.

Why does he keep touching him? I try to draw him back by the shoulder, but he won't budge, continuing to prod Dallas like he's a cow up for inspection.

"What?" Dallas huffs, eyeballing Riley like he's lost his mind.

"About six-three?" Riley repeats.

Smirking, Dallas unloads another wicked peal of laughter. Practically shouting like Riley is deaf, he lets out arrogantly, "Six-*four*. Right here, buddy."

161

His hands close over top of Riley's, drawing them up to the sides of his neck, making me nauseous. "You like that?" Dallas purrs, smiling lasciviously at Riley before giving me a taunting wink and planting his hands on Riley's sides. "If you're sick of railing this little whiny twink, I can show you how a real man fucks. We can even let Harper watch." Glancing over Riley's shoulder, his cold eyes bore into me. "I bet you'd like that Harp. Huh?"

"Leave us alone, Dallas," I get out, gripping Riley's shoulder tighter as the panic chokes my windpipe.

What the fuck is happening? What is he going to do? What is Riley doing?

I watch, trembling as Riley's fingers graze up the sides of Dallas' neck behind his ears, his fingers carding into the base of Dallas' long brown hair, producing an amused laugh from Dallas. The fire of arousal in Dallas' eyes as he canvases Riley's body has me wanting to lurch.

"Aw, Harper," Dallas murmurs, running his hands over Riley's hips. "You got me a present."

"Six-four," Riley mutters under his breath like he's talking to himself and nods. Then louder, to Dallas, he says defiantly, "No, but I did."

His hands clamp onto Dallas' ears. It happens in a flash. Him tugging Dallas' head forward into his. Him bashing his forehead into Dallas' nose. The *crunch* sound of something breaking. Dallas yelling, "Fuck!" and shoving Riley back so hard he slams into me, sending me falling on my ass onto the floor.

Scrambling to my feet, tunnel vision takes over. As Riley regains his footing and his balance, Dallas charges for him, ripping a cry from my throat, but the older couple that we chatted with grab him from behind just in time.

Struggling to shake them off, he succeeds, snarling as he locks his gaze onto me and Riley, "You're fucking dead! *Both* of you!"

Just as my hand grabs a handful of Riley's jacket, his arm swings. His fist slices through the air between him and Dallas. Dallas sways back to deflect, luckily putting him in the clutches of two bouncers that do a better job of subduing him than that kindly couple.

Trying to wrench out of their grip, Dallas laughs sardonically as Riley swings at the air again. "You're such a fucking joke Harper. Really, with this shit?"

Tugging Riley back, my voice finally returns. "He's leaving. He's leaving," I repeat, possibly just as much to reassure myself. "The bouncers are taking him out."

Panting, he turns toward me. The skin above the bridge of his nose is swollen and red. I can tell he'll have a shiner, a tinge of pink puffy skin forming under his right eye from his head butt to Dallas' nose.

"Jesus, your face," I rasp, cupping his cheeks with shaky hands.

"Are you okay?" he asks, squeezing his hands over the top of mine, eyes canvassing my face.

"Yeah. Yes. I…let me go get you some ice."

On shaky legs, I make it to the bar, careful to check that Dallas has been extricated from the building. When the bartender gives me a clean bar towel with a portion of ice in it, I turn around to head back to Riley.

One of the men we were speaking with earlier helped him to his seat and has his hand on his shoulder. They're chuckling, clearly reliving the events of the brawl. The man's partner slaps me on the shoulder, startling me. With his other hand, he fans himself.

"Oh my God. That was the hottest thing I've ever seen," he coos, glancing from me to Riley.

"Yeah," I agree breathlessly. "Yeah, it was."

The ride home is a blur of Riley's head on my shoulder, his cloth of ice pressed to his face, and little groans that make my heart break as I worry his hand in mine like a nervous mother. Guiding him upstairs and into the apartment, I shoo away a concerned Larry, and get Riley to his bed. Prying off his boots and jacket for him, he doesn't protest the assistance although I know he takes pride in dressing himself. When he's down to his t-shirt and boxer briefs, I decide that's enough stripping and leave him to get fresh ice from the kitchen.

When I return, he's laying down with his hand over his face, but turns his head when I sit on the edge of his mattress by his chest. Taking the plastic bag of ice, I gently press it to the place on his forehead where he took the direct hit.

Groaning in protest, he tries to shove it away, so I scold, "Your face is going to be swollen."

"It's freezing my brain," he grunts.

The sight of him in such misery, knowing it's because of me, yanks at my heartstrings. He didn't even bat an eye at intervening. It was like a protective response, defending his mate.

"Riley, you didn't have to do that."

"Yes. I did," he responds with finality.

When he lets out a little moan, it heightens new feelings of useless-ness inside me. "Are you okay?"

"No," he grumbles.

I sigh, helplessly. There isn't anything more I can do for his swollen eye. I both hate and am proud of the fact that his urge to defend my hon-or was the cause of it. "What can I get you?"

Peering out from under his bag of ice, he ventures boyishly, "Kisses?"

The hope is his voice has me chuckling. He's too damn irresist-ible, and kisses? Yeah. Kisses sound like the perfect remedy to this screwed up night.

Leaning down, I press my lips to his warm mouth. His whiskers dust my chin as I tell him thank you without words.

The clacking of ice cubes breaks my concentration on his intoxicating mouth. The cold plastic bag grazes my cheek. Opening my eyes, I find he's moved the compress off his swollen brow.

"Hey," I scold, setting the bag back over his puffy skin. "No ice. No kisses."

"It's in the way of my kisses!"

Snorting, I shake my head at him. "You're a terrible patient."

His lips purse, but he holds the bag where it needs to be. "I prefer the title *noble avenger*."

"My hero," I declare, stroking his chin.

"I don't feel like a hero," he says with feigned dramatic flair.

"You defended my honor. That makes you a hero," I reassure his fishing expedition for compliments.

His shoulder shifts, and I catch his Adam's Apple bobbing. "Yeah, but…heroes get kisses."

Freaking Riley.

Grinning, I decide to accept his challenge. The man does have a point.

Leaning in, I press my lips to his neck, knowing he wasn't antici-pating me going there. Another idea takes root remembering his I'll tell you about mine if you tell me about yours comment at the bar before Dallas showed up. Actually, it's less of an idea rather than the ever-un-checked desire he stirs in me. Drawing up the hem of his shirt, I bring my lips to his chest, over his heart, thanking it for beating for me today. He sucks in an audible breath, sending a rush of giddiness through me. I still can't believe this gorgeous, vivacious man responds to me the way he does. Moving lower, when I reach his chiseled stomach, his fingers weave into my hair.

A satisfied whisper floats to my ears. "I like being a hero."

Smiling against his warm skin, I can't think of any of the reasons why I never let us go this far before, even after the last two weeks we've spent falling asleep together on his couch. Tonight, all logic has been locked outside the door, or maybe it was left back at the bar the second that he bashed his face into my ex's nose, making me feel like Dallas isn't as invincible as I thought. Never once has Riley pushed me for more even though I sense his passion has no off-switch. It's made it difficult to fight giving him more. He's my hero, and heroes deserve special attention.

Slipping my fingertips under his waistband, I meet no resistance. His agile hips lift a second before I even decide to tug down his boxer briefs. His thickened cock bobs free to greet me. I have to suppress a groan at the sight of his naked glory. Fuck, he's incredible. I can't be the good steward any longer. Hell, who am I kidding? We've already shared half a dozen orgasms other ways.

Bending down, I draw the tip of my tongue up his arousal-dampened slit. His intake of breath floods the silence, followed by a ruckus. I glance up just in time to see him toss his ice bag on the nightstand. It misses the wooden surface and lands on the floor with a flop.

Maybe I've gone too far. Face heating, I deflect. "Hey, I said, no ice, no kisses."

"That wasn't a kiss. That was a lick," he rasps accusingly, cupping my face and dragging my mouth back up to his.

Laughing against his lips, I trail my hand down his naked hip and break away. Sliding back down his body, I lower my head and tease, "You mean...*this?*" I lap again, more slowly and swirl my tongue around his tip.

His chest rises and then stills. For a second, I wonder if he's stopped breathing, but then his throat undulates. His croaked voice betrays his foolery, "I'm not sure. I...wasn't paying attention. Better try again."

Grinning, I swirl my tongue around the circumference of his head again. His groan is all the encouragement I need to take his hot length into my mouth.

"Harper. Harper," he chants, weaving his fingers through my hair as I treat his cock like the delicacy that it is to me.

Drawing off, I whisper, "You okay?"

"Yeah," he chuckles. "Who else can I beat up?"

Rubbing his thighs, I place a kiss at the juncture of his hip. "I think I prefer you as a lover not a fighter."

"You and your good ideas," he murmurs.

I don't care that Dallas found me. I don't care that he threatened me and Riley. I don't care that he knows I'm with another man. I'm not his anymore, and I'm happy. This moment is ours, mine and Riley's. Nothing can touch us here but each other. Nothing can take this away. There's only giving, all the affection and spoiling I want to give him, all the laughter he gives to me.

Reaching down, I caress the soft skin of his sac as I invest more motivation in this blow job than I ever have in my life. Drawing off him, I move my mouth to the delicate wrinkled skin and lick the circumference, eliciting more noises that make my hairs stand up on my arms and my own balls tingle. Gingerly, I trail my finger up and down the seam between his impossibly firm ass cheeks, feeling him tremor under my touch. I have no idea what he's up for. How far he's willing to go. What, if anything, will be too much for him, but he spreads his legs wider. His breathing gets choppier.

Moving back to his beautiful erection, still slickened from my mouth, I take him in as deep as I can. His hips move in little jerks like he's holding back using my mouth, which only coils the need inside me, knowing I'm driving him wild. I can feel his shaft thicken and tense against my tongue, a sign he's close.

"Har...Harper," he rasps, tapping my shoulder.

I don't want to let him go. I want to drink every drop down, but when he taps and stutters my name again, I release him, not wanting to push him into things he's not ready for. He reaches for his length, but I beat him to it. It only takes two strokes until he erupts onto his stomach, his abs flexing under the glistening pool he made there.

As he comes down, his breathing evening out, I place tiny kisses around his groin, worshipping any place I can. He took a chance on me when I was a mess, when I needed a chance the most. He let me into his home and trusted me. He turned my world from dark to light, and then he gave me all of himself when I'd have just settled for a fragment. Every kiss I place on his silky skin is a thank you for those gifts.

Sitting up, he reaches for my neck, urging me to his mouth. Kissing my swollen lips, he smiles against them, caressing my face as though I'm his new favorite thing.

"I'll get you something to clean up," I whisper.

"No. Stay right there," he warns, pressing my shoulder like he wants me to lay down.

I comply, watching him stagger off the bed like his legs are made of jelly. His bare ass shines in the moonlight creeping through his patio doors. Reaching down, he retrieves his t-shirt off the floor and wipes himself clean, then prowls back onto the mattress.

Caging me in with his hands on either side of my shoulders, his smile meets my lips. I'm still fully clothed and he's completely naked, but the difference doesn't seem to make him insecure.

Moving to my jaw and then to my neck, his lips leave a trail of hot wet kisses. Gliding my hands over his shoulders, I close my eyes and revel in the soft feel of his hair falling down against my shoulder, his warm skin under my touch.

"Mr. Reid," he whispers, looking up at me. "You have way too many clothes on to sleep in my bed."

"Sleeping, huh? That look doesn't say you have sleeping in mind."

Smirking, he leans toward his nightstand and opens its drawer. "Sighted people...so cocky." Peering through the darkness, I watch as he feels around in the drawer and pulls out a sparkly, purple sleep mask.

Climbing back over me, he hands me the mask much to my confusion. "What's this?"

"To even the playing field," he says, tugging my shirt up until I help him draw it over my head.

Laughing, I toss the shirt aside and inform him, "It's purple with silver sequins."

"I'll have to take your word for that," he says, planting a kiss on my lips.

Feeling for the mask, he tugs it on over my head as I lay dumbstruck. His fingertips slide gently over my brow as he slides the mask into place, sealing out what little light I could see before. All I can hear is his breathing and the rustling of the bedsheets. All I can feel is skin, warm, Riley-scented skin against my skin. My body warms instantly.

Lips press to my stomach. Fingers trail up my chest like he's seeing my body with his hands. A hand taps just below my eye like he's checking to make sure the mask is still in place.

"I feel ridiculous," I whisper, shuddering when his free hand circles my nipple.

"No," he answers. "You feel perfect."

His hot mouth moves over my nipple, covering it. I suck in a breath at the feel of his tongue flicking it to a hard bud.

"What do you think you're doing, Mr. Davenport," I challenge, running my fingers through his hair as my toes curl.

"Learning Braille," he says matter-of-factly, moving to my other nipple.

"With your tongue?" I laugh.

"Mmhm. This one," he begins, lapping the tip of that wicked tongue over my right nipple, making me gasp. "This one says you like it when I do that."

"You're a prodigy," I rasp.

"Thank you," he says cheekily, nipping at the other, sending a jolt all the way to my nuts.

Fuck. He's going to kill me with lust.

Thankfully, his hands make their way to my jeans next, deftly working the button and zipper open. For a man who's always in a hurry, he's deliberately slow at drawing my pants and underwear down my legs, placing little kisses as he goes, discovering every inch of my skin with his fingertips. It's all I can do to lie still, so overcome with emotion from the slow worship.

With the mask blotting out my sight, his careful touch imparts a lesson on fragility into my being, not the scary kind I knew with my ex. There's fragility when people break you, but there's fragility in being put back together too. With every touch, Riley is returning a piece of me I didn't think I'd ever get back.

"Harper," he whispers, his hot breath ghosting my shaft. "I...I want to taste you."

Half-groaning, half-whimpering, I rake my fingers through his hair, barely able to speak. "You don't have to ask."

"I do," he corrects, kissing the skin on my stomach next to the head of my cock, "because I don't think I'll be able to stop."

His wet heat envelopes me, making me want to tear off this stupid mask his ex probably left here, but I agreed. I promised to see what he sees, to feel what he feels. And right now, I hope to hell he felt what I'm feeling as his tongue explores the circumference of my cock. In perfect Riley fashion, he moans, fucking lets out one of his food-devouring moans around my dick. I can feel it vibrate my sensitive shaft, making me cry out and my legs quake. He barely has time to slide up and then down before my flesh goes turgid, giving a knowing twitch.

"Riley!" I warn, tugging at his jaw to release me. He groans in protest, much like I wanted to but pulls off just in time.

Working my length, it's embarrassing that all my hand serves to do is capture my release. A single stroke not even necessary for how turned on I was. Riley crashes to his pillow beside me as I locate my own shirt and hastily clean myself up the way he did. Flopping back onto the pillow next to him, I pant like a third-string swimmer, smiling when his hand glides down my belly, pulling me to his side.

"You're forgiven for freezing my brain," he declares, pressing his lips to my temple. "Wait a minute," he murmurs.

His fingers tug at the elastic of the mask. I didn't even realize I still had it on. Sliding it up, his green eyes meet mine, mischief in them.

"Freak," he mutters.

Chapter 31

RILEY

My head is killing me. If it's the price of having too much fun last night, so be it. I can feel Harper's warm body next to me…in my bed. Right where he should be.

Smiling through the pain, I pry open my eyes, still instinct upon waking up. The light assaults me, sending needles through my corneas. My head throbs, and I wince.

That asshole had a hard head. I hope what I did to his nose makes him uglier than I imagine him to be. Peeling my lids open, the light evens out, more tolerable. Larry's chestnut fur glows under the morning light, spilling in through the patio doors.

Larry.

I can fucking see him.

Whipping my head around, I rise up on my elbows off my stomach and squint when the motion sends a sharp pain through my skull. I see him. I can see him. *Harper.*

My breath catches in my throat. Blinking through the odd overlay in my vision like rain on a window, I take in the sight of the face I've dreamt about, the face I've longed to see. He's gorgeous, so fucking gorgeous.

Short dark brown hair, just like he said. It comes to a peak in the front where his bangs are a bit longer than the rest of his hair on top of his head. Smiling, I take in the way it's sticking up at all angles from what we did last night. I did that. I did that, *and* I get to see it.

There's a pink scar in his eyebrow from where I think that asshole did something to him. I want to reach out and trace it, take away any lingering pain both inside and out, but I don't dare move and wake him. It'd probably freak him out if he knew I could see, and who knows how long it'll last? The doctor assured me again last visit that the damage was irreparable.

There's another nick just underneath the left side of his jaw that I've felt before, and I wonder if it was another gift from that bully. Traveling down his neck, I strain to make out what I can through the blurry droplets distorting my view.

Moving in closer, holding my breath so as not to wake him, I canvas every inch, putting his body to memory. Three little freckles above his right collarbone. Flat brown nipples that I teased last night. There's a mole above his left hip. Gently lifting the sheet, I raise it, not caring what he'd think of being on display. He's seen me bare ass naked. Fair is fair, my dear Harper.

Fine hairs scatter the length of his legs from mid-thigh down to his ankles. Even his damn feet are sexy, I muse. His cock, only half-flaccid tells me he might be waking up soon and the size of what was in my mouth last night.

Eyes burning, I feel like a total perv, but also desperate as the imaginary rain drops start to take over my vision. Moving in closer, I can smell his potent scent, the salty latent scent of our intimate exchange last night. His close-trimmed dark curls around his groin look as soft as they felt. Eyes watering, I strain, staring at the bulging vein that works up to the head of his cock. There's a freckle there, one lone freckle. I want to taste it with my tongue, claim it, let it know that I saw it and that I'll remember it forever.

Dropping the sheet, I settle back down on my pillow and watch his sleeping face. Peaceful. Happy. Gorgeous. *Mine.* As all those images fade and blur, as my head pounds beyond reason, I take comfort in knowing that when everything is black again, they'll still be true.

Peaceful. Happy. Gorgeous. Mine.

Chapter 32

HARPER

It's surreal living with indifference for so long only to wake up to a cuddly mess of emotions. The heat of Riley's body hovering over me as I opened my eyes this morning to him stroking my cheek with tears in his eyes was as touching as it was heart-wrenching.

"What?" I asked.

With a forlorn smile and shake of his head, all he whispered was, "Just wish I could look at you." And then he kissed me like he was sealing a promise.

If he's worried that I couldn't get used to that, he's worrying for nothing. I pulled him into my arms and basked in the sensation of just lying there, wrapped up in each other, appreciated, cared for. I don't know what he'd think of me if he could see me, but I wish I could grant him that wish just to give him something he wants.

And now…at the most inopportune time, the man is pushing post-wake up cuddling a little too far. "Riley, I'm going to burn myself. Seriously, not even Larry begs for this much attention," I complain, carefully sliding the sheet of cinnamon rolls into his oven.

"It's Barkus," he corrects me. "Barkus Maximus. And yes, he does. That dog is needy as fuck. You're not the one who's had to sleep with him the last few months," he adds, trailing his lips across the nape of my neck. "He gets me up at two every morning to go outside and piss on the patio. I think he's killing that potted ficus."

Does he even know what he's doing to me? "Come on," I complain on a laugh, trying to ignore the delicious shiver he sends down my spine. "Your mom and dad are going to be here soon, and you promised you'd make the frosting."

"I'm on it!" He defends, releasing me to return to his work at the island counter.

Sighing, I throw the dirty cooking utensils in the dishwasher and wipe down the counter. He warned me his mom and dad were coming for brunch today, but he strategically waited to warn me until after we got out of bed this morning. His bed that now smells like sex.

Thanks, Riley. I'm not supposed to be your caretaker or anything.

He says I worry too much, and that if he'd told me sooner, I'd have been fretting about it. Well, damn it...he's right. I've met Leigh Ann. She was a doll. She liked me, but that...was before I made her son come, before I corrupted his straight morals.

I asked if he planned on telling them, not because I want to, but because he looked way too excited about the prospect of them coming over to eat with the two of us. Kind of like he wants to show me off. It's sweet, really, but also holy-shit-I-don't-know-if-I-can-do-this level nerve wracking. He's coming out to his parents? Because of me?

"Riley, are you sure you want to tell—" I don't get to finish the sentence, snared by the sight of his bare ass peeking out above his drooping gym shorts. There's at least two inches of his cute butt crack showing. What the fuck is he doing?

Head lowered, it almost looks like he's...looking at his cock. He's supposed to be mixing up the icing for the cinnamon rolls.

When he turns around, I'm greeted with a proud smile and...an icing covered-cockhead. Pinching my eyes closed, I press my fingertips into them, telling myself not to smile.

"I think I might need some help with this after all," he says, gravely.

His mother needs a medal. I swear. Shaking with repressed laughter that I refuse to let loose lest I encourage his antics, I force out a dramatic breath.

"*What*...are you doing?"

"I thought maybe we should taste it to make sure it's okay." Sighing as though he's carrying a burden, he adds, "You can go first."

"Your parents will be here in like half an hour," I inform him.

Squeezing my shoulders, he bares his teeth impishly. "I know, so we have thirty minutes alone."

"No," I try to sound firm.

"I'll come really quick," he reassures me. "Like so quick, you won't believe it."

"That's...the least sexy thing I've ever heard."

"I'm serious."

"So was I."

"Uhn. Come on. I don't want to be walking around with a hard on the entire time my parents are here and knocking shit over with it."

"You have a really high opinion of your...image," I deadpan.

Gasping. "Ouch! That hurt," he exclaims, his smile betraying his claim of offense as he runs his hands up and down my arms. "This is totally your fault, by the way. You smell like cookies and then threw cinnamon rolls in the mix. I didn't stand a chance."

He's not going to quit, and the thought of him with a hard on for me in front of his parents does terrify me. At least, that's what I tell myself, drooling over the sight of his icing covered cock as I drop to my knees.

"Oh my God," he groans, his fingers splaying through my hair. "I didn't think that'd actually work."

Choking on a laugh around his sweetened cock, I give the side of his ass a little swat. "Ooh," he grunts. "I'm almost there. I can't wait to lather you up. How's my frosting taste?"

Scoffing, I pop off him. "Like cock and powdered sugar. What do you think?"

His laughter stops abruptly at the sound of a knock at the door. Our widened eyes lock, my heart jumping into my throat.

"Fuck," he mutters. "The cookie monster."

"Oh my gosh," I mutter, tugging his shorts up with one hand, wiping the frosting off my lips with the other.

"Wait. What are you doing?" he asks, catching my wrist before his waistband clears the iron rod still pointing at me.

"I'm going to go wash my face in the bathroom," I whisper. "You can let them in."

Why is his lip pouting? Oh, fuck no. No way. Is he for real?

"But I'm almost there," he whines.

"You can't be serious! They're right outside the door!"

On cue, another knock resounds, so I gesture for emphasis like an idiot. His hips shift back and forth, waving his hard cock in front of my face.

"I'm going to knock *so much* shit over with this thing. I want them to know I like you, but this isn't how I imagined showing them," he tries whining, kneading my shoulders like a cat.

"Oh, brother. You...you're horrible," I seethe at how easily he can manipulate me.

Taking him in, I bob like my life depends upon it because...well, because he makes me an idiot, and the mental image of him actually knocking things over with his erection in front of his parents is something I don't want to live through.

"I will so get you back, baby. I swear," he pants.

"Riley!" Leigh Ann calls through the door after another knock. "Are you okay in there?"

I whimper in panic, questioning my sanity, while moving at the speed of light up and down his hot, sweet shaft.

173

"Yeah," he groans in response. "I'm coming!" Glancing up at him, I arch a brow, wondering who that sentiment was for, but then I feel him stiffen in my mouth. "Oh, shit! I *am* coming!"

Drinking him down I decide is easier clean up than wiping up the kitchen or our clothes or my hair. As soon as his last spurt hits my tongue, I hop to my feet, snapping his waistband up with me when I go. Scrambling down the hallway, I race into his bathroom like a tornado with swollen lips. Slamming the door shut behind me, I burst out laughing and can't stop, even when it becomes painful to breathe.

"Harper, don't you want any of these cinnamon rolls you made?" Leigh Ann asks, offering me the platter.

"Um, no, thank you. This breakfast casserole you made is delicious though."

"Oh, I used to make it for the boys for breakfast on Sundays, and the leftovers would last them through Tuesday morning. Saved me from cooking for a few mornings every week."

"Brent is…two years younger than you, Riley? Right?" I try to sound normal as he smirks at me while slowly licking frosting off his thumb.

"Yeah. That's when we found him on the doorstep. Right, Ma?"

"Ha. Ha," Leigh Ann quips, setting a cinnamon roll on her plate, making me fidget.

Worse yet, Riley reaches for my hand, taking it in his. His father notices when he looks up from his plate. His fork stops halfway to his mouth. He looks from me to Riley and my heart hammers against my chest, but then his jaw continues chewing. He goes back to focusing on his food, and I wonder if that's where his son inherited his appetite.

"So, what do you guys think of Harper?" Riley asks, making my face burn.

Fuck. This is it.

Four months. I've barely known him four months, dated him, if that's what we're doing, for even less. To this day, Dallas' dad probably still thinks I was just his roommate, rather than the man he shared a bed with and professed to not be able to live without.

Leigh Ann looks from our joined hands to me with her mouth agape in evident surprise. I don't know her well enough to know if the smile that brightens her face next is feigned or genuine.

"Well, I think he's wonderful. Don't you, Charlie?" she says much to my relief.

Charlie eyes our hands again and then glances suspiciously at Riley. Still chewing, he points and waggles his fork between us. "Is this…one of your pranks, Riley?"

"What?" Riley makes a disbelieving sound, while my stomach drops realizing the verdict still isn't in on Mr. Davenport's thoughts.

Charlie finally stops chewing and straightens up when he meets my nervous gaze and catches my thumb anxiously rubbing Riley's knuckles.

"You're serious?" he asks, looking to his son.

"Yeah, Dad," Riley says earnestly, squeezing my hand. "I'm totally serious. I really like him." Flashing me a smile, he draws our hands up, kisses my knuckles and adds, "A lot."

Charlie processes for a second and then lets out an amused puff of breath. Looking me in the eye, he holds up his coffee like he's making a toast. "Good luck, son. My best to you."

Riley beams, clapping him on the shoulder. "Thanks, Dad."

"Wasn't talking to you," Charlie says matter-of-factly, returning to his breakfast casserole.

Just like that. Just like not a thing in the world could befuddle him. I don't understand it.

When my jaw stops flapping open at the easy acceptance, I finally remember to breathe again. And Riley? Riley erupts into laughter.

Later, when I'm washing the dishes with Leigh Ann, I can't stand the lack of discussion. Riley's in the living room with his dad, elaborating on Larry's many talents. I didn't know the list was so long or that some of the "talents" were even list-worthy.

As Leigh Ann passes me another dish to dry, I find some of the courage Riley wears so effortlessly. The only mother figure I've ever talked about my sexuality to was mine.

"Does it…bother you?" I hedge. When she looks at me in confusion, I elaborate what I thought was the obvious. "Me…and Riley."

Drying her hands, she turns to me with a sad smile. "My son came out of the womb with a smile on his face that's rarely left it since that day, but," she pauses, glancing into the living room with a fond expression, "I've never seen him this happy, truly, genuinely, bone-deep happy." Cupping my cheek, her eyes look as glassy as mine feel. "Whatever you're doing…keep doing it."

Chapter 33

HARPER

I doubt Leigh Ann meant running my soapy hands up and down Riley's back in the shower was one of the things I should keep doing, but I'm not ready to stop. I'm not ready to stop his tender touch from gliding all over my skin either.

"See?" he says smugly. "Told you I needed help."

Burying my face in his neck, I hide my smile. "You showered just fine for months before this."

"Maybe I wanted to find out if you had anymore VRT tricks you've been holding out on me," he teases, his hands circling over my ass as his tongue traces my jugular.

"Well, your shower is white, so it might be good to find shampoo products that come in a black bottle to provide more contrast," I suggest, but it comes out all choppy as his slick cock brushes against mine.

"Bor-ring," he grumbles at my ear.

"I never said my job was exciting."

"I'm officially insulted. Your *Yelp* review is going to be one-star for that comment."

"You know what you're implying isn't what I meant," I clarify, kissing his mouth.

"Mm. Regardless, you might have a point. I'm more than happy to offer you more excitement," he purrs, trailing his fingers across my ass and grinding his hips into mine.

My laughter is cut off when his middle finger trails down between my ass cheeks, the tip of his finger brushing over my pucker. My heart rockets, my cock kicks, and…and I stiffen, holding my breath. How can I want the touch, but be terrified of it as well? This is Riley. It's not Dallas.

Clenching, I reach back and slide my hand over his wrist, feeling horrid for faking a lover's caress. I can't. I just can't yet. Will I ever be able to find pleasure there again? Will I ever be able to give him pleasure?

"That's…you don't have to do that," I caution.

"It sounds pretty good in your books," he whispers, licking a drop of water underneath my chin. "Tell me what you like, and I'll try it."

My stomach turns in on itself. *Him.* I like him, so why can't my body cooperate? Why can't my nerves cooperate? How do I tell him I'm afraid without him thinking I'm afraid of him?

"I…don't really like that," I explain, delicately.

"Oh." The loss of confidence in his caress as his hands move to my sides, cripples my heart. "Sorry," he murmurs, placing a chaste kiss on my lips like I'm as fragile as I feel.

Eyes watering, I hate that it feels like I'm failing him, like I'm denying him something two lovers should easily share. I've let myself become so lost in the euphoria of how I feel, all I've done is put a bandage on a festering wound.

I knew this was coming. I just hoped that when it came, I'd be ready. It was too much to hope that he'd be the one to ask to stop. I've actually hoped for it, anticipated it, expecting his foray into gay intimacy to take a turn at some point. I'd have understood. I'd have felt the loss but wouldn't begrudge him for not being able to embrace a complete one-eighty in his sexual preferences.

Of course not though. It's Riley, boldly going where he's never gone before, no fear. And then there's me. How can I be afraid of being that intimate with a man who makes me smile just knowing he exists in the world? I really hate Dallas. I hate that he's taken this away from me, from Riley.

"I'm sorry," he repeats. "I thought…the whole prostate thing…that maybe…maybe I could make you feel good," he stammers.

Cupping his face, I hold my lips to his, my chest aching from his intentions. He already makes me feel better than I ever have, and he still wants to give me more. How can I ever be the man he deserves?

I don't even have another job lined up. The few apartments I've found online within the budget of what I've saved from Riley's contract, leave much to be desired. In a few weeks, I'll be unemployed with no other option than to ask him if I can stay until I find more work. Going to Daniel's broom closet isn't an option, not with my ex lurking around with a grudge.

Pushing away all the things I can't give him, I determine to give him what I hope I can. Brushing my thumb across his lower lip, I reassure him, "Don't be sorry. I have a suggestion. Why don't we try something and…you can let me know what you think?"

His chest heaves against mine like the sound of trying anything with me turns him on. Fuck. I wish I wasn't so broken. I wish I'd met him before I gave myself to a man that chewed me up and spit me out.

"Okay," he agrees.

Urging him to turn around, I start with kisses to his shoulder blades, running my hands down his slickened outline to his hips. He shudders underneath my lips when I blaze a trail down his spine. Dropping to my knees, I press a kiss to each globe of his ass.

He sucks in a breath, hanging his head, the water falling off the long tendrils of his hair into his face. Running my hands up and down his thighs, I wonder if he's ever thought of this, or if this is the moment that he'll decide male-male intimacy isn't for him.

"You okay?" I whisper, pressing little kisses to the underside curve of his ass.

"The only way I could be more okay is if you were narrating this like one of your books," his voice floats down, thick with lust.

"Kind of hard to talk and use my mouth at the same time."

"Hm. Noted."

Bending down, I lap my tongue across his sac, while tracing every line of his sculpted legs. He's a freaking work of art on top of being the most lovable man I've ever met.

"Harper works his skilled tongue…across Riley's balls," Riley's voice calls out, an octave deeper like he's narrating my ministrations.

Chuckling, I press my lips to the back of his thigh and pinch my eyes closed, so I don't ruin the moment by losing it over his shenanigans. "I don't think they use the word *balls* too often."

"Hey, this is my audiobook. I can have balls if I want."

That earns him another lick, which produces a suction of breath that makes me proud for derailing him. The water cascading down the curve of his ass, dribbles onto my face as I reach between his legs and stroke him. His cock kicks in my hand as I trail kisses up the edge of his seam.

"Riley's cock bucks in approval when…Harper's talented hands claim his *very* well-endowed, throbbing, engorged member," he pants, pressing his hands to the wall.

Fucking Riley. If I'm going to do this, I need to do it now before he distracts me too much.

Trembling with both apprehension and arousal, I draw my lips to the tight crevice between his cheeks. Cupping gently, I spread them slightly and draw the tip of my tongue up his channel, passing over the warm, wet skin of his pucker. It twitches underneath my tongue. He flinches in surprise, but then lets out a deep groan. That sound and the taste of him has me swallowing a moan.

Drawing back, I circle his ass with my palms, waiting, anxious. "You…stopped narrating," I point out. "Does that mean you didn't like it?"

Clearing his throat and panting, his feet inch farther apart astride my knees. His hips tilt back, and he sighs, leaning into the wall. "And then," he pauses to swallow, "Riley forgot how to spell his name."

Smiling, I basically hug his ass, wrapping my arms around his waist and pressing my cheek to him. "Spelling is overrated."

"I think I might remember *one* word."

"What's that?"

"M-o-r-e."

More? Yeah. I can gladly give him more. Sighing in relief, I retrace my last move, eliciting another satisfied sound from him.

Dallas never let me or wanted me to do this to him. I forgot how enjoyable it could be to give as well as receive. One day, I hope our exchanges won't include my subconscious comparisons about Dallas. I don't want him in the room, don't want him haunting my headspace anymore. I want a life that's all mine, a love that's not tainted by the past.

I blocked his number after the incident at the bar. While I'm terrified, he'll somehow find out I'm no longer reading his messages like an obedient whipping boy, the defiant act is a piece of freedom, one that will allow me to focus my attention on the worthy man in front of me.

As Riley's moaning turns to needy whimpers, echoing off the shower stall, the sounds help keep my worries at bay. Him. Him. I don't know if I have addictive behavior, if that's what got me into my mess, but I'm completely addicted to him.

Working my tongue in careful circles, I knead the results of his gym workouts in my hands, inhaling his steam-enhanced scent. His hips are rocking into my mouth. He's given up on narrating, so I must be doing something right.

Reaching down, I have to squeeze away the pain in my cock when he cries out as the tip of my tongue breaches him ever so slightly. I'm going to come just listening to him lose his mind.

"Aw, fuck. Harper. Harper, baby. What are you doing to me?" he pants. "Don't stop. Please, don't stop."

Fearless. Insatiable. How did I get so lucky? Tasting him deeper, his heat clenches around my tongue. Just as I reach between his legs to bring him relief, I'm met by his eager hand.

"Baby, jerk yourself. Please. Want you to…come too," he pants. "I want to picture it."

The man and his good ideas. Moaning in relief, I let my hand fly over my aching shaft as I suck and swirl my tongue into his twitching entrance, cognizant to let my forearm bump the back of his calf so he can feel what I'm doing to myself. His muscles quake around my face. I can feel the vibrations of him stroking himself in earnest.

My wet kiss sounds mix with the echoes of his throaty groans and panting, making every inch of my skin go taut. I want to live here on my knees for him. I want to go to sleep and wake up to the sounds he's making because of me. I don't know how long I'll be able to fake being the man he deserves, but in this moment, it feels like I am that man.

He cries out, his hole clenching around my tongue in violent spasms. His body collapses into the wall. I chase him with my mouth, still tantalizing, still teasing as he comes, and I burst from sending him over the edge.

When I finally release his sensitized pucker, his ass offers a divine resting place for my cheek as I catch my breath. I run my hands up and down his thighs, chuckling at the way his muscles are quaking.

He pushes off the wall, turns around looking as though he just ran a marathon. Dropping to his knees in front of me, I'm about to embrace him in a hug, but he puts all his weight forward, toppling me back onto the shower floor. Luckily, I catch myself with one palm to the tile and ease us down.

Laughing, I kiss his temple. "Are you okay?"

His wet hair brushes against my chest as he nods with a little grunt, his fingers idly stroking my nipple. "And then," he says breathily, "Riley passed out in a very sexy way."

Chapter 34

RILEY

"I talked to Rob while you were doing your laundry," I tell Harper, nuzzling the side of his head where he's sitting between my legs on my patio lounger.

In the week since my parents' visit, the late summer weather has transitioned to Fall, bringing a chill. Tucking the throw blanket tighter around us to stave off the crisp evening air, Harper tilts his head toward mine.

"Oh, yeah? How's he doing?"

"Good. I told him we finished our app. He's going to come over and take a look at it."

His body rocks in my arms on a puff of breath. I know that critical sound of his. Squeezing him, I press my lips behind his ear. "What? What was that for?"

"Nothing just…you keep calling it *our* app. I didn't do anything. You're the one who designed it."

"Uh, you input all the data and code," I object.

"I typed what you told me to type," he says dryly.

"You gave me the idea," I counter.

Sighing, he squeezes my knee under the blanket and then murmurs, "I'm proud of you."

Although it's said genuinely and with affection, I sense it's an attempt to end the conversation. "Why does that feel like you're not proud of you too?"

Sighing, he fidgets in my arms, telling me I've gotten to the heart of the matter. "Riley, I…I was happy to work on it with you, but let's face it. I could never invent anything. All I know is VRT, and I didn't even have to work hard for that knowledge because of growing up with my mom. I just…I have no skills. I haven't ever really accomplished anything and don't know that I ever will."

Is he shitting me? Sitting up, I turn his shoulders to look at me. "How can you say that? You taught me about contrast and how to shave with one hand as a guide so I don't cut my jugular. I didn't know about that knife guard thing you put on my cutting board, or Braille, or the guide dog process, or even think to wear sneakers around the apartment to quit stubbing my toes until you came along."

"Those are things you could have read about or any VRT could have shown you."

"Harper, you have a gift. You help people. Don't sell yourself short."

"I used to go to the community center and volunteer to help people with low vision there, but I haven't gone since…since I moved out of my apartment. I don't even have a place to live yet or know if Marcy can find another position for me by the end of the month."

Frowning, I don't like the sound of any of his dilemmas. "Did you like helping out at the community center?"

"Yeah, but…I just feel like a fake now."

"How so?"

"How am I supposed to help people in need when I might not even have a home or a job in a month?"

His words twist my heart over the way he feels about himself, about us, and the possibility of him not being here. Rubbing his jaw, I work my thumb across his lower lip. "You have a home…here."

"Riley, I can't be a freeloader."

"Then pay me rent when you start working again, if it makes you feel better."

"I would. I absolutely would, but it's not that. I…I can't live here. We just started…whatever we're doing, and…I haven't been on my own in three years. Before that, I lived with Daniel. Before that, with my mother. I've never been on my own actually. I…need to be independent, or I'll feel like I'll never be responsible."

"You're the most responsible person I've ever met," I counter in disbelief.

Squeezing my arm, he chides, "That's not what I meant. Well, actually…it is. I can't be nervous about everything all the time. I need to learn to be scared on my own even if I'll hate it."

"I don't want you to be scared," I say, hating the thought. "Have you thought about going to therapy?"

"They have a counselor at the community center. I was thinking I could talk to her, maybe go do some volunteer work again too."

"That's good. You've been through a lot, and if helping people makes you feel better then you should do that too."

He stays quiet, not commenting. It makes my stomach flip at the unresolved parts of his concerns. "And *us*...are you saying you don't want to do this anymore?" I hedge.

"No. I didn't mean that at all. You're the best thing that's ever happened to me."

"Then why do you want to move out? I mean, I get the whole independence thing. Believe me—you know I do, but Chicago cost of living sucks. You can still be independent and stay here. I'm not needy or demanding." I'm glad I finally made him laugh, but that wasn't supposed to be funny. Nipping his earlobe, I digress, "Okay, fine. I'm *somewhat* needy and demanding, but I can tone it down and give you your space."

"I don't want to tone you down at all. I like you the way you are."

Hugging him, I whisper, "Then why make it harder for yourself with the stress and financial burden of finding another place and commuting when you already have all these other things to go through? Let me go through them with you...*here*. Will you think about it? Please?"

It takes him longer to respond than I'd like, but I keep my mouth shut, finally exhaling when he says, "Yeah. I'll think about it. Thank you."

Squeezing him, I coo smugly, "Yes! My boyfriend's going to think about it."

"*Boyfriend*, huh?"

"Do you prefer the title *noble avenger*?"

"No. *Boyfriend* will do."

Chapter 35

HARPER

My session with Rosalyn at the community center was as difficult as I thought it would be, but I'm also filled with a new sense of hope. I'm glad I came after spilling my woes to Riley when he was trying to be romantic and let me stargaze on his roof the other night. Instead of his incredible progress making me regret the lack of my own, now I can say I've done something to let his example inspire me. It helped that the universe decided to be gracious yesterday and send me a text from Marcy.

Apparently, Mr. Boswell finally retired from my last place of work at the senior center, and the new management wants to take on another VRT. While I'm excited that they'll hold the position for me until Riley's contract is up at the end of the month, I've spent the day agonizing over the countdown to my time with him. *Live-in caregiver* has been a nice excuse up until now to avoid the inevitable question— what are we doing?

Packing up my bag for the evening, I tell the other community center volunteers who are wrapping up for the evening goodnight. Being here makes me feel like my old self, but an even better version of him. I got to help an elderly man who recently started losing his vision but relies on state aid and doesn't have many resources for the help he needs.

Combined with Rosalyn's advice, being of use to that kindly man has me feeling...restored. Rosalyn said to be aware of my negative thoughts, to identify what creates those negative thoughts, and to stop blaming myself for what happened. Easier said than done, but I want to navigate in that direction for so many reasons.

When I told her about my relationship concerns regarding Riley, she advised me to consider putting as much energy into keeping the good things in my life as I had the bad in the past. Riley is without a doubt a good thing. The thought of staying with him no longer makes me feel

184

like I've failed at adulting, but rather could possibly be the first smart decision I've made in a long time, the first decision for myself.

Boundaries, Rosalyn said. I'll need to have boundaries, so I don't let a relationship take over my life again. It's comical to try and deny that my relationship with Riley hasn't consumed me, but I think it's in a healthy way, a way where I feel safe and cherished, a way that lifts me up. I'm his equal, not subservient.

Walking to his car in the parking lot, I jingle the keys in my hand with a smile on my face. I feel lighter than I have in a long time, years even. The thought of going home—*home*—and making Riley feel lighter too by telling him I've decided to stay ripples giddy excitement through me, knowing I can give him what he wants without any doubts.

I think that's the most valuable lesson I took away from my therapy session tonight—making someone else happy shouldn't mean you have to make yourself miserable. Four months ago, I'd have been embarrassed to admit this realization to Riley, but now I can't wait to get home and share my progress with him. I can't wait to see what he's named Larry today, if he's sitting on the roof ledge, or if he's racing to the bathroom because he got into the energy drinks again.

Pulling out my phone, I send off a quick message to him.

ME: Be there soon. What are you up to?

RILEY: Looking up frosting recipes.

Snickering, I slip the key into his car door lock. A scrape of footsteps on the pavement behind me has me tensing. Not tonight, I chide myself for my hypervigilance. Tonight is going to be a good night. Tonight, there's nothing to be afraid of.

Positive thoughts.

The breeze blows the scent of alcohol and a familiar cologne, sending the hairs on the back of my neck to attention. A voice taunts at my back, making my pulse jump, "Hellooo, *Harper*. I knew I'd find you here eventually."

Chapter 36

RILEY

"Rita, what time is it?"

"*It is ten-twelve p.m.*"

"Where the hell is he?" I mutter, raking my hands through Bartholomew's fur.

I should have gone with him. I know how important independence is to him, but I could have gone for moral support. I could have sat quietly in the hallway like a harmless fly on the wall just in case he needed me at any point. I can sit quietly. I've been doing it all night.

What if his session didn't go well? What if he had a bad emotional break through? Why isn't he answering my texts anymore? Is my fucking voice-to-text broken? He said he'd be home *soon*. That was over two hours ago.

The lock on the door rattles, making me bolt off the couch. Thank fuck. I've stress eaten so many *Better Cheddars*, I'm not going to be able to crap for a week.

"Hey! I was starting to think you were out buying a cat to scare Bartholomew away," I jest.

"Hey, sorry," his tired voice comes out barely above a whisper.

Rounding the couch, I make my way toward him. I barely need to rely on sounds anymore to locate him, sensing his presence always seems to be enough, like my heart will take me where I want to go. Okay, it's probably that I've gotten that good at echolocation, but my theory sounds more romantic.

"How did it go?" I ask, hearing the keys drop on the counter.

"Good. It…went good. I…I got hung up. Sorry, I'm so late."

"It's okay." I soothe, stepping closer, not liking the meek tone in his voice.

It almost sounds like he's slurring, but I don't smell any alcohol. I'd be happy for him if he was able to let loose for a drink with some friends, but there's something sad in his voice. Reaching out to embrace him, I'm surprised when instead he captures my hand, squeezing it. It's trembling and cold.

"Do you want to listen to a movie or just go to bed and let me try out my new frosting on you?"

His chuckle is faint and broken. It almost sounds like he's panting. "No, I…actually," he stops to swallow. "I've got quite the headache. I think…I might go lay down in the spare room. Then I…I won't wake you if…if I have to get up for some aspirin or s-something."

"Harper?" I tug my hand from his when I realize the way he's clutching onto mine feels more like he's holding me back…holding me back from getting close to him. And he just fucking stuttered and slurred. "Are you alright?" I ask, reaching for his face.

His hand comes up, deflecting mine. "Y-yeah. I'm f-fine."

"You are not fine. I can hear you," I counter, using my other hand to clasp onto his shoulder.

"*Hngh!*" He yelps, flinching when my palm connects with the distorted feel of his shoulder.

"Harper, what the fuck?" I gasp, cupping his face only to pull back like it electrocuted me when I feel heat, swollen heat, and a damp substance that can only be blood. "What happened?"

Moaning, he cradles his dislocated arm, trembling underneath my touch. "D-Dallas," he croaks. "I'm sorry."

"What?" I shout but regret it as soon as I feel him flinch again. "Where did you see him, baby?" I ask, guiding him to the couch.

"The…c-center. He…was at the center, waiting…waiting out by the car. I'm sorry."

Tripping over the coffee table, I stumble to my knees in front of him when he drops down on the couch. Canvasing his legs, I work my way up, afraid to touch him, yet desperate to comfort him. There's never been a more inopportune time to not be able to see than right now. I don't even know where he's hurt, where to not touch him to prevent causing him more pain.

My heart is in my throat. Tears choke my sinuses. I want to rip something in half, and I know exactly what it is that I want to destroy. What did that fucking psychopath do to my man?

"Baby, did he…did he…" I can't even say the words. I don't want to traumatize him anymore than I think that bastard already has in the past.

"No," he croaks. "I…p-passed out. Hit my head…off the car. Just… just woke up an hour ago."

"Jesus," I whisper, now understanding why he's so cold. He could have laid there and bled to death, could have gone into a coma from his brain swelling. He could have been in a wreck on the way home.

"Tell me what's hurt," I plead, fighting everything in me not to touch him. The way he's shaking, I can tell it's more from pain than the cold.

"F-fine. I'm fine, Riley. Just—"

"You're not fine," my voice breaks. Heaving in frustration, I raise my fingertips. "Baby, I'm going to touch you. Okay? I need to know what's wrong."

Trembling, I dust my fingertips over his forehead. There's a gash in his hairline. A dried substance, still sticky in some places runs from his hair down to his eyebrow where I can feel the encrusted blood. His eye…it's so fucking swollen I doubt he can see out of it. Rocking back and forth, his stuttered, shallow breaths are pained with each inhale, each exhale. I make it to his jaw, his mouth. A crescent of puffy skin greets my fingers, his lips swollen under my touch as he makes a quiet anguished sound that kills a piece of me.

The way he's holding his middle, clutching his dislocated arm to his stomach, I fear there's more damage underneath his gritty, mussed shirt. "I'm going to call an ambulance," I tell him, rising to my feet.

"No! No, I'm…f-fine," his voice waivers as he clutches my wrist with a weak grip.

Eyes wide, I can't even believe what I'm hearing. Did he come to me like this after his last beating from that fucker?

"Can you lay down?" I whisper, helping to guide him back onto the cushions. Larry whines from the floor at the other end of the couch, mirroring the noise my heart is screaming. Placing a kiss on Harper's forehead, I assure him, "I'm going to go get you some ice."

Chapter 37

RILEY

It's been two days since the ambulance took Harper to the hospital. I want to hear his voice. I want a different memory than the last one I have of it, him whimpering a defeated sounding refusal when the paramedics showed up, realizing I had called 9-1-1.

He shut down when the police officer arrived, asking him questions as the paramedics were loading him onto the gurney. I, however, was happy to supply the name of the person responsible for treating him like less than a human being.

Inhaling a gulp of cool air on the rooftop, I feel Larry nudge my calf with his nose, signaling he's done watering my plants. "Is he going to be mad at me?" I ask him.

That asshole belongs in jail where he can't hurt anyone else ever again, where Harper doesn't have to live in fear. And Harper...he belongs here with me where I can show him how much he's taken over my heart, my entire world. He belongs where I can make every day the life his gentle soul deserves to live.

"Hey, it's getting cold out here," Rob says, joining me on the patio.

He came as soon as I called him. Good old Rob. Mom offered to come too, but I asked her to check on Harper at the hospital instead, so I could stay with Larry. Harper said not to, that he'll be home today, but someone needs to be with him, so I got ahold of his friend Daniel the night of the attack by calling that bar he works at. His reaction was pretty much the same as mine, and he thanked me for diming Dallas out to the police.

"I can't even feel it," I say idly, staring through the afternoon light over the city, my mind on the other side of town.

"Come on in, man. You'll get sick, and then you won't be any good to Harper when he gets home."

Rob's advice gets me to return inside. He hasn't said a word about my evident concern for Harper. He's not as stupid as our other friends think. I'm sure he's guessed my feelings by the way I wept in his arms when he arrived.

His hand grips my shoulder, and he shoves a soda at me in the kitchen. "He'll be alright," he reassures me. "He's tough. I can tell."

"Yeah." I nod, popping the can lid open. "Just...I...I'm worried." I don't add, *about us*.

Mostly, I'm worried about Harper's state of mind. Witnessing what happened to him the other night first-hand, and remembering the way he was when I first met him, something foreboding makes me wonder if all the progress he's made will take a one-eighty. How much shit can one person go through before it breaks them?

"You really love him, huh?" Rob ventures.

Smiling, I chew my lip and nod. "Probably sounds crazy, huh?"

"Mm, no. I mean, I figured you were bound to fall in love with someone other than yourself sooner or later."

Chuckling, I make to swat his arm, but my heart is so full, I end up clapping him on the shoulder instead. Pulling him into a hug, I mutter, "I love you too, man."

"Uh, well, you're not exactly my type."

Our laughter is cut short at the sound of the door unlocking from the outside. My breath catches in my throat, knowing I'm only seconds away from that sugar cookie scent.

The sound of Daniel's voice helping Harper inside hits me first, but then I catch Rob's barely audible whisper. "Jesus."

It's not the reaction I want to hear from someone looking at Harper's appearance ever, but it lets me know how bad he must look. Holding back until he gets inside, and Daniel gets the door closed, I make my way to him.

"Hey," he murmurs when I get close.

"Hey," I parrot, gently gliding my hand up his non-injured arm and pressing a kiss to his temple. "How are you feeling?"

"Okay. Just...tired. I...I think I'll go lay down."

"Sure."

I think nothing of it, making my way toward my room, assuming he's following, but when I hear his footsteps heading in the opposite direction down the hallway, a sickening feeling churns in my gut. Following the sounds of Daniel helping Harper to his old room, I wait at the bedroom doorway, hearing him get settled.

"Do you need anything?" Rob asks, coming up beside me.

"No. No, I'm good. Thanks for stopping by."

"Yeah. Call me if you need anything. Okay?" Stepping into the room, I hear him address Harper. "Hey, Harper. I'm glad you're back. I hope you mend up quick."

"Thanks, Rob, and…thanks for staying with him."

"Yeah. No problem."

I resent being talked about like I needed a babysitter but remind myself that maybe Harper was just as worried about my emotional state as I was his. When Rob leaves, I wait for Daniel to exit the room and call out to Harper.

"I'll be right back. I'm just going to walk Daniel out."

He answers with a little grunt, bidding Daniel farewell. Following Daniel, I wait until we're in the kitchen to make sure Harper won't hear our discussion.

"How's he doing?" I ask.

Daniel heaves a sigh. "Fucked. Totally fucked up in the head."

Well, if I wanted someone to sugar coat things for me, I asked the wrong guy. It's for the best though, I tell myself, bracing for whatever else he can let me in on. I don't want to be coddled with lies and half-truths.

"The concussion?" I venture, my throat thick around the words.

"No. Just…with Dallas' bullshit all over again. I was happy for him, so fucking happy. After you two got together, he was starting to remind me of how he was in college. Happier even. I had my doubts at first. I was scared as hell for him, thinking he was making a mistake getting mixed up with another guy. No offense," he emphasizes.

"None taken."

"Well, but he was good, you know? And now everything's his fault again and…and…"

"What?"

"Nothing. Just…you should talk to him, remind him how good he felt, but give him some time. Don't…don't take anything to heart he says right now. He needs to get out of his own head."

I don't like the way that sounds one bit. Why does it feel like I've been voted off an island? Thanking Daniel, I lock up behind him and make my way to the bed that isn't mine, isn't ours.

It's quiet as a tomb when I step inside. Inching my way toward the bed, I call out, "Are you awake?"

He doesn't answer, but I know the sound of his breathing when he sleeps, and that's not the sound I hear right now. What the fuck is going on?

Bending a knee, I climb carefully onto the mattress so as not to jostle him. Laying down beside him, I find his uninjured hand. When I close my fingers over his, he grips them.

"Hey," I whisper.

"Hey." That broken, quiet voice isn't Harper's, shouldn't belong to Harper.

"You're going to be alright," I assure him. "I'll have Bogart bring you breakfast in bed. I'll fasten a tray to his back, and I promise I won't burn down the kitchen. When you feel better, we'll get you back in my big ass bed, and I'll give you backrubs every night for six months."

"Riley," he chokes out.

I'm used to him pretending to chide my stupid jokes, but the way he says my name this time…it's sad and cautionary.

"I start my new job next week," he says before I can inquire about his mood.

"Yeah. Yeah, I know, but if you're not up to it by then, can Marcy tell them to move your start-date back?"

The pillow jostles with the shake of his head. "No. I…I need to go. I don't want to put it on hold because of…because of this."

"Yeah, but…I mean, if you needed a few extra days, I'm sure they could hold it for you. Right?" I reason.

His grip on my hand loosens, and he slips his out, tucking it away under his side. "I can't keep putting things off because of my bad decisions. I need to work. I need to earn money for an apartment."

My throat closes up, but I force the words out. "So…you're moving out?"

"I asked Daniel to go look at a few places for me that I found online."

That answers the question, but not exactly how I wanted it answered. When I don't respond, he must realize a rebuttal is on the tip of my tongue, because he elaborates.

"Riley, I need to be on my own, and you don't need to look after me. You shouldn't have to."

"What if I want to look after you?" I rush out, panic rising in my chest.

"This…this won't work. I've got nothing to offer anyone. We can't—"

"We can't *what?*"

His body tremors against mine, and then I hear it, a sniffle. His sniffle turns into a sputter. He's crying.

Running my hand up and down his arm, I soothe, "Hey. Hey, it's alright. We'll figure it out. You don't have to worry about this shit right now. I'm not kicking you out just because your stupid contract's up. I told you, you don't have to go anywhere."

"Riley, please," he sputters. "I have to go. I…I'm not trying to hurt you. I swear. Can…can we talk about this later? I can't do this right now."

Do this? This? What the fuck is *this? I'm* a *this,* an issue on an agenda, a box to tick off in single-handedly destroying his own life?

No. I'm supposed to be one of the good things, the things you keep, not the things you discard, I want to tell him.

"I just really want to be alone." He sniffles again, sounding muffled like he's hiding his face from me in the pillow. "Please?"

All I can think as I blink stupidly at the darkness in the room, at the heat of my lover in front of me, shying his face away from mine is that I love him. I love him so much that I'd give him anything. I just wish that *anything* wasn't the absence of me.

Chapter 38

HARPER

Larry nuzzles his nose into the folds of the comforter and huffs at me again. I know what he's saying, go talk to him. Go talk to Riley.

But I can't. I need to talk to him, but I don't want to have that talk yet, the talk that I have to make myself have with him.

We've barely said more than a few sentences to each other the last few days, mostly him asking me how I'm feeling and if I need anything.

You.

The answer my heart cries out each time he asks is *you*. And that's the crux of it.

When I came here, I thought it was to assist a person with low vision who needed help. Riley didn't need any help. Riley just needed a friend. One of us did need something though and still does, it just isn't Riley.

I've stayed in this room, essentially hiding from him as long as I can. Prying myself out of bed, I wince at the soreness in my shoulder, my face. At least he doesn't have to see the marks that look like someone took a cheese grater to my cheek from when I hit the pavement. I will be eternally grateful for whatever ruckus noise I heard when I hit the ground that startled Dallas enough for him to take off, believing we'd been happened upon and cursing that he couldn't finish what he started.

I find Riley on the couch in the living room, folding laundry. Taking in the sight, I let out a humorless breath. As if I needed more proof that he doesn't need me.

"Harper?" he asks, his hands freezing mid-air.

"I'm here," I tell him, making my way to the couch.

"Feeling better?" he asks.

"Yeah. Yeah, I'm good."

His grimace says he doesn't believe me. The serious expression twists my heart. I've broken his happy-face. Everything around me is left in a wake of desolation. There's no way love can thrive with me. No matter that Daniel tried to convince me otherwise at the hospital, Riley's low spirits are just further proof that I need to do what's right. He deserves someone who can soar as high as he does. The weight of the black marks on my soul from Dallas will never let me be that man.

"I can make you some breakfast," he offers rubbing the place above my knee.

"I'm good. Thank you though."

Frowning, he draws his hand back like an animal that senses danger is near. I hate that I'm the danger.

"I...I think I found a place. They said I can move in Saturday if I want."

"Okay," he says slowly, setting aside the shirt he was folding. He's quiet for a moment, his nostrils flare. "So, you're still going?"

"Yeah. We really...rushed into this, and it's...it was wonderful, but... with all my crap with Dallas I've been just avoiding reality, I think. So...I think I should go. It's for the best."

"Best for who?"

I'm practiced at avoiding arguments. When someone asks a loaded question like that, I know it doesn't lead to resolution. It leads to them getting their way. Riley's way is tempting beyond reason, but it's not what I need to do, so I ignore the question.

"Um. The agency said they can send someone new over Monday."

"Larry and I will be fine," he says testily. "I'm done with caretakers."

Done with caretakers—me. I'm the caretaker. He's done with me and my stupid drama, just as I figured. It still stings.

"Right. Well, still. I...I can stop by once a week to go through your mail if you like."

"Why are you doing this?"

Does he seriously think I want to abandon him? That just because I'm starting another job, I won't worry about him after everything we've shared? Or does he think I'm babying him?

"Because I care," I assure him. "I know you can manage most everything by yourself, but I just...I want you to know I'm still around if you need me."

"I don't need you, Harper."

And there it is. The cold hard truth. My lip trembles, my emotions welling near the surface. "I know."

"I don't *need* you. Not in the ways you think." Turning his body toward me, he grips my hand. "I need you to be happy. I need you to laugh at me and with me. I need to know when you're sad so I can hold you and cheer you up. And I need you to stop finishing the job that asshole started. You said the other day that you've got nothing to offer anyone. That's *him* talking. That's not what I think and not how you should think about yourself. Nobody should beat you up anymore, including yourself."

His selfless sentiments warm my heart but break it a little at the same time. People lament that they met someone too late. I think it's just the opposite in our case. I met Riley too soon. I got so swept up in his affections and mine for him that I never truly worked on healing. Dallas' beating the other day only reinforced how careless it was of me to let myself believe that Riley was the answer to all my prayers.

Wiping my eyes, I nod. "Yeah. You're right, but those are things *I* need. You really don't need me, Riley. You're just...a good guy."

His eyes telescope my face rapidly. Reaching forward, he cups my cheeks. "That's not true," he whispers in front of my mouth before kissing me. "I need a lot of things."

"You drove a motorcycle, survived a bar fight, learned Braille, and can use a stovetop without burning yourself. You don't need me."

"I need you to help me get undressed," he whispers pressing a kiss to my tear-stained cheek.

Sputtering, a sharp pain slices through my chest, knowing how much I'm going to miss his zany flirt game. "You can do that too."

"But it feels better when you do it."

Rubbing his stubble with my thumb, I shake my head in frustration, trying to find the right words to convince him that as good as it feels, we're all wrong for each other. "Riley, you aren't...weren't gay."

"I'm not straight apparently either."

Scoffing, I can't help but laugh at that remark. "How do you know you're even attracted to me? You don't even know what I look like."

"Looks aren't important."

"I know, but they always went along with attraction for you before. I mean, you'd never been with a man until me. I might be physically repulsive to you if you could see me. I think you just...needed company."

"Really?" he says, rearing back, looking affronted, and rightly so.

I've known plenty of low vision and interabled couples who were happily married, regardless of knowing the other's physical looks by sight. But I'm not them. I'm *me*, and Riley is...*Riley*, a word that's become equivalent to perfection in my vocabulary.

"I'm not saying this to hurt you. I swear. I'm trying to be honest to both of us and call it what it is. We were both...lost."

Pursing his lips, he stares at me, his chest rising and falling. "You've told me what this is for *me*. What was it for *you?*"

"Riley..." I trail off, the determination in his stance making me feel cornered into losing the battle I promised myself to win for the both of us.

"What was this for *you?* What am *I* to *you*, Harper?"

If my heart wasn't bleeding already, it is now. I love him. I love him with every sad, miserable, aching fiber of my heart, but that's the problem. If I tell him, he'll want me to stay when I'm the last thing he needs. If I don't tell him, I'm hurting his misguided belief in what he feels right now.

"I can't do this," I rush, standing up, my adrenaline kicking into overdrive from all the times I left the apartment to avoid a fight with Dallas.

He's not Dallas. I know that, but I'm not good at winning arguments, so I head toward the door to grab my jacket.

"I…I've got to meet Daniel," I tell him to ease the blow, so it doesn't look like I'm just leaving to avoid him even though I know that's exactly what I'm doing. Coward. I'm still and always will be a coward.

"There's a mole on your left hip the size of a pencil eraser!" he calls out, making my arm freeze halfway through donning my jacket. "You've got a scar at the edge of your right eyebrow."

Sighing, I pinch my eyes shut to fight back more tears. His recounting of sweet memories when he touched my face and body are not the image I need to be reminded of right now.

"Riley," I warn, pleading for him to not make me be cruel by reminding him that he still can't truly know what I look like.

"Your hair is a shade darker than Larry's fur," he continues adamantly. "There's a constellation of beauty marks above your right collarbone, and one lone one on your buttcheek."

Larry's fur? How could he know what color Larry's fur is? And my mole is raised, but not my beauty marks. He wouldn't have felt those…

"I…I don't have a freckle on my butt," I blurt, gaping at him.

"You do," he says, his voice dropping. "It's down low, on your right cheek."

"How? How…"

"But my favorite one is the one on your cock, right about…here," he adds, tapping his finger to a spot on the fly of his jeans, to a spot where I do have a freckle on my cock.

My heart wallops a resounding thump as he stares right at me.

"Did…can…can you see me?" I sputter, half-weirded out, half-hopeful.

He shakes his head, his shoulders sagging ever so slightly. "Only once. It had come and gone periodically, but…I got to see you in bed one morning."

He saw me? He saw me, and I missed it. All I can do is sniffle, watching the corner of his mouth tick up.

"You're hot, by the way," he adds.

I know he said it already, but the signal from my brain to my mouth finally connects. "You saw me?"

197

He answers with a single nod.

"Why didn't you tell me?"

Stuffing his hands in his pockets, he shrugs. "I didn't want to get your hopes up that I'd get my vision back."

"But you could. Did you tell the doctor? You could still—"

He cuts my words off by raising his hand and shaking his head. "He knew, Harper. He said it was just a matter of time."

"But…you never know," I rationalize, knowing vision problems aren't a cut and dry issue, especially when the result of an infection and subsequent trauma. "Can you see anything now?"

"No. It's all blurry light and night blindness again."

I can't give up on the possibilities for what this means for him, even if they're fleeting. Desperately, I explain, "You can tell me when you can see, and I'll take you anywhere you want to go."

"Then you should stay or take me with you because that's where I want to be."

I walked right into that, didn't I? Pinching my eyes closed, I'm back to square-one, but now it's even more painful.

"I can't, Riley. That's the nicest thing anyone's ever said to me, but I can't. I need to stand on my own two feet—"

"With someone who can see?"

"No. With no one. And you need to live your life, one that doesn't revolve around cheering me up. You're amazing. You'll meet someone with your energy, someone who's not afraid of everything—"

"You've thought this all through. Huh?" he says gravely. "No changing your mind?"

It would be easier to say *no. Forgive me. Forget every stupid thing I've just said,* but that won't do either of us any favors. That won't make me not afraid of the dark, afraid of every noise around the corner. It won't make me a capable man that can be an equal to a partner instead of a sad, jittery, liability.

"I'm sorry. It's what I have to do."

Chapter 39

HARPER

"Madison and I split my former caseload that she'd been trying to handle since…since I left," I explain to Daniel as we unpack the dishes that I bought at a resale shop. "And Mr. Boswell retired, so basically, I'm back to the same pay at my old job, while only having to do half the work, and without a jerk for a boss. It's…good."

I've been back at the senior center for a week and in my tiny new one-bedroom apartment a day longer. Everything *is* good.

It is. It will be.

Now that I finally got around to getting some dishes, I won't have to live off take out. I had a mattress delivered a few days ago, so I also don't have to sleep on the floor with my duffel bag as a pillow any longer. I'm doing things…on my own. Living, on my own.

It's slightly terrifying. Okay, it's incredibly terrifying, but each day I hear a voice in my head, one that sounds like a stronger version of my own, saying, you did it. You're doing it. You *can* do this.

A part of me, the part that's curled up in a ball and living in the giant hole in my heart, tells me there's a voice across town that was willing to tell me those motivational sentiments too. It's a battle every minute of the day to ignore that voice.

I miss him. I worry about him. In spite of the latent soreness of my most recent presents from Dallas, the most painful wound is wondering if I broke Riley's heart along with what remained of my own.

No, Harper. No.

He was straight. He was lonely. He was lost. We bonded. You're like a boring old man, and he's rambunctious—he even said that.

And to complete the mantra, I seal it with the final reminder I've told myself each hour since I stumbled back to his apartment a bloody, swollen mess. You can't take care of him because you can't even take care of yourself. Look what Dallas did to you. Could you stop him or anyone from doing that to Riley?

I'm aware the words wax negative, the kind of thoughts Rosalyn told me to identify and remove from my mind and vocabulary, but I have to allow them. I have to allow these few to keep me from being weak and running back to a beautiful man that I'll surely, eventually disappoint in every possible way. Riley doesn't deserve any more disappointment.

"So...things are...good," I advise Daniel, realizing I trailed off. "They're...good."

Sighing, he straightens up from a box on the floor, hands on hips, arching a brow. "You said that already. You don't need to convince me."

Jerk. Can he ever use kid gloves with me?

Lifting my chin, I muster the tone of confidence I want. "Well, they are. I'm...I mean, it's nice to finally have my own place, one where I don't feel like I have to follow a schedule or worry that if something's out of place, I'll have to pay for it later."

Trembling at my own words, the odd sensation of sticking up for myself, I watch Daniel's stubborn expression morph into concern. Moving to the counter, he sets a stack of bone-colored plates down. I can't help but notice how little they contrast against my white countertop and chide myself for not picking a darker color in case...in case Riley ever comes over. Right. Not going to happen.

"Did you hear anything from the police?" Daniel ventures more delicately.

Swallowing against the constriction in my throat, I nod. "When they called the other day, I asked...when he'd get out. They said they charged him with aggravated assault on the account of my injuries."

"Did they give you an order of protection?"

"No. I declined it."

"Why the hell would you do that?"

"Because then he'd have my address. They have to list the addresses the person is supposed to stay away from like my residence and place of work. I don't...trust him not to have one of his friends pay me a visit, if he found out where I live, or him even."

Daniel nods, popping a sheet of bubble wrap. "Good call."

"So...they said he'll have an arraignment in a few weeks, and they'll determine bond or stipulations of his release."

"They're fucking releasing him?"

Scoffing, I grab the plates and stack them in one of my few kitchen cupboards. "It's the new laws, Daniel. The system is full. As long as someone isn't a flight risk, they want them out of the jail to free up room. I'm just lucky they're so backed up that he can't get an arraignment for a few weeks."

"Fucking Illinois," he grumbles. "Are you…mad that Riley called the cops?"

Face heating, I'm ashamed to admit that I was at first. I know he did it with good intentions. I know people have faith in the legal system to do the right thing. I know he has no idea that reporting the incident has probably only pissed Dallas off more, but I also know Riley, like Daniel, is braver than me. It's why I left. I need to learn to be like that.

"No. I know it was the right thing to do."

"Good. Good, I'm so glad to hear you say that."

The praise only reminds me of how frustrated and ashamed of me Daniel probably was the last time I had trouble. One day, I won't bring the few people in my life anymore problems.

"Be careful, please," I caution him. When his brows pinch together and he sucks in a breath to argue, I hold up a hand. "And save the whole I'm-not-scared-of-him and he-can-fuck-off comments. You're my best friend. If anything ever happened to you because of me, I'd never forgive myself."

Lips pressing into a thin line, his nostrils flare. "I appreciate the sentiment, and you know I feel the same way about you, but I just want to make it clear that if he ever tried anything…it wouldn't be because of you."

I open my mouth to refute that claim, but this time he cuts me off.

"No. If I don't get to cuss him out, you don't get to do that." He points at me. "You don't get to blame yourself for someone else's actions. You don't make him do the fucked-up shit that he does. That's all on him."

Sighing in defeat, I nod for the sake of ending the discussion. Somewhere in the back of my mind, I know he's right, but feeling that way, freeing myself from responsibility of Dallas' carnage isn't that easy.

My phone pings on the opposite end of the counter, filling me with relief for the distraction. I can't imagine who it would be, which is a sad reminder of how isolated I let myself become living with Dallas. I had co-workers, acquaintances I met at Daniel's bar and the community center that asked to hang out, and I always declined. The fear of Dallas' jealousy was too great to risk making new friends.

My breath catches, reading my screen.

RILEY: I have an appointment next Thursday at nine a.m. I know you'll probably be working, but do you think you could take off to come with me?

"What is it?" Daniel asks, making me realize I'm standing here frozen, gaping at my phone.

"It's…from Riley. He wants to know if I can take him to an appointment next week."

"Are you going to?"

"I…he could have his mom go with him," I suggest, cringing at the thought of not seeing him. I want to see him. I want to do anything he needs me to do, but I remember the way he avoided me the last few days I was at his apartment after our talk. He left several times for hours with Larry all by himself. Once, he came back with a fresh haircut. Another time, he left in a dress shirt and slacks. I have no idea what he was doing, but I know the point of the lesson was to reinforce that he doesn't need me, that he can do anything he wants without me. So, why is he asking me to accompany him now? Maybe it's an olive branch, one I can use as a way to ease the blow of me leaving.

"No grown man wants to take their mommy with them to a doctor's appointment," Daniel grouses, shoving some mismatched coffee cups onto one of my shelves.

Rolling my eyes, I tell myself I really need to find time to have a serious conversation about his issues with his parents. It was a delicate subject we discussed only a few times in college and have hardly ever broached since then. I'd take him to see Rosalyn with me, if I knew he wouldn't go kicking and screaming. That's on my list of things to do in my new life, be a better friend. To give more than I take.

"Yeah, well, not everybody doesn't get along with their parents," I manage, feeling brave.

He answers with a scoff. "Lucky everybody else."

"So, you think I should go?"

When he doesn't answer, I turn around. Standing with his arms crossed, leaning against my tiny kitchen counter, his perturbed gaze is leveled at me.

"What? What's that look for?"

"Harper…are you happy here? Like really happy?"

What the hell is this about?

"I just moved in. How am I supposed to know if I'm happy or not yet? I don't even have my dishes in the cabinets yet."

Rolling his eyes, he groans in frustration. "Dude, my place sucks. We know that, but I'm happy there. Okay. This place…it sucks even worse. It's not you. It's like a lonely little isolation box for you to hide from your feelings."

"What? What are you talking about?" And why is he trying to destroy the first sense of responsibility I've managed to accomplish?

"You can't even turn around in the bathroom without bashing your elbow on something."

"Neither can you at yours!" I counter, starting to get mad.

"I found a cockroach under your bathroom sink."

Pursing my lips, I can feel anger rising in me. I've been too afraid to be angry, but ever since Dallas found me in the parking lot, it's been creeping up on me, surprising me. "Everyone has cockroaches at some point."

"Forget I said anything. It's not even about what the apartment looks like. I'm happy for you. You did it. All by yourself. That's what you wanted, but now what?"

"Now what...what?"

"Great. You're here. You're on your own. What do you see your life being like now?"

This is starting to border on cruel. Why is he doing this?

"I'm going to live my life," I stammer. "I'm going to...to do things better."

"Alone?"

"For now," I defend, befuddled by his attack.

"For now, or forever? Because I'm scared that you're just going to hole up in here like a hermit after work every day or use that community center you go to as an excuse for a personal life."

"What...what are you talking about? You've always said I date assholes. That guy in college that cheated on me, Dallas... And you hate straight guys. Riley was straight. Why are you flipping it all around all of a sudden?"

"Was he straight when he repeatedly wanted to *keep* sticking his dick in you and putting that smile on your face you had?"

Flushing, I have to look away. I did smile with Riley, all the time. Of course, Daniel would assume we'd had sex after seeing us getting cuddly at the café that morning weeks ago. It's just one more thing I fall short on. I can never be a lover to him. The thought of being intimate in that way again, terrifies me. I have no doubt it was headed in that direction. Part of me was even looking forward to it. The rest of me though...the part that remembers how much it hurt, how things took forever to work right again after Dallas violated me, that part gets nauseous over the idea. Riley's straight. I'm gay. Of course, he'd assume I would be able to do that with him at some point.

"What's your point?" I huff, trying to control my voice.

"My point is, you're an idiot."

Is he serious? I know I'm an idiot, but considering what I'm going through, what I've been through, I think I'm allowed to be a little bit of one, but I didn't expect my friend to label me as one so easily.

Absorbing my anger and shock, his frustrated expression twists. "And...I'm an idiot too...*sometimes*," he concedes, only baffling me further. "Yeah, straight guys aren't my favorite, but…Riley was different. I could tell. I mean, it's *you*. What guy wouldn't be into you?"

All my anger falls away. Daniel gets zero points for being eloquent, but I'll award him a bonus for that compliment.

Sighing, he leans on the counter and gestures with his hand. "All I'm saying is you were happy, like stupid happy. I see it all the time at the bar. Most of the time, I see people looking just for a quick fuck, but sometimes I also see those couples that look at each other like…like the world only exists for them. Like they're the only two people in the room. You guys looked like that, and for the first time in a long time…I wasn't worried about you."

Watching him run his hand agitatedly through his hair, my sinuses feel like they're filling up. There's not enough air to breathe.

"You can stay here alone and work on your fifty-seven-step program or whatever it is you think you have to do to flush Dallas out of your system, but then what? What happens when you finish all those steps? What if Riley's gone? What if you don't meet another Riley? Will you regret it? Will…fucking Cockroach City have been worth it?" He finishes, waving his hand at my humble abode.

A tired gust of air leaves my lips. I'd laugh at his metaphors if I had the energy because I can't disagree. "I'll…I'll go," I tell him, shrugging my shoulders.

Staring at me remorsefully, he sighs. "Good."

When he leaves, I work up the courage to reply to Riley.

ME: Absolutely. I'll be there. Just let me know what time.

RILEY: 8 a.m. My apartment. Thank you.

My heart skips at his quick response, at the thought of him eagerly awaiting my answer. Will it be awkward? Of course, it will. I'm always awkward. Thinking back now, it makes sense why Dallas was drawn to me, singled me out. I was an easy target.

Negative thoughts, I remind myself, brushing the idea away. Moving to my bedroom, I pick up my duffel bag off the closet floor to stow it away but feel something weighing it down at the bottom. Reaching inside, I discover a stack of underwear I forgot to unpack.

Fishing them out, I head to the used dresser I bought and pull open the top drawer. Setting the stack on top of it to smooth out the fabric into a semblance of order, a flash of white catches my eye below the inside of the waistband. It's an older pair of my boxer briefs, worn and faded. The tag shouldn't be that pristine. There's a QR code on it. It's one of Riley's fabric tags.

When did he do this?

Pulling my phone out of my pocket, I bring up the prototype of his clothes-reader app that we installed on both of our phones. With bated breath, I hover my phone's camera over the tag, knowing it means I might get to hear his voice in a second as soon as the scan is complete.

"Harper's sexy ass boxer briefs," his mischievous voice comes over the speaker, making me laugh and my cheeks warm.

"They're not," I whisper. "They're absolutely not."

But…he probably knew that. That was the whole point. I believed terrible lies from Dallas, but I rejected the ones I thought were good lies from Riley.

Picking up the underwear, I'm treated to another tag on the pair below them. Instantly, a picture of him in the laundry room or sneaking into my room to do this forms in my head, making me smile.

"Another boring pair of underwear that Harper makes look sexy. Dear underwear, you're welcome."

And the next…

"Briefs. Color—a dark shade of Riley-wants-to-take-them-off-with-his-teeth."

When I come to the last pair, I'm reluctant to hit the scan button. I don't imagine I'll be hearing this playful timbre in his voice next Thursday. This will be the last I get of it. I appreciate what Daniel said, his encouragement. I understand the whole concept of Cognitive Behavioral Therapy that Rosalyn introduced me to, but there's a certain amount of realism no one can change. I can't be the lover or the man Riley deserves. No, I'll probably never meet another Riley. I don't want to. I only want one, but the one I want absolutely won't be there by the time I go through my "fifty-seven-step program", as Daniel put it. He's too fucking perfect for anyone to pass up. There's a comfort in knowing at least I picked a good one this time. Maybe I finally did something right. Maybe, if I'm lucky, he'll let me be his friend.

Hitting the scan button, I hold my breath.

"Mr. Reid…why do these smell like sugar cookies?" the app broadcasts his voice over my phone's speaker.

Healing, Rosalyn said. Part of recovering from abuse is healing and allowing yourself to grieve. So, I bury my face in my hand and weep over the self-inflicted abuse I gave my heart. This time, it's okay to cry.

Chapter 40

HARPER

Remembering the casual way Riley always made me feel, I dressed in a comfortable sweatshirt and jeans, thinking it would help me relax for this reunion. He's wearing gray dress slacks, a crisp white dress shirt, silver tie, and gray suit jacket. If I thought he looked good in casual, cleaned-up Riley knocks that out of the park.

"Thanks for coming," he says, letting me in. "Let me just get Larry's harness on, and I'll be ready."

Larry? He calls him Larry now? Did I break his funny bone so badly that he has no interest in his ridiculous dog-naming game anymore?

When we make it down to the garage and in his car, we get Larry settled in the backseat. The way he's whimpering and trying to stick his nose over the driver's seat to lick my ear is already breaking my heart. I didn't know Larry was sentimental. Maybe that was why having a relationship with Riley never stood a chance. I always saw myself as temporary because that's what I was, a temporary employee.

"This should only take about an hour or two," Riley explains, holding a leather briefcase in his lap.

"Where are we going?"

He gives me the address, but doesn't elaborate. I don't feel like I have the right to ask him anything, so I just drive, trying not to lose my head over the scent and heat of him so close to me again.

"You look...good, by the way," I tell him, desperate for any conversation, any kind sentiment I can leave him with if this turns out to be the last time I see him.

"Thanks," he says with a chuckle, fidgeting with his tie. "So do you."

My cheeks warm at the playful compliment. It's typical Riley, insinuating that I'd look good no matter what and no matter that he can't see me. It's awful being reminded of what you threw away, of what you can't have. I want to grab ahold of Daniel's words, want to beg him for another chance, but the past week has still left me drawn up short on confidence. What can I possibly give this wonderful man who lights up any room he walks into?

When I make it to the address Riley gave me, I pull into the parking garage and help him and Larry out of the vehicle. Riley seems to know where he's going, selecting the seventh floor elevator button on his own, making me wonder why I'm even along for the ride.

"Doctor appointment?" I venture, doubting the guess since so far the listings look like we're in a business complex.

"No. Just a meeting with some old colleagues."

"Oh." I'm just as lost as I was when I arrived at his apartment.

When the elevator doors open to a lobby with a silver reception desk, the words Mol Tech on the wall behind it give me pause. Riley told me that was the name of the company that he and Rob worked for. My nerves hit me in full force. If he's bringing his app idea in the hopes of getting his old job back, and I'm along to watch Larry while he's in a meeting or interview, I don't know if I can deal with his disappointment if they turn him down. I didn't imagine that today would be an incredibly happy affair, but I sure as hell don't want to see him hurt any more than what I've recently caused.

"Riley! How are you?" the woman behind the desk greets enthusiastically.

Grinning, he returns her sentiments and introduces her to Larry with the familiar gusto I've missed. It's a brief display of the man who stole my heart and makes me smile. Of course, anyone who worked with him here probably adored him. How could they not?

"Hey, Harper," a voice calls to my left. "How've you been?"

I'm surprised to see Rob walking down the hallway that leads to offices and conference rooms. He's wearing a dress shirt and tie, making my sweatshirt and jeans start to look shabby. I've never seen him spiffed up before either and suddenly wish I'd asked Riley dress code instructions.

"Good. I'm good. It's nice to see you," I reply.

"Are they ready?" Riley asks him.

"Yeah. Yeah, everybody's in there. You guys ready?"

Riley concurs. I'm left gaping, however, wanting to know what it is I'm supposed to be ready for, but they start walking down the hall. As we approach the glass wall of a conference room, I can see one of those long polished oval tables that seats like twenty people. There's six people seated at it, four men and two women.

My steps slow as we near the door. Glancing down at the stupid Home Reach logo on my faded green sweatshirt, I want to run and hide.

"Is there a break room or something I should wait in?" I ask to either of their backs as they start through the entrance of the conference room with Larry.

"What?" Rob asks, looking confused.

Riley turns around and grips my shoulder. "No. Come on. I need you in here with me."

"Oh, um. Do...do you want me to go sit in a corner and watch Larry or something?" I ask quietly so as not to embarrass him in front of what I assume are former co-workers and supervisors in their fancy dress apparel.

"No, Larry'll probably want to sit up front with us," he says with a small smile.

I assume that was one of his little playful comments, but I notice now that he looks nervous. I assumed his subdued behavior since we left his apartment was because of his discomfort with being around me, but now that I can see he's apprehensive about whatever's going to happen in this room, I'm nervous for him. I should have gotten over my guilt and awkwardness and asked more questions. I don't want to embarrass him more than I probably already have in ratty sneakers and a tacky sweatshirt.

Flashing a nervous smile and a small wave to the strangers who eye me curiously, I follow Riley and Rob to the front of the conference room. There's a cart on wheels to the side of a projector screen up front. A young woman comes in and stands to the side of it, giving Rob a nod. There's what look a lot like the clothing label printers I ordered for Riley on the cart, and I notice the second shelf has various shirts folded up on it.

Oh, God. He's pitching his app idea.

Fuck. Why didn't he tell me?

Scanning the room, my first instinct tells me to find a trash can in case I need to throw up. He was so excited about this. I assumed he was just going to use it for himself at home. I know he mentioned telling Rob, but I have no idea how pitching technology works. I figured after Rob came over and checked it out, he'd take it from there, refining it in a proper...office or tech place. Wherever they normally program and test apps. Fuck. I have no clue.

As the young woman rolls the cart behind the chairs down the table, she stops to shut the conference room door. The resounding *click* sends another wave of panic through me. I'm trapped. This is happening. Oh, please, let this go well for him.

It was one thing to think he might be trying to get his old job back and anticipate his misery if he was turned down. It's entirely another to know he's pitching the app that I single-handedly entered the code for, me, Harper Reid, who has never programmed anything other than my cable box in my life. What if I screwed something up that we missed?

Rob offers for me to take one of the two chairs at the head of the conference table. Gratefully, I sit down, my knees quaking. Larry ambles over and rests his chin on my leg likely sensing my distress. Petting his soft wavy fur helps calm some of the butterflies.

"Good morning everyone," Riley calls out, one hand tucked in his pants pocket looking casual, confident, and refined all at once as he stands off to the side of the projector screen. Rob is sitting in the corner in front of a laptop with a smile on his face. Apparently, he'll be running a slide show. Glancing at the words on the screen behind Riley, my heart lodges in my throat.

There's a picture of our app on a phone and a clothing label maker next to it. Above the images is a logo for the app and the hardware. *Olivia—vision reader app.*

My mother. He named it after my mother. I'm going to have to add crying to the list of ways I'll probably embarrass him today.

"I know there's some old faces here—Jeff, Tara. Thanks for setting up this meeting. I know I've been gone a while, and I'm told there's some new faces here too who didn't have the incredible pleasure of working with me," Riley continues eliciting a round of laughter from the room. "So, I'll introduce myself. I'm Riley Davenport, former assistant head of app design at Mol Tech. I'm blind. I like short walks on my rooftop. My favorite food group is pizza, and I have an ugly dog named Larry."

Another round of laughter, this time including mine, chips away at what I only likely imagined was a sense of stuffiness in the room. He's in his element, a small smile on his face, his movements so fluid as he casually gestures with his free hand.

"This is Harper Reid," he continues, motioning to me. "He's a vision rehabilitation therapist, which basically means he teaches people with low vision how to see without their vision. There's more ways than you might realize, and I was lucky enough that he was the VRT that had the misfortune of being assigned to me."

Misfortune? Nothing about my time with him was a misfortune. I know he's teasing, but my emotions are running high, hearing what I imagined he practiced at home on his own. His secret trips out of the apartment, the day he left in a dress shirt—it all makes sense now. He was preparing for this, setting it up all by himself to prove he doesn't need anyone's help.

"Harper came up with the idea for what I named the *Olivia* reader after his mother who was legally blind. He's just finding out that I named it that, so if he looks emotional, leave him be or Larry will have words with you later."

His colleagues chuckle, and I'm met with more than one emotional smile from them. My face burns, being the center of attention. Imagining what my mother would think of this makes my eyes water. I have to bite the inside of my lip to keep it together.

With a nod from Rob, the assistant starts to pass out the phones, label makers, and shirts to each attendee in the conference room. I give a start when a hand settles on my shoulder.

"You doing okay?" Riley asks, leaning down.

"Yeah," I whisper back.

Squeezing my shoulder, he returns to his place in front of the room before I can add any of the sentiments that are running through my mind like *thank you, you're amazing, I miss you, I'm sorry, and I love you more than anyone else can ever possibly love you.*

Because I do. I finally got to see what real love between a couple feels like, is supposed to look like, and I'm so lucky that I got to learn that lesson from him out of all the people in the world.

Riley continues his presentation with the ease of a practiced show-man. Relating some amusing tales that involved the two of us makes my insides glow reminding me that I got to be a miniscule part of something special, something special that involved a special man. Watching the re-action on his face as he listens to the sounds of his colleagues operating the beta equipment fills me with relief for him. Their cooing and excite-ment bring that pleased little smirk to his lips. He should be proud.

When he's finished, everyone claps, and I'm left unsure of what to do or where to go next. I've nervous-petted Larry for so long, he's proba-bly going to have a bald spot on the back of his neck. As Riley speaks animatedly to Jeff and Tara, whom I've discerned are the heads of the company, two other attendees approach me and start asking questions about VRT, my mother, my time with Riley, and even Larry.

When the hubbub is over, Riley lets me know it's time to leave. On the elevator ride down to the parking garage, I study the anxious way he's chewing his lip, leaving me afraid to ask about the feedback he got from his bosses.

"That was amazing, Riley. You were amazing," I finally tell him.

"Yeah?" he asks, glancing at me with one brow arched.
"You liked it?"

"It was incredible. How you put all that together, the way you delivered everything, you...you're impressive. You should be proud of yourself."

"Proud of *us*," he corrects with a constrained smile, looking back to the number panel of the elevator. "I'm sorry if it caught you off guard. I wasn't sure that you'd show up if I told you what the meeting was about, and I really wanted you to be here to see it."

Swallowing against the lump of guilt in my throat, I kick my toe at the carpeted floor. "I'd have probably chickened out, so I'm glad you didn't tell me, but I'm really happy you invited me. Thank you, and…it was really sweet that you named it after my mother."

Flashing me a quick smile, he fidgets with his tie. "So, how's the new apartment? Did you get all settled in?"

The small talk continues intermittently on the ride back to his building. I get us parked and don't even ask if he wants company on the ride up to his apartment. I don't want our time together to end, while at the same time I know I should count my blessings and leave. It's been both the most perfect day and saddest day of my life. Just when I think I can't possibly care more about him, he does something like this, and I'm still me who has to do the right thing—give up a gift that I can never be worthy of.

"Do you want to come in?" he asks when we get to his door.

I shouldn't. I don't want to lead him on. I had hoped to at least get the privilege of being his friend, but I know if I walk in that apartment there's the wonderful chance that he might ask me for more again. There's also the very real chance he's accepted what we discussed and agrees that us not being together is for the best. I really don't want to find out either way. I want to stay safe in the limbo of this happy day.

"Um, for a bit. If you want me to."

Nodding, he finagles his keys and lets us in, releasing Larry. I feel like an unwanted guest in a place I had started to think of as home. It's clean, everything still as in place as when I left it, signifying how little my assistance was needed. He's the most capable man I've ever met, sighted or not sighted.

He offers me a drink, but I decline, then immediately regret it, realizing it would buy me a few more moments in his presence. Licking his lips, he sets his soda down on the island counter, leaning back against it.

"You didn't ask me what they thought of our design," he says.

"Oh, I didn't know how that worked, if they'd give you feedback right away or review something privately before they made a decision."

"They loved it, Harper. Jeff and Tara are going to put it into production immediately."

A happy laugh escapes my lungs. "That's great. Congratulations."

"Same to you."

Scoffing, I pick at the back of the couch where the kitchen meets the open floorplan of the living room. "I didn't do anything. What do I need congratulations for?"

Frowning, he unfolds his arms and shoves them in his pockets. "You helped me come up with the idea. You helped design it and test it. I wouldn't call that nothing."

"Yeah, well, I was happy to help. It was a fun learning experience, and now if I ever see a client using the Olivia app, I can smile to myself, knowing it's named after my mom."

He studies me for a moment, making me want to squirm. Did I offend him? What should I say? Should I cut my losses and leave?

"What are you going to do with your half of the proceeds?" he asks.

"Proceeds?"

"Yeah." He shrugs, taking a sip of his soda. "You were the co-designer. You get half of the proceeds."

"Riley," I choke out. "No. I don't need anything for that. You were paying me to work here for you. It was my job to help with whatever you needed. I can't profit from this."

And just like that we're right back where we left off with the dreaded words help and need as he frowns at me. Why is it when the last thing you want to do is hurt someone, you hurt them at every turn?

"Well, I can't take your half, knowing you came up with the idea and did most of the work, so that's a dilemma for you to work out on your own. Larry wants a few new chew toys, and I was thinking of getting a hang glider," he adds casually like he's inspecting his nails.

"Riley," I complain.

"Harper," he counters, leveling me with a patient look.

Sighing, I stare stupidly at the floor. I missed his stubbornness but right now it's not helping matters.

"If you're worried about what to spend it on, I've got a suggestion," he offers.

"Yeah, what's that," I say, trying to sound like I'm not enjoying humoring his benevolence.

"You could build a little audio narration studio for yourself so you can record all those romance novels you like so much."

"Yeah. Because I have as much experience narrating as I do with designing apps."

"No, actually, you have more. All those years you read to your mom. You're basically an expert."

"Riley, I…"

"It's just a thought," he cuts me off, shrugging. "Since it's something you love so much, and it makes you happy. I mean, who in their right mind wouldn't do something that they love and makes them happy? Plus, you have a great voice. It made me fall for you, and if you can make a straight guy fall for you, I think you'd be a hit as an audiobook narrator."

I don't know if it's a dig or a compliment. Riley's not one to dispense cruel veiled messages the way Dallas used to do, but it's difficult to believe he'd still want anything to do with me.

When I don't answer, he adds, "You could practice. Say…come over and read to me and Larry every day." When he shoves off the counter and steps toward me, the message is no longer unclear, and my heart unfolds. He still wants me.

"I could…order something other than pizza when you visit," he murmurs, taking another step. "And nobody uses that spare room, so we could set up audio recording equipment in there to test out and see if you like it. Plus, I…still owe you some motorcycle lessons."

"Riley," I choke out as he reaches to cup my jaw.

"I miss you," he whispers.

"I miss you too," I confess.

"Then…can we try again?"

Fuck. Fuck. Fuck.

Chapter 41

RILEY

I don't know what else to do. If this doesn't work, the only other thing I can think of is camping out with Larry outside his apartment door, but then I'll look like a stalker and more terror is the last thing he needs. He's so quiet. What's going on in that silly head of his?

"Riley, I want to but, I can't. I can't take care of you. I can't even take care of myself."

When is he ever going to stop seeing me as a patient? What we had was more than Stockholm Syndrome. I know it in my bones.

"I don't need you to take care of me. I just need you to be happy."

"I know you don't, but a partner is supposed to be able to take care of their significan other. And being happy isn't that simple."

"Being happy is the simplest thing there is. You just have to let yourself. You just have to tell yourself you deserve to be," I emphasize, cupping my other hand to the side of his face, hoping it helps the words sink in.

"I can't," his voice cracks. "Riley, I'm...I'm not enough. I can't give you enough."

"I don't want anything."

"I mean *I can't*... I can't even let you fuck me," he warbles and a hot tear hits my thumb. "I...he hurt me. Okay? He hurt me *there* and...and I'm scared. I'm not scared of you, but the thought of it now just... You deserve to be with someone you can experience everything with."

My teeth are in danger of cracking over that asshole who manhandled him, but I've got to stay calm. I knew he was struggling with things, knew it even though he did everything he could to hide it, but how can he think that physical intimacy is a deal breaker for me?

"I don't want to fuck you," I inform him.

"Do you...still want to be with women?"

That brain of his. My God, it's like talking to Larry sometimes. Where does he get these ideas?

Finishing what I started before he cut me off, I soothe, "I don't want to fuck you because what we do together isn't fucking. I want to make love with you, and I don't care how we do it or when we do it or if we ever don't."

Taking his hand, I place it over my chest and hold it there. "This thing inside my chest? Do you feel that? It bangs on my ribs like it's trying to break out of a cage whenever I'm with you or without you, whenever I think of you. Let me let it out, Harper," I plead. "Please? It's yours already anyway."

His broken weeping sounds crack my heart in half. His head lowers, so I do my best to wipe at the tears with my thumbs.

"You don't care?" he asks. "What he did to me? I mean, you don't care that this is what's left of me?"

"What's *left of you?* Baby, anyone can be a victim, but not everyone can be a survivor. You're a survivor," I insist, cupping his face again to look at me. "So, quit thinking that there's nothing left. There's more Harper here now than there probably ever was. Stronger, kinder, wiser, and even more compassionate if that's possible."

Sputtering, he sniffles, but at least it sounds like he's calming down. Maybe I've made a dent.

"I wish I could see myself the way that you do," he whispers.

Shaking my head, I'll never understand how someone so kind and wonderful can have such a low opinion of their worth. "You taught me how to see. I honestly don't know why God gave me eyes before you came along, because I didn't use them for a damn thing until I saw you."

He sucks in a shuddery breath. I'm holding mine as his hands settle on my shoulders. I can feel his heat in front of my face. His dampened lips press against mine in a chaste kiss that I hope to God isn't a goodbye.

"Riley?" He lets out with a defeated sound, resting his head on my shoulder. "I've got nothing to give you though."

"How can you say that?" I whisper, wrapping my arms around him, grateful to have him close again. "You have the only thing I want. *You.* Just you. Your kind heart, your jokes, your laughter, your smiles, your beautiful fucking intelligence. Your patience."

"Riley," he says again, drawing his head off my shoulder.

"Hm?"

He's staring at me, hovering just in front of my face. Sniffling, he whispers, "How are you real?"

I don't care if it takes as long as I live. I'm going to make sure he knows I ask myself that same question about him every day.

Cupping his face, I place a kiss under his tear-stained eye. *"We're* real." Another kiss. "We're real," I repeat, sealing the oath. *"Let us* be real."

His hands sift into my hair, pressing my mouth against his. He kisses me like I'm the air he needs to breathe.

Gasping, his words tumble out in a rush. "I love you. I love you so much it hurts. I thought I had to stop it before it hurt me even more, but it only made it hurt worse being without you." As his head drops to my chest and he clutches onto me, I close my eyes, absorbing the gift of his confession. "I'm sorry I hurt you," he whispers, pressing a kiss to my neck. "I'm so sorry."

Crushing him in my arms, I breathe a breath of relief when he clings to me just as tightly. "It's okay. Tell me when it hurts too much, and I'll make it better. Please just don't ever run away again."

"I won't," he assures me, peppering my face with kisses. "I won't."

We kiss and kiss, gentle hands gliding up and down, healing wounds, cementing promises. It's slow and affectionate, savored touches, holding. And then he takes my hand.

When he stops in my room at the side of my bed, I ask, "Do you have to go into work today?"

"No. I took the whole day off. Can I…just hold you for a while?"

"You can hold me forever," I tell him, kissing his nose. "Why don't we get some sleep?" I suggest even though I know the sun is shining through the windows.

He helps me with my tie and buttons, and then I help him. Equals. Lovers. No scorecard of who is more helpless than the other.

We crawl under the covers, and I almost want to laugh at the sound of our relieved sighs exhaled in unison. His smile presses to my chest like he's grateful the wait is over too, that we figured our shit out. Within minutes, he's asleep in my arms, his wrapped around me. It's dark, but I'm no longer in the dark. I have my light back, and he's going to be okay.

Chapter 42

RILEY

This novel is doing nothing for me but creating background noise. Harper insisted on going to his therapy session at the community center alone again just like the last few, so I needed a distraction. He's so fucking brave. How he thinks anything else of himself is beyond me. I'm the one lying here awake, afraid to fall asleep until I know he's home safe.

I'm aware it will take time for him to heal from both his physical and emotional trauma, but the transformation since he moved back in three weeks ago has been nothing short of mesmerizing. His confidence, his determination, the way he holds nothing back now, expressing his feelings to me like he's no longer afraid of repercussions for his opinions—it feels like he's actually living. He's the guy I fell in love with, but rejuvenated.

The morning after the app presentation when I told him those exact words for the first time, he asked, "How can you love me at my worst?"

I laugh now at my reply. "If this is you at your worst, I wouldn't stand a chance with you at your best."

And I don't. I learned the most glorious secret of the universe—what it's like to truly be in love. It's a fall that never ends. It's a plummet where everyone is blind.

The sound of the apartment door opening is an instant muscle relaxer. Thank fuck. He's home.

"See, Larry?" I scratch behind his ears. "Told you he'd be fine. Go get him. Go get Harper."

Scrambling off the bed, Larry lands on the floor with a graceless plop. I can hear his excitement by how many times his tail *thwaps* against the walls on his way into the kitchen. He never moves that fast for me. Larry knows the good ones, I guess.

"The money's in my back pocket," I call out. "If you can get it out, you can leave the pizza on the end of the bed."

217

A bubble of happy laughter floods through my bedroom doorway. "Hey, you're still up?"

"Larry wanted a bedtime story," I inform him, stopping the audio-book on my phone.

"Hm, I think Larry might have a bit of an obsession." His voice grows closer. "What are we going to do with that dog? He'll corrupt you."

Huh. That almost sounds like...flirting.

"Did you have a good session?" I venture.

"Yeah. Yeah, I did. They're all good one way or the other."

His knee slides onto the mattress next to my hip. I can smell the chaotic city on him, but the undertone is that pure sweet Harper scent. I miss it on my pillow at night, since we agreed on boundaries and to actually go on dates.

Our day outings before always felt like dates, but let's face it, we lived together, and then we were in a relationship. He needs proper woo-ing, and I've been game to give it to him. The other part of Harper sleeping in his old room since he's been back is so he can do things on his terms, knowing a hundred percent they're his choices with no pressure.

That's why it surprises me when he murmurs, "You want some company tonight?"

"Uh, are glitter pens an inappropriate writing utensil?"

Snickering, he rises from the bed, followed by the distinct sound of his belt buckle unfastening. "I'm glad we both agree on the answer to that one."

He seems so at ease tonight. I'm afraid to ruin it by asking what occurred to bring about this newest leap. Crawling out of bed to help him, I can't restrain my curiosity. Whatever happened, whatever breakthrough, I want to know so I can help him hold onto it.

Unbuttoning his shirt, I brush my lips against his neck. "That must have been some session. You seem..."

"Happy?"

"Yeah."

Kicking his pants off, he lets his arms hang at his sides so I can strip off his shirt. "I am," he confirms, running his palms up my chest. "I realized something."

"What's that?"

Rather than answering, he cups my face and steals my breath with a toe-curling kiss that doesn't end until his weight tumbles down on top of mine and my back hits the mattress.

Panting for air, I tease, "Okay, now I gotta know."

He goes quiet, gazing down at me, brushing my jaw with his thumb. Maybe my teasing was ill-timed. Did I hit a nerve?

His lips dust mine, feather light. "I realized...I love you more than I'm afraid of anything."

The brutal honesty squeezes my heart, but he doesn't stop there. "I realized I love you more than I'm ashamed of my past. I love you, Riley," he whispers, pressing his lips to my cheek.

For once, I don't have a flirty comeback. Tracing his face as a tear streams down mine, I can barely get out the words we've said before. "And I love *you*."

His thumb brushes my tear, and I imagine him smiling at me lovingly. When his arms snake around my back and he lowers his weight on top of me, I sigh at the sweet reunion of body to body. He's holding me so close.

It's strange, the difference in his love making, an incredible strange. I can tell now how cautious he was before, always holding back like he was taking something from me that he shouldn't or was as nervous as I was like any two new lovers. Right now, though, his foot trailing up and down the outside of my leg, his hips slowly moving like a steady wave of the ocean over mine, and his long languid kisses, it's a passion unleashed. It's a transferring of souls. He's open, completely open. He's letting me see all of Harper, the one he kept locked away inside, protected from all the world had thrown at him.

When his lips suck on my collarbone and his hand squeezes my cock, I gasp for control that I don't have anymore. We've regressed to kisses and cuddling since he's been back. I wanted to give him time to process what he needs to process, but I still want everything with him. I want him carved on my soul, but I don't want him doing things because he thinks they'll please me.

"We don't have to," I trail off. "If you need time, I've got all the time in the world."

"I want to," he rasps in my ear, tugging down his boxer briefs and then mine so we're skin to skin.

He's rock hard and leaking, gyrating his pelvis into mine, sucking on my earlobe, making my eyes cross. Reaching down between us, he cups and rolls my balls. Holy fuck.

Remembering the concerns he voiced that day of our app presentation, I'm hesitant to make the request, but if he doesn't stop touching me like that, I don't know what I'll do. "Harper, would you...want to make love to *me?*"

He draws back, looking at me. Damn it. I put him on the spot. Why did I say that? He had a perfect night, and I just dumped a huge decision on him.

"Riley, we don't have to do that just because I said—"

"That's not why I asked," I reassure him. "Not at all. I just…I want you…that way, but please believe me I don't need it. I don't need it at all." Rubbing his back, I want to swallow my tongue. "I'm sorry. I didn't mean to ruin the mood."

His lips brush against mine, and he whispers, "You didn't ruin anything. I just…didn't think that was something you'd want."

After I exhale in relief, I run my fingers through his hair. "Well, I liked your tongue that time in the shower."

"Um, I'm not trying to scare you, but my cock is a lot bigger than my tongue."

"Conceited much?"

Chuckling, he reaches for the lube in my nightstand, making my pulse zing. "I've only done it a few times a long time ago," he admits. "How about we try something else first and see how that goes?"

"Challenge accepted," I tell him, my heart skipping a beat in nervous anticipation.

Luckily, I've listened to enough romance books that I think I know what he's implying. The thought of even just his fingers inside me has my nuts drawing up tight.

Planting a hard kiss on his mouth, we separate to shuck our underwear from our legs. Standing in the darkness, I kick my boxers to the floor. He's swung his legs over the side of the bed to shed his own shorts. His bare knee is warm, brushing against my thigh.

I can't resist the slide of his smooth skin against mine, so I draw my knee up next to his hip, and then the other, straddling him.

Months ago, I'd have never thought of sitting on a man's lap, but the stories I've heard have left me dreaming about being on his. There's something about the thought of Harper being in charge that turns me on like never before.

"You're sure?" he whispers, sliding his hands over my hips.

"Yeah. I trust you."

Chapter 43

HARPER

I trust you.

Three little words. Three words I was never able to think about Dallas. Someone trusts me, and I trust him completely. I trust the person that matters the most to me in the entire world. And it's not a dream. I'm going to give him everything he wants, even if I still can't believe that what he wants is me.

"I'm not going to lie," I tell him, drinking in the sight of him in the moonlight. "You have the most beautiful body I've ever seen. It was difficult to not check you out."

Chuckling, he slides his arms around my neck and murmurs at my lips, "*Bad* caretaker."

The idea that he'd think the gift of entering his body would bother me is laughable. I never imagined it would be something a former straight guy wanted, but he always surprises me. My only trepidation is that my lack of experience topping will affect the amount of pleasure he receives. Just the thought of opening him up with my fingers makes me anxious for him, but he's right. We have all the time in the world. I believe that now.

Flicking open the bottle of lube, my breath catches as he settles the warm svelte skin of his ass onto the tops of my thighs. Slickening my fingers, the privilege it is to be the one who gets to share this with him resonates within me. The honor of that amount of trust overshadows any lack of confidence. I *will* make this good for him.

As I draw my fingers through his crease, his hitched breath ghosts my face. His eyes close, morphing his expression into complete concentration on my touch. That's Riley, always giving all of himself.

"What do I do?" he asks.

"Nothing," I whisper, planting kisses on his Adam's Apple as I trace the tight circumference of his ring.

"I don't want to do nothing. I want to do lots of things," he pants, kneading the muscles in my shoulders anxiously.

"You can do one thing."

"What?"

"Breathe out," I advise, pressing the tip of my finger to his circumference.

Except, he brings his fist to his mouth and coughs, so I wait. I want this to be sensual, memorable, romantic. Circling my finger around his ring, I press a kiss to his jaw and skirt back over his entrance. When I apply pressure, he turns his head and coughs into his fist again.

"You okay?"

"Yeah," he whispers, pecking my lips.

I hope he's not getting sick. The Chicago winds have grown more frigid, and he still spends a lot of time on his rooftop.

Attempting round three, I make for his mouth as I press the tip of my finger to his entrance. Just as my lips are about to connect with his, he turns his head and lets out one more forceful cough into his fist.

It's odd. It sounded…voluntary, no noises of chest congestion.

"Riley, are you…coughing on purpose?"

"Well, yeah," he agrees readily, weaving his other hand into my hair.

"Why?"

His lower lip presses into his top one. "Well, to relax the prostate," he says matter-of-factly.

"What?"

"You know like when you go and see the doctor or in the movies when veterans talk about military medical entrance exams, how you're supposed to turn your head and cough when the doctor does the finger in the butt thing for the prostate exam?"

Holy shit. Is he serious?

Pinching my eyes closed, I drop my forehead to his chest and grip his hips. It takes everything in me not to bust up laughing at his naïveté.

"What?" he asks. "You've never heard of that? When they check your prostate?"

My shoulders shake on a stifled laugh. "Riley, that's not to check the prostate. They do that to check for hernias."

Frowning, he blinks at me. "Seriously?"

"Yeah. You don't…need to do that. Just push against me when I push."

"Huh," he lets out, sounding baffled. "I figured they just didn't put it in your books because it'd kill the romance."

I can't hold back a chuckle any longer. "Well, you didn't kill anything."

"Smart ass." He smirks, holding my head for a long kiss. "Alright, check my hernia. I'm good to go."

"Your pillow talk is so sexy," I quip, tracing my way back to his seam.

Snickering, he rests his forehead against mine. A look of concentration clouds his features when my finger slips inside him. He sucks in a breath, making me go still, but then he releases it, relaxing around me. All the affection I feel for him unfolds around my heart, discovering this act he's never shared with another soul. Knowing that I'm the first man he's ever been with, the depth of his feelings for me hit home.

Gently, I press and feel inside his heat, hoping I find what I'm looking for. When the pad of my finger grazes over that spongy bundle of nerves, he lets out a low moan, his mouth hanging open.

"Ah, shit," he gasps.

"Okay?" I whisper, studying his face with bated breath.

"Uhn," he groans, undulating his hips and letting his head drop to my shoulder. "F-yeah."

Smiling into his hair, I shudder at the sound of his aroused slurring as he continues to move, seeking more. Working his P-spot, I can feel him relax into a puddle of bliss in my lap, on my hand. His breath catches when I edge a second finger to his entrance.

He rises up, looking at me. Cupping my face, his breath ghosts my lips, and I'm in awe, watching him ease down onto what I'm offering. I've never felt so wanted in all my life.

"Fuck, Harper."

Whimpering, we both get lost in a battle of trying to swallow the other's sounds. Mine say, you healed me. Thank you. I'm going to love you forever.

His body relaxes more and more, his undulations becoming needy and abandoned. Pride swells in my chest, knowing I'm bringing him this much pleasure.

Panting, his hand snakes between us. My cock, aching and leaking, gives a jolt when he palms it, brushing his thumb over the tip.

Drawing back, he gasps, "*This*," squeezing my cock, "need *this*. Please."

It surprises me how much I want to give it to him, having always preferred bottoming. Seeing him quaking though, hearing him unraveling, sends a powerful urge through me to claim him, to give him what he's asking for. I only hope he doesn't regret it once it's happened.

"Okay," I whisper, withdrawing from him and kneading his ass.

He twists like a rabid contortionist toward his nightstand, nearly toppling off my lap. Laughing at his aroused urgency, I brace his hips until he comes back with a small box of condoms that he tears open with his teeth like I'm going to disappear if he doesn't get them out immediately.

He's been so patient with me, so tender, never asking for anything. It makes this intimate request even more special.

Watching him open the condom and bring it to my cockhead, my pulse skips when he pauses, staring down at where he's bracing my sex with one hand. A puff of air leaves his lips.

"What?" I ask.

"Nothing. It's just funny."

"My cock?"

"No." He chuckles, sliding the latex down my shaft, making me suck in a breath. "Putting one on someone else," he elaborates and then kisses me. "I like getting you ready."

Smiling against his mouth, I grab the bottle of liquid and place it in his hand. With a pleased smirk, he lathers me up, tortuously like he's delighting in teasing me.

"Alright," I huff in amused frustration, stopping his wrist when he twists his grip around the head of my cock, making my balls want to explode. "I'm ready, if you are."

Cupping my face, he smiles at me with nothing but love. "I think I've been ready for you my whole life."

Riley. My Riley.

When he rises up, I neither keep him waiting nor rush. Drawing the head of my cock back and forth through his channel, his choppy breath mingles with mine in anticipation.

I don't know how he imagined doing this, but he seems content straddling me, and he can go at his own pace this way. Offering up my aching erection, I hold the tip to his entrance and watch each miniscule change in his expression.

Holding his breath, pushing, sinking, easing past my cockhead, blowing out a shuddery breath. A stifled groan. Baring his teeth. Closing his eyes and pressing his forehead to mine.

His hot insides scorch that little bit of me that's breached him. Clutching his hips, it's all I can do to hold back as he trembles, adjusting to my intrusion.

"Stop, if you want," I whisper.

His forehead rattles against mine, refusing like the daredevil he is. Reaching between us, I take his waning erection in my grasp, hating that I know it means he's not enjoying this like he was moments ago. Stroking him and swirling his fluids over his dome, I feel him exhale in relief, feel his tight heat loosen around me.

Pressing his face into the side of mine and clamping his arms around me tight, he moves his hips, slowly working me in, an agonizing welcome.

By the time he's fully seated, we're both panting, quivering. He lets out a feral groan, collapsing his head onto my shoulder, fisting my hair. All I can do is anxiously rub his sides and press little kisses to his shoulder, waiting for him while trying to will away my need from the pressure of him around me.

And then…he moves. It's just a brief undulation, him rising, drawing me nearly out of his channel, then hugging me back in deeper. My cock throbs, sending shards of tingling pressure to my balls.

The moan, the fucking moan he lets out from deep inside goes on and on as he moves again and again. I can't believe he's mine and that he's giving this to me.

Pausing, he moves his mouth to mine and whispers, "Harper."

"Yeah?"

"Harper. Harper," he chants between sloppy kisses.

"Baby, you okay?"

He huffs like I asked a ridiculous question. "Why did you wait so long to do this to me?"

I don't think I'll ever get tired of the way his words surprise me. Rotating my hips up into him for a tease, I grunt, "I didn't know you'd want it."

"Fuck. Your lap is my new favorite place."

Laughing—he'll always have me laughing at the most inopportune times. "Riley, you have no filter."

"Sorry," he pants.

"No," I reassure him with a kiss. "It's my favorite thing about you."

Grinning like he's proud of himself, he straightens up and puts more determination behind his thrusts, driving me mad. His cock bobs, slapping against my stomach. I want to stroke him, want to watch him go over now, but I don't want it to end.

Pausing, he seats himself and carves out my mouth with his tongue. There's so much pressure, deep inside him. I feel like we're one, this love, this big accepting, understanding love. Leaning back, he braces my shoulders, unfolding his legs.

What is he doing, and how is he that flexible? Baffled, I watch him wrap his legs around my waist, hugging me to him with his body.

"I didn't know you were part spider monkey," I joke.

"See? Told you I was highly trainable."

When I rock into him, he groans. His legs tighten around me. I need to move. It's too much, his channel clenching me for so long, but I don't want to criticize his technique, and I'm not strong enough with my sore shoulder to lift a grown man up and down on my lap. When his heels dig into my ass, I catch a look of concern on his face.

"Shit," he mutters. "That was stupid."

"What?"

"Now I can't move," he laughs nervously.

"Hold on to me."

Wrapping my arms around him, I push myself up with some effort. Turning us, I let his weight pull us down to the mattress until his back rests on the bed. Sighing in relief, I'm able to move again inside him as I settle my knees under his thighs.

"That felt hot," he rasps. "I bet it looked hot."

"So hot." I chuckle, flicking the tip of my tongue across his lower lip.

His smile slips away. He brushes my cheek with his thumb, gazing into my eyes. I know. I know exactly what he's feeling. I don't know why I ever doubted it. He says I taught him how to see again, but he did the same for me.

Moving slowly, I savor every breath, every sound, every brush of our lips. It's a lover's dance I've never known. All the hurt, the longing, the self-doubt is gone, replaced with a warmth in my chest, replaced by a future I have all my faith in.

"Babe, so full. Like you're everywhere," he pants against my lips. "Missed you. I fucking missed you."

A tear slips down my cheek, the kind I'll never mind shedding. "Missed you so much," I tell him.

And it's true. In the three weeks of healing, of finding myself, of becoming the man I want to be for him and myself, saying goodnight and sleeping down the hallway while longing for his arms was a battle. I wanted to return to him whole, even though I knew he would have taken me in pieces.

Head reared back, neck straining, his cry untethers the cord I can no longer hold back. We go over the edge together, his release painting our stomachs, a warm branding of our passion. Clenching around me, his body greets my own convulsions as my vision clouds while I pulse in relief inside him.

I don't know how long we lay there like that, coming back to Earth, little jolts of our bodies eliciting sated sounds. His hand is lazily combing through my hair. I've found that sleek patch of skin at his hip juncture my thumb can't seem to stop stroking. His heartbeat is steady beneath my ear on his chest.

I'm not sure why life hands us the turmoil that it does, if it's meant to challenge us for a reason, if it's supposed to mean something. Marcy told me once, after her husband passed away, that if you go looking for answers, you'll spend your life searching instead of living. I believe that now, although I still had to find some answers in myself.

I spent a lot of time thinking about what Riley said a few weeks ago and came to this conclusion: Dallas made me a victim, but *I* made me a survivor. The latter choice was all mine. I was lucky though. I didn't have to search for many answers. They found me when I knocked on a door six months ago with only a duffel bag and granola bar to my name. I just had to tell myself it was okay to believe them.

Pressing a kiss to Riley's lips, I withdraw from his heat, causing us to both exhale at the loss of the intimate bond.

"Let me go get rid of this. I'll be right back," I tell him, placing a kiss at his temple.

Eyes closed, lips parted, he lets out a drunken-sounding grunt that makes me smile. Sated looks good on him.

When I return from the bathroom and offer him a cloth, he cleans himself up lazily and then tosses it on the floor like it took what was left of his energy. It's surreal to see him so depleted.

Crawling in under the covers next to him, he rolls into me, draping his arm over my waist. "Are you staying?" he asks, sounding surprised.

"Yeah. That okay?"

Nuzzling into my neck, he sighs a happy sound. "Yeah. Larry's had his eye on your room anyway."

Wrapping my arms around him, I smile at the insinuation. "Did you give up on finding him a new name? You've called him nothing but Larry for weeks now."

He's quiet for a moment, and I wonder if he drifted off to sleep that quickly, but then he shrugs. "I don't want him to ever think I want him to be something he's not. He should know I love him just the way he is, and that it's okay to be *a Larry*."

My arms tighten around him instinctively, my heart skipping a beat. Pressing my lips into his soft, loved-up hair, I whisper, "He knows now. It's why he loves you so much."

Chapter 44

RILEY

The distinct sound of Harper's sleepy footsteps in the hallway, make my hand flinch just as I crack the next egg on the side of the frying pan. The yolk running down my fingers and the sizzle noises emitting from the stovetop tell me I missed my target.

"Damn it, Larry," I mutter to the audience at my feet. "You were supposed to be my look out. No bacon for you."

"What's going on in here? I thought I was dreaming I was at a diner."

"Go back to bed. It's not ready yet."

Of course, his footsteps don't retreat, but I smile when his arms wrap around me from behind. His chin rests on my shoulder, his stubble, tickling my cheek.

"Were you going to serve me breakfast in bed?"

"Nah, but I was going to give you a raspberry on your stomach to wake you up when it was time to eat."

"Mm, that's very thoughtful."

"That's my middle name."

"I thought your mom said it was *Eugene*."

"You're going to trust a woman who eats your cinnamon rolls?"

His laughter tickles my ear. "There was nothing wrong with those cinnamon rolls. I was just...self-conscious that she'd somehow figure out what happened during the baking process."

"Serves her right for getting here early."

Without a word, he guides the hand I'm wielding the spatula in an inch to my left. That's Harper, thoughtfully giving without making a production or being pushy about anything. Applying pressure to the bottom of the skillet when my egg timer goes off, I feel the weight of the egg and carefully flip it, hoping the yolk didn't break. I was never good at making eggs over-easy when I could see. I don't know how in hell I manage it now.

I'm guessing I was successful by the way I feel his arms tighten around me and his smile press to my neck. "You know," he begins, "You're always telling me how proud of me you are, but I don't think I've told you enough. You amaze me, every single day. I don't think there's anything you can't do. You should be so proud of yourself, Riley, for everything you've accomplished this year."

Things came easy to me before I lost my sight, so compliments were in rare supply. I think everyone just assumed I excelled at everything, so nothing was truly an accomplishment since it didn't look like it took much effort. The fact that this bit of praise is coming from Harper swells my chest with pride. I don't care if flipping a damn egg impresses him, I'll take it. And truth be told, I probably never would have attempted it again if it wasn't for him.

Squeezing his hand where it's resting against my stomach, I challenge, "Well, I can't bleach my light fixtures, but I'll get there."

He chuffs, amused by the silly stories I regale just to make him laugh. I can't believe he remembers all the dumb things I tell him, but I guess that's part of what love is.

Shutting off the burner, I lift the eggs out of the pan and feel for where I left the plates. Harper looks on, neither interrupting nor offering to help. I've learned that's also part of love.

When you know your partner is struggling or could use a hand, the natural instinct is to want to give them assistance. Sometimes, however, it's just as important to stand back and let them succeed or fail on their own. It's the only way we truly learn.

Smiling at my small victory, I turn around and hand him his plate, proud to be feeding my man. I'm thanked with a kiss before he moves to the stool at the island counter where I join him.

"Speaking of accomplishments," I tell him, reaching for the pile of mail that came yesterday and setting it in front of him. "We got our first payment for the Olivia app."

"*We?*" he queries.

Rolling my eyes, I ignore him and nudge the checks I felt come in the mail closer to him. "Are you going to open yours?"

"They sent individual checks?"

"Partnership. Remember? Am I going to have to take you to a memory institute and have you checked out?"

Smirking, I can practically hear the grimace of protest on his face as he sighs. The rustle of paper makes me smile though. Baby steps. His audible gasp has my heart leaping in excitement for him.

"Holy shit, Riley," he whispers.

"Are you going to rethink your profession now?" I tease.

Sputtering, he stammers, "I…this…I can't believe the number of zeros. I think this is more than I've earned in five years."

Setting my coffee cup down, I level him with a serious expression. "You're going to leave me now, aren't you?"

"Why would I do that?" he laughs.

"Young, attractive, well off. You've got the world at your fingertips."

"What about you?" he challenges.

"Nah, you're stuck with me."

"Good," he chuckles, leaning over the counter to kiss me. "I'm still not comfortable taking this."

"Well, that's one discomfort I'm going to have to ask you to live with. So, what are you going to do with it?"

"I…I have no idea. Put it in the bank, I guess."

Rebel. He's such a rebel. I stop my internal teasing though when he adds, "Maybe I could go take motorcycle lessons and get my license though."

"Really?" I grin.

"Yeah, so I can take my boyfriend out for a ride before he sells his bike."

The thought of the wind in my hair again, but with the added sensation of being wrapped around Harper sends a rush of giddiness through me. How hot would he look driving my bike? I can see it now.

"Well, if you get your license, I'm not fucking selling it," I declare, making him crack up.

"Yeah, I guess you won't have to worry about affording this place anymore," he says. "I'm happy for you."

His words remind me of my lamentations over my financial situation. Our app is going to do well, but who knows if I'll ever make another one. As soon as the proceed payments stop, it's back to being on disability stipends for me for the rest of my life. I don't need the money right now and probably won't for years, but the thought of being idle doesn't sit well with me and is something I've given a lot of thought over the last few weeks. While Harper was finding himself, I guess I was busy finding the new me also.

"Actually, I was thinking of selling this place, maybe buying a house in a small town closer to my parents. Do you think you could handle living closer to Leigh Ann's cookie delivery service?"

I hold my breath, waiting in the silence. I've never been one to be able to hold back what I think are good ideas. Harper will always be a part of my good ideas as far as I'm concerned, so I need his approval on this one, but hope it's not too much pressure on the delicate balance he's just found.

"I think…that would probably save her on gas," he finally says. "With what she'd save in fuel, she could probably afford more ingredients to bake even more cookies."

Exhaling in relief, I reach out and grab his hand, smiling when it grips mine back tightly. "Exactly! See, I like the way you think."

Rubbing my hand with his thumb, he murmurs, "Are you still worried about money…for when you get older?"

He knows me so well. "Nah, I've got another idea. I want to go into a new profession, but I might need your help, if you're willing to stick with me."

Interweaving our fingers, he draws my hand up to his lips and kisses my knuckles. "Riley, you're absolutely stuck with me."

I think the grin on my face will probably stay there all week, the last bit of my apprehension flying away. It feels like the final hurdle we had to overcome, the forever hurdle.

My romantic boyfriend ruins the moment though by hedging, "Um, maybe I should ask what the new profession is first though."

"Smart ass," I scoff, giving him a gentle cuff on the chin. "No. You'll love it. I'm going to write romance novels."

Okay, why is he so quiet? It's a brilliant idea. I'm practically an expert now for how many I've listened to.

"Romance novels," he repeats. "Like…what kind of romance novels?"

"The best kind, of course. I was thinking of specializing in witty bromance with demisexual themes and bi-awakenings. Show all those straight guys what they're missing, plus I want to give people hope. There's too much angst in the MM genre. And I want to write a few about just two gay guys or two bisexual guys figuring their shit out and falling in love. What do you think?"

"I think," he pauses, soft laughter floating across the counter, "I think that's a great idea, but what do you need my help for?"

"Well, I'll need a proofreader…and a narrator."

"Ah ha. I knew there was a catch."

"What? You have something against narrating books with an overuse of the word *balls* in them? Because I promise to never use the word *impaled.* Remember? We already had that discussion over that one book we listened to a while back and agreed on that one. Plus, now that I've experienced an impaling, I can totally vouch for the *unsexiness* of that word."

Shifting on my stool, I warm at the tingle of the welcome soreness in my ass, still feeling the memory of Harper there last night. He can so impale me any time he wants to. My man is fucking brilliant in bed.

Laughing, he gets up. To my right, the dampening of the background noises of the apartment tell me he's rounding the counter. My pulse kicks, wondering if he's actually going to shut me down and write my idea off as a silly Riley pipe dream, but his arms wrap around me.

"You know what? I'll gladly proofread and narrate *all your balls*, but don't be disappointed if my performance affects your ratings."

"No way. That voice of yours, it'll only make the story better," I tell him, reaching my arms up behind me to drag his mouth down to mine. "So, should we get pen names or a stage name, in your case?"

"What happened to letting everyone be the Larry they were meant to be?"

"To protect our privacy so we can *Larry it up* at home. What about this for me, *Buck Boomer*."

"I am not calling you fucking *Boomer*." He laughs.

"Think about it for a while. It might grow on you. It's got a nice ring to it."

Epilogue

HARPER

Eighteen months later

"Harper, you know I don't like tattling on him, but you asked me to tell you if he was ever at it again. Well, I caught him out there this afternoon for about an hour," our neighbor calls over the fence that adjoins our yards.

Sighing, I pinch my eyes closed and fight the smile that wants to appear. "Thanks Fabi. Did he do any damage?"

"I think you can say goodbye to your daylilies for the year, but they're perennials, so they'll be back next summer."

"Alright. Thanks."

Walking up the steps to our porch, I put the key in the door and unlock it. Larry's nails click against the hardwood flooring in the hallway as he comes to greet me. Scratching under his chin, I have a word.

"What were you two up to today? Didn't I tell you to keep him out of trouble?"

He snorts at me as if to say, "You actually think that's possible?"

I don't understand how this dog failed guide school, but then again, the guide school had never met one Riley Davenport. Larry guided him out of the darkness just not in the traditional way, and sometimes still not in the ways that a true guide dog should. They're perfect for each other.

Walking toward the sounds of a man's voice narrating a steamy sex scene in the kitchen, I know I'm close to finding my man. I've informed him there are other genres of audiobooks in the almost two years we've been together, but he's become a bit obsessed with romances. Who am I to judge?

I'm greeted by the sight of a very delectable naked ass, the bow of Riley's apron tied above it as he mutters to himself over the vegetables he's chopping on the cutting board.

"You're damn right he's the one, Max. You fucking idiot. I could have told you that six chapters ago! Run Jack. Run! You can do better!" he growls at his phone where it's on the counter broadcasting a novel.

Shaking my head, I try to wipe the smirk off my face so as not to encourage him. I know he won't see it, but I swear the man can smell when I'm smiling. Maybe he just knows how much I love him and that there's always a smile on my face.

"You know, it's rude to stare," he calls over his shoulder.

"Really? I kind of figured that was the goal of your get up."

"You like it?" he shakes his ass. "I was out sunning all afternoon. I needed to cool off."

"Yeah," I drawl, slinking my arm around his waist and pressing a kiss to his neck. "I heard. Fabi said you were on the lawnmower again."

He stiffens in my arms, but then his hand slides over my forearm, his fingers interlacing with mine. "Babe, you want our yard to look like shit?"

"I want you to not hurt yourself or mow over a neighborhood child."

"Our yard is fenced in! If some feral kid gets in, that's their fault, and I had my cane. I know where the fence is. It's really not that hard to cut grass, once you know where the boundary line is."

"Well, she worries about you just like I do."

"If she wants to worry about something, she should worry about keeping Fifi from squeezing under our fence."

"Fifi was over here again?"

"Mmhm, and let's just say we're probably going to have to discuss parental rights with Fabi in a few months from the way things sounded. I didn't know Larry had that much stamina."

Oh, no. Guide dogs are usually spayed or neutered, but Larry never was an official guide dog, and Riley's been adamant about letting his boy keep his manhood. The only thing as ugly as Larry is Fabi's Glen of Imaal Terrier. Picturing their potential offspring, I drop my forehead to his shoulder.

"You're kidding me. Why didn't you stop them?"

"I'm not a cock blocker! And how would that look to my readers if I broke up a love match?"

"Riley, I don't think your readers will stop buying your books if you keep two dogs from procreating."

At least he gave up on the Buck Boomer pen name idea. His initial visions of grandeur over his potential novelist success faded enough that he stopped worrying about a level of fame that would disrupt our privacy. He just writes as plain old Riley Davenport, although the world like me discovered there is nothing plain about Riley Davenport. Embarrassingly enough, Leigh Ann Davenport is his biggest fan, which he enjoys reminding his father of immensely. Poor Charlie.

"They'd know if I posted it on my *Larry Out Loud* podcast," he counters. "Besides, it's the principle of the thing, Harper. Where's your sense of romance?"

Trailing my finger down his bare spine, I hook it through the loop in his apron tie. "It got distracted by this bow above your ass. Isn't cooking in the nude a little unhygienic?"

"Pfft. Everything we do in this kitchen is unhygienic."

"True," I admit, knowing he has a point.

"I was getting into character. I have an idea about a chef who cooks in the nude when he's at home."

"Oh, yeah? What's the angle?"

"Uh, well, that's as far as I got so far," he adds, the brief lack in confidence making me smile at the crack in his invincibility.

"Well, it's something," I reassure him.

"How'd it go at the recording studio today?"

"Great. We finished up, now they just have to do the mastering, and then my twelfth audiobook will be born."

Spinning around, he squeezes the shit out of me and presses a kiss to my mouth. "Yes! Congrats! I still can't believe you narrated an Eagan Brannigan novel."

"Co-narrated," I correct.

"Whatever. We're so having sex while we listen to that."

"Okay," I agree with a laugh.

No way will that be happening. I don't want to listen to myself talking to another narrator while I make love to my boyfriend.

"So, does that mean you'll be home all day tomorrow?" he asks hopefully, returning to his dicing.

"No. I was going to work a shift at the community center in the afternoon."

"Ugh. Why does my boyfriend have to be a saint?" he grumbles even though I know he's proud of me for continuing to volunteer there even after I quit working at the senior center.

He's always eager to come along when I ask him to do a guide dog demo with Larry, further evidence of his support. He might also have a bit of a thing for peacocking.

"Why? What did you have planned?"

"Research," he says innocently.

"What kind of research?"

"The best kind. It's for my book."

"Ah. Do I have to wear an apron?" I ask, skimming my hands up and down his sides.

"No. You're the obnoxious handyman who lives next door."

Fucking Riley. I don't even care that means our toolbox is probably already in the bedroom. Pinching my eyes closed, I chuckle into the back of his neck. "Of course, I am. No offense, but that sounds like a bad porno."

"Really?" he perks up. "Yes! I knew I was onto something!"

He's so happy, not that he ever isn't, but I want to keep him riding this wave. Heart skipping, I take his hand, urging him to turn around.

"Can you leave this for a minute and come with me? I want you to listen to something I recorded the other day."

Grabbing a towel, he wipes off his hands and then reclaims my hand, leaning in for a kiss. "For you, I've got *two* minutes. What is it? A steamy scene? 'Cause dinner might be just a memory if you make me listen to that right now."

Rubbing my thumb over his knuckles as we head toward my home recording booth, my stomach flips. We've both come so far. Sometimes I wonder if this bliss-filled bubble will burst, but remind myself that's part of the old doubts creeping in. I'm well aware life will have hardships, ups and downs, but I know now that the downs won't be insurmountable because this wonderful man will be there with me through them. And if the downs ever involve something happening to him, they'll just be the price to pay for all the incredible moments we've had.

Seventeen months ago, during the first Christmas we spent together, I got a visit from the police I never would have expected. Dallas was found dead outside of Daniel's bar one night. The cause of death: blunt force trauma. There was finally a fight he didn't win, an adversary he didn't best. The questions from the police were cut and dry, obligatory, asking me my whereabouts, my alibi, since I was still listed on our apartment lease with him. Of course, and luckily, I had been with Riley.

It's strange; sometimes I still think about him, but it's no longer fear I feel. It's pity. I never imagined feeling pity for a man who caused me so much torment. What a waste of a life though. He never got to have what I have. Love, true love reciprocated. I don't know if he was even capable of it. I realized allowing yourself to be loved is more difficult than people think. I know enough about it, how it almost cost me Riley. It's one instance where it's okay to be greedy—he can give me all the love he wants. I'll gladly take it and cherish it.

Guiding him to the extra chair in my recording booth, I wait until his bare ass is situated in the leather chair, smirking at the sight he makes. I fucking love this goofball so much the emotions choke me sometimes. Taking my own seat, I roll my chair closer to his, bring up the track I prepared a few weeks ago that I've been waiting for the right moment to share, and press *play*.

"Harper sat the love of his life down in the recording studio and hit play, a nervous jitter working its way through his veins as he gazed upon Riley. Never had he seen such an attractive man, one who could make any article of clothing look like it was meant just for his body."

Snickering, Riley wriggles his brows at me, running his thumb under the neck strap of his apron. Smiling, I reach my sweaty hand into my pocket and pull out the small velvet box, grasping his hand with my other one.

"Riley had changed his entire world, his entire view of life. He brought him light when all Harper saw was darkness. He brought him love when all Harper thought was left in the world was fear and misery. Most of all, he brought him hope when he'd always only dreaded what was to come each day.

How could he ever repay Riley for a gift like that? What could he do to let him know that every morning when he woke up now, he couldn't wait for their tomorrows? He wanted all of them with this silly, sexy man who still made his head spin and his heart flip every time he looked at him.

They already lived together with their ugly dog, named Larry, in a cute little house that they bought the year prior. Harper and Riley both had dream jobs they loved as much as each other. How could you top that? And why chance ruining it by making more requests? But that was the thing...Riley had taught him not to be afraid to take chances. If you don't, you might miss out on something great, and what could possibly be better than asking Riley to spend the rest of his life with him? So, Harper took a breath and looked at the face of the man he loved and asked him..."

The tears in Riley's eyes, his slack jaw from when he figured it out a few moments ago, make my own eyes go glassy. His grip, tight on mine, tells me what his answer will be before I even ask the question, but I'm still trembling.

"Riley, would you do me the honor of becoming my husband?"

The sound of the shaky breath that rushes out of his lungs as he sniffles, makes tears spill over my eyelids. Lurching forward out of his chair, he throws himself onto me before I can even think to present him the ring in my hand. His mouth crashes down on mine, and I help haul his bare ass onto my lap.

"Fuck yeah," he whispers between sloppy, urgent kisses. "Fuck yeah."

Laughing, crying, I kiss him with all I have, wiping away his tears while he wipes at mine and our lips battle like the two stupidly happy fools that we are. His mouth gravitates to my neck, and his fingers start anxiously working the buttons on my shirt, making me laugh.

Peeling my shirt open, he whispers over my lips with a brilliant smile, "Dinner is so fucked, *Mr. Boomer.*"

RILEY'S PLAYLIST

1 **Dirty Deeds**
Performed by AC/DC

2 **Seeing Blind**
Performed by Niall Horan & Maren Morris

3 **Fall Into Me**
Performed by Forest Blakk

4 **If You Could Read My Mind**
Performed by Gordon Lightfoot

5 **I Believe (When I Fall in Love With You)**
Performed by Stevie Wonder

01:30   04:03

DEAR READER

Thank you for reading *Until I Saw You*. I hope this story brought you some hope, smiles, and a few laughs despite the sensitive subjects that were covered. I understand that not everyone who has dealt with vision issues and/or abuse will have the same experiences throughout their ordeals or recovery. I can only hope yours and their journeys end as happily as it did for the main characters in this book.

As the topics covered in this story are very dear to my heart for personal reasons, a portion of this book's earnings will be donated toward charities helping victims of domestic abuse and the vision impaired. Thank you for helping me support them.

ACKNOWLEDGEMENTS

Christie and Yael, you helped me make the loving moments of this story extra sweet and special. Thank you for your romantic hearts and keen eye for detail.

These wonderful beta and sensitivity readers helped to polish my story and hunt down errors I overlooked. I am forever in your debt: Cathy, Tracy Ann, Meagan, Kassandra, Rachel, Emma, Larissa, Marge, Deb, and Keren.

To my incredible team of ARC readers, I am so grateful for your enthusiasm for my work and your dedication in making time to early read and review, good or bad, to help spread the word about my books. I couldn't do this without you.

Leigh Ann and Fabi, thank you for letting me highjack your names for two special ladies in this story. To the Bun Squad, thank you for all the brainstorming, *Larry* names, and the laughs.

BOOKS BY DIANNA

MM ROMANCE

The Shutout

You Again: Men of Olympus Book 1

Tough Love: Men of Olympus Book 2

Until I Saw You

MF ROMANCE

A Fair Warning: A Grand Valley Novel

Printed in Great Britain
by Amazon

46455867R00138